Silver Bullets

Silver Bullets

The 25th Anniversary of Crippen & Landru Publishers

Twenty-five years of the best mystery short fiction from Crippen & Landru.

CRIPPEN & LANDRU PUBLISHERS
Cincinnati, Ohio
2019

MISTRESS THREADNEEDLE'S QUEST by Kathy Lynn Emerson first appeared in Malice Domestic 12: Murder Most Historical copyright © 2017. Reprinted by permission of the author.
MR BO by Liza Cody first appeared in as a separate holiday booklet given to friends of Crippen & Landru Publishers copyright © 2009. Reprinted by permission of the author.
A BATTLE FIELD REUNION by Brendan Dubois first appeared in Alfred Hitchcock's Mystery Magazine copyright © 2016. Reprinted by permission of the author.
MURDER ON THE BRIGHTON RUN by Amy Myers first appeared in Ellery Queen's Mystery Magazine copyright © 2016. Reprinted by permission of the author.
A RUN THROUGH THE CALENDAR By Jon Breen first appeared in Ellery Queen's Mystery Magazine copyright © 2007. Reprinted by permission of the author.
THE FLYING FIEND by Edward D. Hoch first appeared in Ellery Queen's Mystery Magazine copyright © 1982. Reprinted by permission of the author's estate.
THE SPARE KEY by Edward Marston first appeared in Ellery Queen's Mystery Magazine copyright © 2005. Reprinted by permission of the author.
CHANGE THE ENDING by Terrence Faherty first appeared in Alfred Hitchcock's Mystery Magazine copyright © 2011. Reprinted by permission of the author.
READER, I BURIED THEM by Peter Lovesey first appeared in Ellery Queen's Mystery Magazine copyright © 2018. Reprinted by permission of the author.
THE CHATELAINE BAG by Bill Pronzini and Marcia Muller first appeared in Ellery Queen's Mystery Magazine copyright © 2011, Reprinted by permission of the author.
THE TEST by HRF Keating first appeared in Ellery Queen's Mystery Magazine copyright © 1969. Reprinted by permission of the author's estate.
WHAT THE DORMOUSE SAID by Carolyn Wheat first appeared in. A Hot and Sultry Night for Crime, copyright © 2003. Reprinted by permission of the author.
A MATTER OF HONOR by Jeremiah Healy first appeared in Ellery Queen's Mystery Magazine copyright © 2006. Reprinted by permission of the author's estate.
DEATH ROW by Michael Z. Lewin first appeared in Alfred Hitchcock's Mystery Magazine copyright © 2008. Reprinted by permission of the author.

All other materials copyright © 2019
All characters in this publication are fictitious and any resemblance to real persons, living or dead, is purely coincidental.

All rights reserved.

No part of this publication may be reproduced, stored in a retrieval system, or transmitted, in any form or by any means, without the prior permission in writing of the publisher, nor be otherwise circulated in any form of binding or cover other than that in which it is published and without a similar condition including this condition being imposed on the subsequent purchaser.

For information contact:
Crippen & Landru, Publishers
P. O. Box 532057
Cincinnati, OH 45253 USA

Web: www.crippenlandru.com
E-mail: Info@crippenlandru.com

ISBN (softcover): 978-1-936363-38-4
ISBN (clothbound): 978-1-936363-37-7
First Edition: July 2019
10 9 8 7 6 5 4 3 2 1

CONTENTS

INTRODUCTION by Douglas G. Greene	7
MISTRESS THREADNEEDLE'S QUEST by Kathy Lynn Emerson	11
MR BO by Liza Cody	21
A BATTLE FIELD REUNION by Brendan Dubois	37
MURDER ON THE BRIGHTON RUN by Amy Myers	61
A RUN THROUGH THE CALENDAR By Jon Breen	77
THE FLYING FIEND by Edward D. Hoch	87
THE SPARE KEY by Edward Marston	101
CHANGE THE ENDING by Terrence Faherty	113
READER, I BURIED THEM by Peter Lovesey	125
THE CHATELAINE BAG by Bill Pronzini and Marcia Muller	141
THE TEST by HRF Keating	157
WHAT THE DORMOUSE SAID by Carolyn Wheat	163
A MATTER OF HONOR by Jeremiah Healy	187
DEATH ROW by Michael Z. Lewin	205
A CRIPPEN & LANDRU CHECKLIST	215
AFTERWORD by Jeffrey Marks	222

Introduction

Early in 1994, my brother and I put our collection of L. Frank Baum and Oz books at to auction, and the result was that we had enough money to complete our children's university education. And, to get to the point, I had a small amount left over, with which I bought a word processor – and began Crippen & Landru.

I had long collected mystery short story volumes, believing (with Ellery Queen. G. K. Chesterton, and others) that the short form included the purest detective stories. I was disturbed that so many fine stories had never been "bookformed," and in the early 1990's commercial publishers rarely published short story collections. I even made a list of authors and series characters who deserved to have their tales preserved as books. When I had a few dollars left over from the auction, I decided to start Crippen & Landru to specialize in publishing single author short story volumes..

The name was taken from two infamous murderers, Hawley Harvey Crippen and Henri Désiré Landru. It was only after the publishing company was up and running that my wife belatedly pointed out that both were wife-killers. Later, however, Jacques Barzun told me that he didn't believe that Crippen actually murdered his wife, so I was semi-saved. Whatever the case, the name sounded to me like a publishing house – and both Landru & Crippen were frequently mentioned in detective stories of the 1920s and 1930s. Of course, many people didn't get the allusion, and for years we received letters and e-mails addressed to Mr. Crippen or Mr. Landru.

Rather ironically, our first publication was John Dickson Carr's *Speak of the Devil*, which was a radio play not a short story collection. This was followed by a Margery Allingham collection, and two volumes by contemporary authors, Marcia Muller and Edward D. Hoch. All four books sold encouragingly, and the fact that current authors were willing to trust stories to us meant that we were on our way.

Eventually, we published more than 100 volumes over the next twenty-three years. Our books ranged from private-eye writers (Bill Pronzini, Ross Macdoaald, and others) to classical, fair-play authors (Ellery Queen, Michael Innes, and others), from major writers (Michael Gilbert, Margaret Maron, Peter Lovesey, and others), to writers no longer well-known (Charles B. Child, Joseph Commings and others). The complete list of our publications can be found at the end of this book – and many of our authors have contributed stories to this anniversary volume.

Eventually we published two series of books. Our "Regular Series" was (and still is) made up primarily of current writers, with some copies being signed and numbered by the author, and bound in full cloth. Each of these books included something special – an additional story in a separate chapbook or a page of the author's typescript. Other unsigned copies were bound in stiff paper. The other series is "Lost Classics" – books by authors of the past whose contributions to the genre have been unfairly forgotten. These too are published in both cloth and trade-paper.

Our publications have received many compliments:

"This is the best edited, most attractively packaged line of mystery books introduced in this decade. The books are equally valuable to collectors and readers." [*Mystery Scene Magazine*]

"The specialty publisher with the most star-studded list is Crippen & Landru, which has produced short story collections by some of the biggest names in contemporary crime fiction." [*Ellery Queen's Mystery Magazine*]

"God Bless Crippen & Landru." [*The Strand Magazine*]

"A monument in the making is appearing year by year from Crippen & Landru, a small press devoted exclusively to publishing the criminous short story." [*Alfred Hitchcock's Mystery Magazine*]

But years began to take their toll on the publisher, and by 2016 I was considering ways to shut down the company. I mentioned this to my good friend, Jeff Marks, and he offered to take over. I agreed with alacrity. Jeff is well-known as an officer of the Mystery Writers of America and a major writer about the genre; author of biographies of Craig Rice and Anthony Boucher.

With his energy and his knowledge, he is the perfect person to continue Crippen & Landru.

Doug Greene
Norfolk, Virginia
June 2019

Mistress Threadneedle's Quest
by Kathy Lynn Emerson

I first met Doug Greene at Malice Domestic. I introduced myself to him because we both had a connection to the English department at Old Dominion University. I had no idea that he'd recently started publishing collections of short mystery stories. I had not yet had any of mine published and I certainly never imagined I'd write enough of them to fill even a slim volume, but fast forward a few years, to another Malice, this one shortly after one of my stories appeared in Alfred Hitchcock Mystery Magazine. *One of the highlight of that conference was Doug's request to keep Crippen & Landru in mind when (not if) I was ready to bring out a collection of stories. I think I'd written five by that point. It was his confidence in me that inspired me to keep writing them. I'm very slow at writing short. I doubt I'd have written many more, let alone ended up as an Agatha finalist in the short story category, if not for his encouragement. Thank you, Doug, and happy twenty-fifth anniversary to Crippen & Landru. The following story first appeared in the Malice Domestic anthology* Mystery Most Historical.

London, 1562

On the day of Edward Sturgeon's funeral, I stood in my garden, staring at an upper window in his tall, narrow house. It had been a fine, large casement, made up of dozens of small, expensive triangles of colored glass held together by H-shaped lead rods. Now blackened wood and missing panes told a terrible story. I was at the same time fascinated and horrified. I could not look away.

Sturgeon had been standing just inside that window when he'd been struck by lightning. His death was quick, but it must have been excruciatingly painful. The stable boy who bore witness to his passing said Sturgeon looked as though he was wrapped in exploding fireworks. By the time the flames were extinguished, it was too late to save him.

You may well ask how such a thing could happen. Some said it was an act of God. Others called it a portent of disaster—a strange, unnatural death. I believe I am the only one in all of England to suspect that Edward Sturgeon was most foully murdered.

I am Mistress Dowsabella Threadneedle, childless relict of a prosperous mercer. I married beneath me, having been born the daughter of a knight. In my widowhood, I live in considerable comfort in a house in Catte Street in the parish of St. Lawrence Jewry. Most of my neighbors are well-to-do merchants of one sort or another. Edward Sturgeon was the richest of them all, not only a goldsmith, but a moneylender, too.

Even as I ruminated upon the strange manner of his death, the Goldsmiths of London were bearing his body in solemn procession from their guildhall to the churchyard. From where I stood, I could hear the wailing of professional mourners and imagined them in their new black gowns, tearing at their hair and weeping.

Inside the Sturgeon house, the new-made widow grieved in seclusion with her kinswomen and closest female friends. The spouse of the deceased never attends the funeral. I have no idea why this is the custom, but it was the same for me two years ago when my beloved Richard was taken from me.

Although I knew I would be welcome to mourn with Mary Sturgeon, I did not go to her. When we'd first met, she'd made it all too plain that she would value my acquaintance not because of any pleasant characteristics I might possess, but solely because my gentle birth made me desirable to know. I am related by blood to certain persons who have influence at the royal court. My husband benefitted from those connections, which brought additional custom to his mercery, but I am not inclined to ask my cousins to do similar favors for anyone else.

Instead of entering the Sturgeon house, I returned to my own. I would bide my time before confronting Mistress Sturgeon. I had much to ponder before I took action.

Why, you must be asking, did I imagine that a crime had been committed? No one has the power to call down lightning from the sky, let alone direct it at a specific target. Even the most powerful necromancer would be hard put to accomplish such a feat.

To explain, I must first tell you that my husband indulged me to a degree most people would find peculiar. Having been taught the skill at an early age, I had already developed a passion for reading by the time we wed. Knowing this, he made it his habit to gift me with books instead of jewelry. Thus have I acquired all manner of reading material, but in particular I am partial to the tales of brave knights, impossible quests, and strange happenings. As a widow with control over my late husband's entire fortune, I continue to purchase such stories. Anyone who hopes to persuade me to speak on his behalf to one of my kinsmen at court, or keep me sweet for any other reason, is encouraged to find an appropriate token in one of the booksellers' stalls in Paul's Churchyard. So it was that, about a year before Edward Sturgeon's strange death, I acquired a slim volume entitled The Sorcerer Knight.

This is the story of an arrogant knight's attempts to turn base metal into gold, raise the spirits of the dead, and find lost treasure. All these things defy both the law of man and the law of God, and when the knight seeks to call down the power of a storm by holding a sword over his head, he suffers divine retribution. He is struck by a bolt of lightning and dies.

I know for a certainty that Edward Sturgeon was familiar with the story. He was the one who presented me with the book.

The more I thought about the knight's tale and compared it to what happened to Master Sturgeon, the more convinced I became that the circumstances of Sturgeon's death were suspicious. If for no other reason than to ease my conscience, I felt compelled to investigate.

* * *

A week after the funeral, I paused once again in the garden. I studied the scorched and boarded-over casement for a long time before passing through the narrow alley between the houses. Like a proper visitor, I went to the door of the house that now belonged to the widow and was admitted by one of her maidservants.

Mary Sturgeon herself received me in an upper room at the front of the house. The faint smell of smoke still lingered in the air but we both ignored it.

"How kind of you to call." She seemed surprised by my visit.

"I have brought a gift to cheer you in this sad time," I said, presenting her with a small packet.

Her forced smile turned genuine as she opened it and found a sampling of the best my late husband's mercery had to offer—assorted ribbons and tassels and a decorative border for the front of a French hood. The latter was made of the finest black silk and garnished with jet beads.

"You are most generous, Mistress Threadneedle."

"It was the least I could do, Mistress Sturgeon. Even the deepest mourning allows for a few adornments." I glanced at the sewing abandoned beside my hostess's chair. She had been attaching a length of black cord to a black sleeve. "Shall I work on its mate?" I offered, catching sight of more of the same cord wound into a ball and tucked into a corner of her sewing basket.

I reached for it, but she stayed my hand, delving into the basket herself and producing a smaller segment of the cord, together with a needle and a short length of black thread. She was still rummaging after I had seated myself and taken up the materials she'd provided.

"What do you lack?"

She gave a nervous laugh. "I am unable to locate any pins. I have been more distraught of late than I realized. I forgot that I needed to buy more."

It was a trifling matter, but odd all the same. Pins, whether small fine ones or long dress pins, are customarily purchased a thousand at a time.

Together with Mary and her two maidservants, I sat and stitched. I offered news of the royal court, where there had been a recent outbreak of smallpox. A goodly number of highborn ladies in the service of Queen Elizabeth had been afflicted and those who survived were likely to be scarred for life.

Mary Sturgeon had little to offer in return, save that the butcher's wife had been delivered of twin sons. "They say twins are unlucky, but surely it is better to have two at a time than be barren." She sounded wistful and then, too late, remembered that I was also childless.

I let her comment pass unanswered, for to tell you true, I look upon my barren state as a blessing. Too many women, burdened with fatherless chicks, are pressured into remarrying and once again become little more than a husband's chattel. Now that it had been forced upon me, I prized my independence. I especially liked being answerable to no one but myself when it came to how I spent my money and managed my property.

After a little silence, I began, by a circuitous route, to approach the subject that had brought me to Mistress Sturgeon's door. "Will you need to replace your roof? I have heard that when the steeple of St. Paul's was struck by lightning last year, molten lead poured down onto the street below."

"There was no lead in my roof to melt. The tiles are scored but intact."

"I did not realize anyone had climbed up to inspect them," I said. "You must not think I spend all my time spying on my neighbors, but a ladder that tall would be most conspicuous."

"There is a trap door in the garret that gives access to the roof," she said. "It is not difficult to open and go through. Thus I have seen for myself that the roof does not need repairs. Only the window must be replaced."

I executed a few more careful stitches before I spoke again. "Did your husband stand at that window every time there was a storm?"

"Oh, yes—the more fool he!" Color rose in Mary's cheeks as she spat out heated words. "He said thunderstorms made him feel alive.

Mistress Threadneedle's Quest | 15

He lived to watch lightning flash across the night sky. He had no one but himself to blame that such an ungodly habit killed him!"

Her anger at her late husband struck me as natural. He had been both careless and arrogant. "Sensible people are afraid of thunder and lightning, as well they should be."

Some believe thunderstorms are sent by the devil. Others see them as an expression of God's displeasure. Either way, almost everyone agrees that it is best to stay indoors with the shutters closed during violent storms.

"Edward thought himself sensible," she said. "He laughed at the superstitious things people do to repel lightning."

I nodded. Everyone knew such remedies. "I cannot see that planting houseleeks on the roof or draping mistletoe over doors and windows offers much protection."

"And most foolish of all, or so Edward always said, is the belief that ringing church bells during a thunderstorm will drive away the devil. What more likely place, he used to say, than a church with a tall steeple to be struck by lightning? And what more dangerous occupation than bell ringer? It was his frequent observation that lightning seeks out the highest point in the landscape."

"I suppose that is why he thought himself safe. Your house is no taller than any of those surrounding it."

"He tempted fate. Worse, he mocked God." Mary Sturgeon's fingers flew faster and faster as her voice rose. Her two maidservants shrank away from her. "He paid the price for thinking too well of himself."

Sturgeon had been accustomed to having his own way. That was true enough. He'd trampled anyone who stood in his path. By one means or another, even threats of violence, he'd forced choices upon lesser men, and upon some women, too.

I reached for the sewing basket to retrieve more thread. My nose wrinkled as I caught a whiff of singed fabric. It was not coming from the room at the back of the house, the one where Edward Sturgeon had died. Instead, it seemed to emanate from within the basket.

Frowning, I bent closer. Surely the widow would not have kept any of the clothing her husband had been wearing when he died.

"What is it you need?" The sharpness in her voice made me jerk upright.

"Thread," I said.

She provided me with more and we all resumed stitching.

It was soon after that exchange that the glazier arrived.

When Mistress Sturgeon left the chamber to supervise his work in the other room, I seized the opportunity to examine the sewing basket. The smell was as strong as I remembered and led me straight to the roll of silk cord. I plucked it out to study more closely.

The outside was undamaged, but when I unrolled the cord, I at once found evidence of scorching. I might have attributed Mary Sturgeon's frugal reuse of expensive decoration to her upbringing—her father had been naught but a yeoman farmer and it was said that, because of her beauty, Sturgeon married her without a dowry—had I not noticed a second oddity. A great number of pinholes showed in the fabric. The pattern they made suggested that someone had inserted dozens of them, overlapping, all along its length.

Pondering this curious discovery, I returned the cord to the sewing basket. I looked up in time to catch the maids exchanging a look. For once, I was glad of my superior birth. I had no power to enforce my will, but I could speak with convincing authority.

"You will say nothing to your mistress of anything you see me do this day," I said. "Do you understand?"

Identical nods answered me, although one maid was short and stout and the other tall and thin.

"Do you know what happened to the pins?" I felt certain they had seen the same thing I had.

The tall girl shook her head so vigorously that she nearly lost her cap. The other young woman worried her lower lip and tried to avoid meeting my eyes.

I waited, my hands busy with the sewing but my full attention on the maids. After a lengthy silence, my patience was rewarded. The one who had been gnawing on her lip spoke in a whisper.

"Threw them down the privy, she did."

"Why?" Pins might be a paltry expense to someone of Edward Sturgeon's wealth, but a frugal housewife would not carelessly discard so many of them, especially one who knew what it was to scrimp and save in order to afford the cheapest sort.

"All blackened and bent, they were." The expression of distaste on the maid's plump face convinced me that she'd had a good look at them.

"How did they get that way?" I asked.

Neither maidservant dared offer an opinion.

I felt certain that the pins were somehow connected to Sturgeon's death, but how had they been used? I pictured in my mind the illustration that accompanied The Sorcerer's Tale—the knight with his sword held high. Swords are made of metal, and so are pins, but how could pins draw down lightning from the sky?

I glanced toward the door through which Mary had disappeared. I had no business following her, but if I wished to examine the window before it was repaired, I had to do so at once. I set aside my sewing and stood. If all else failed, I could use that sad old excuse of needing to use the privy. The Sturgeons, having money enough to afford such a luxury, had a small chamber for that purpose right in the house. It could not be reached by passing through the room where Edward Sturgeon had died, but that was a minor concern. I could always claim, with some truth, that I had not visited Sturgeon's house often enough to be sure of the way.

The glazier, closely supervised by the widow, was busy measuring when I entered. Neither noticed me at first, giving me the opportunity to study the casement from the inside. It was easy to picture Sturgeon there in the opening. He'd been accustomed to stand in the center, one hand braced on either side of him. Braced, I realized with a jolt, on the lead bars that framed each section of the window.

If it was not just the height of a steeple, but the lead roof and the bells within that attracted lightning to churches, then surely it was not a good idea to touch metal of any kind during a thunderstorm. Even so, this house was nowhere near as tall as a church tower. I was still missing a piece of the puzzle.

I learned no more that day, and although I had the most dire suspicions about what had happened to Edward Sturgeon, I still did not understand the mechanics of it.

That night I read the story of *The Sorcerer Knight* again.

The next day, I accosted the thin maidservant as she crossed Sturgeon's garden on an errand for her mistress.

"What else did your mistress throw away after your master died?" I asked her.

She cast a guilty look toward the house. "It means naught," she whined.

"Let me judge that." I resisted the urge to seize and shake her.

"Rope. A length of thin, fine rope."

"Was it blackened, too?"

She nodded, but before I could ask anything more, she fled.

* * *

That evening, I invited my neighbor to sup with me. Afterward, I sent the servants away and fixed her with a steady gaze.

"At some time when you felt certain you would not be seen," I said, "mayhap in the dead of night, you climbed through the trapdoor to the roof and tied your husband's sword to the chimney. Then you attached a length of silk cord, bristling with pins, to the sword, let the other end down beside the window, and fastened it to the lead frame."

She had to swallow hard before she could speak. "What madness is this?"

"Not madness. Murder. And your victim was the one who devised the means of it. You took note of his observations about lightning and put them to good use."

"No one will believe a word of this." Her bravado was touching, if ill-founded.

"Perhaps not, but I might convince the church courts to charge you with sorcery."

"You can prove nothing!" She sprang to her feet. "And in my turn, I will accuse you of foul slander."

I rose, too, blocking her way to the door. "Just tell me why. Why did you want him dead?"

She started to laugh. "How can you ask? He was a cruel man who stopped at nothing to get his own way. He cheated his customers, lent money at a usurer's rates, and mistreated women."

I sighed. "Yes, he did."

"He deserved killing, and it must have been God's will that he die." She was frantic now, determined to convince me of the rightness of her actions. "How else could a sword and a few pins smite him? It was as you said. I listened to his speculations about storms and swords and steeples and tall trees and I devised a plan. When I heard distant thunder that afternoon, I was ready. All I had to do was attach the lower end of the cord to the window. He came into the room just as I finished and flung wide the casement. In the next moment, God struck him down."

Emotions flickered, one after another, across her pale face. Remorse was not one of them, nor was sorrow.

"I never thought it would work," she whispered, more to herself than to me. "I expected he would beat me when he discovered that his sword was missing."

I led her to a padded bench and tugged on her arm until she sat beside me. After a moment, I said, "You are fortunate the house did not catch fire."

"That was God's will, too."

Her voice was stronger and more confident again. Well, why not? She had the right of it. I could prove nothing. She had removed most of the evidence. The rest was now firmly affixed to the sleeves of her mourning gown.

"You have nothing to fear from me," I told her. "I have no intention of going to the justices to accuse you, or to the church courts, either. What would it avail me? No one would believe such a fanciful tale."

"You have powerful friends." She regarded me with wary eyes. "You could cause me a good deal of trouble. Why are you willing to forget what you know?"

"Because your husband deserved to die. He preyed on the weaknesses of women left alone in the world. Once one yielded her virtue to him, he expected her to yield in all things."

She heard the bitterness in my voice and knew my truth, just as I knew hers. At first, Edward Sturgeon had offered sympathy and kindness . . . and a book about a sorcerer knight. But in the end he had been greedy and demanding, angling to take control of my fortune as well as my body.

Had his wife not killed him first, I'd have had to murder him myself.

MR. BO
by Liza Cody

I first met Doug Greene at a Bouchercon. His reputation for being a good guy preceded him: a friend whose opinion I respect pointed him out to me. (Could it have been in a bar? Surely not!) "That's Doug Greene, the short story specialist," my friend said. "You'll like him." He was absolutely right.

I love reading and writing short stories, but it is a limited market. So understandably I was thrilled to my bones when Doug asked me for a collection. There's no room for bullshit or padding in a short story; it's a very pure form that demands quite a lot from both readers and writers. I suspect they aren't the easiest things to sell either. So I've got to give many thanks to a guy who specialises in publishing them, and who is also a dream to work with.

As well as publishing single-author collections he occasionally brings out an anthology which celebrates the life and work of an author he loves. I've been lucky enough to contribute stories specially written for a couple of those too. Both of them were launched at very posh venues in England — which is how I happen to know that, as well as all his other wonderful attributes, Doug looks really cute in a tux.

I wrote Mr. Bo as a Christmas story for Doug in 2009. I warned him that I couldn't do anything about sleigh bells or glistening snow — I wasn't a jolly Santa sort of writer. He seemed to know that already and he accepted the somewhat dystopian family story I offered him. Bless his heart.

My son Nathan doesn't believe in God, Allah, Buddha, Kali, the Great Spider Mother or the Baby Jesus. But, he believes passionately in Superman, Spiderman, Batman, Wolverine and, come December, Santa Claus. How this works out—bearing in mind that they all have super powers—I don't know. Maybe he thinks the second lot wears hotter costumes. Or drives cooler vehicles, or brings better presents. Can I second guess my nine year old? Not a snowball's hope in Hades.

Nathan is as much a mystery to me as his father was, and as my father was before that, and who knows where they both are now? But if there's one thing I can congratulate myself on, it's that I didn't saddle my son with a stepfather. No strange man's going to teach my boy to "dance for daddy". Not while there's a warm breath left in my body.

I was eleven and my sister Skye was nine when Mum brought Bobby Barnes home for the first time. He didn't look like a lame-headed loser so we turned the telly down and said hello.

"Call me Bo," he said, flashing a snowy smile, "All my friends do."

So my dumb little sister said, "Hi, Mr. Bo," and blushed because he was tall and brown-eyed just like the hero in her comic book.

Mum laughed high and girly, and I went to bed with a nosebleed —which is usually what happened when Mum laughed like that and smeared her lipstick.

Mr. Bo moved in and Mum was happy because we were "a family." How can you be family with a total stranger? I always wanted to ask her but I didn't dare. She had a vicious right-hand if she thought you were cheeking her.

Maybe we would be a family even now if it wasn't for him. Maybe Nathan would have a grandma and an aunt if Mr. Bo hadn't got his feet under the table and his bonce on the pillow.

I think about it now and then. After all, some times of year are special for families, and Nathan should have grandparents, an aunt and a father.

This year I was thinking about it because sorting out the tree lights is traditionally a father's job; as is finding the fuse box when the whole house is tripped out by a kink in the wire.

I was doing exactly that, by candle light because Nathan had broken the torch, when the doorbell rang.

Standing in the doorway was a beautiful woman in a stylish winter coat with fur trimmings. I didn't have time for more than a quick glance at her face because she came inside and said, "What's up? Can't pay the electricity bill? Just like Mum."

"I am not like my mother." I was furious.

"Okay, okay," she said. "It was always way too easy to press your buttons." And I realised that the strange woman with the American accent was Skye.

"What are you doing here?" I said, stunned.

"Hi, and it's great to see you too," she said. "Who's the rabbit?"

I turned. Nathan was behind me, shadowy, with the broken torch in his hand.

"He's not a rabbit," I said, offended. Rabbit was Mr. Bo's name for a mark.

We were all rabbits to him one way or another.

"Who's she?" Nathan said. I'd taught him not to tell his name, address or phone number to strangers.

"I'm Skye."

"A Scottish Island?" He sounded interested. "Or the place where clouds sit?"

"Smart and cute."

"I'm not cute," he said, sniffing loudly. "I'm a boy."

"She's your aunt," I told him, "my sister."

"I don't want an aunt," he said, staring at her flickering, candlelit face. "But an uncle might be nice." Did I mention that all his heroes are male? Even when it's a woman who solves all his problems, from homework to football training to simple plumbing and now, the electricity. I used to think it was because he missed a father, but it's because you can't interest a boy in girls until his feet get tangled in the weeds of sex.

I fixed the electricity and all the lights came on except, of course, for the tree ones which lay in a nest on the floor with the bulbs no more responsive than duck eggs. Nathan looked at me as though I'd betrayed his very life.

"Tomorrow," I said. "I promise."

"You promised tonight."

"Let's have a little drink," Skye said "to celebrate the return of the prodigal sister."

"We don't drink," Nathan said priggishly. He's wrong. I just don't drink in front of him. My own childhood was diseased and deceived by Mum drinking and the decisions she made when drunk.

"There's a bottle of white in the fridge," I said, because Skye was staring at my second-hand furniture and looking depressed. At least it's mine, and no repo man's going to burst in and take it away. She probably found me plain and worn too, but I can't help that.

She had a couple of drinks. I watched very carefully, but she showed no signs of becoming loose and giggly. So I said, "It's late. Stay the night." She was my sister, after all, even though I didn't know her. But she took one look at the spare bed in the box room and said, "Thanks, I'll call a cab."

When the cab came, Nathan followed us to the front door and said goodbye of his own free will. Skye was always the charming one. She didn't attempt to kiss him because if there was one thing she'd learnt well it was what guys like and what they don't like. She said, "I'll come back tomorrow and bring you a gift. What do you want?"

Now that's a question Nathan isn't used to in this house, but he hardly stopped to think. He said, "Football boots. The red and white Nike ones, with a special spanner thing you can use to adjust your own studs."

"Nathan," I warned. The subject of football boots was not new. I could never quite afford the ones he wanted.

But Skye grinned and said, "See you tomorrow, kid," and she was gone in a whirl of fur trimmings.

* * *

Mr. Bo used to buy our shoes. Well, not buy exactly. This is how he did it: we'd go to a shoe shop and I'd ask for shoes a size and a half too small. Mr. Bo would flirt with the assistant. When the shoes arrived I'd try to stuff my feet in and Mr. Bo would say, "Who do you think you are? One of the Ugly Sisters?" This would make the assistant laugh as she went off to find the proper size. While she was gone, Skye put on the shoes that were too small for me and slipped out of the shop. Then I'd make a fuss — the shoes rubbed my heels, my friends had prettier ones, and Mr. Bo would have to apologise charmingly and take me away, leaving a litter of boxes and shoes on the floor. It worked the other way round when I needed shoes, except that he never made the Ugly Sister crack about Skye. I hated him for that because although he said it was a joke I knew what he really thought.

The only time he paid hard cash was when he bought tap-shoes for Skye.

He'd begun to teach us dance steps in the kitchen. "Shuffle," he'd yell above the music, "kick ball-change, turn … come on girls, dance for Daddy."

* * *

The next day Nathan didn't want to go out. His friend came to the door wanting a kick-around but ended up playing on the computer instead. I didn't say anything but I knew he was waiting for Skye.

At the end of the day there was nothing I could do but make his favourite, shepherd's pie, and read Harry Potter to him in bed. I could see his heart wasn't in it.

I wasn't surprised — Skye had been taught unreliability by experts — but I was angry. She'd had a chance to show him that a woman could be as good as Batman and she'd blown it. All he had left was me and I was not the stuff of heroes. What had I done in the past nine years except to keep him warm, fed, healthy and honest? Also, I made him do his homework, which I think he found unforgivable. I thought I was giving him solid gold, because in the end, doing my homework and passing exams were the tools I used to dig myself out of a very deep hole. But how can that compare to the magic conferred upon a boy by ownership of coveted football boots? At his age he thought the right boots would transform his life and give him talents beyond belief. Magic boots for Nathan; dancing shoes for Skye.

* * *

Mr. Bo tried to teach us both to do the splits. Maybe, at eleven or twelve, I was already too stiff. Or maybe, deep down inside, I felt there was something creepy about doing the splits in the snow-white knickers and little short skirts that he insisted we wear to dance for him. Either way, I never managed to learn. But Skye did. She stretched like a spring and bounced like a ball. She wore ribbons in her crazy hair. Of course she got the dancing shoes.

One evening he took us to the bar where Mum worked, put some money in the juke box and Skye showed off what she'd learnt. Mum was so impressed she put out a jam-jar for tips and it was soon full to overflowing.

Now that I have a child of my own I can't help wondering what on earth she was thinking. Maybe she looked at the tip jar and saw a wide-screen TV or a weekend away at a posh hotel with handsome Bo Barnes. Or was she just high on the free drinks? Once, she said to me, "Wanna know somethin', kid? If you're a girl, all you ever got to sell is your youth. Make sure you get a better price for it than I did. Wish someone tol' me that before I gave it all away." Of course she wasn't sober when she said that, but I don't think sobriety had much to do with it; it was her best advice. No wonder I did my homework.

* * *

Skye showed up when Nathan had stopped waiting for her. "C'mon, Kid," she said, "we're going shopping."

"You're smoking." He was shocked.

"So shoot me," she said. "You have dirty hair."

"So shoot me." He grinned his big crooked smile.

"Needs an orthodontist," she said. "I should take him back to L.A."

"Over my dead body," I said. "Nathan, get in the shower. Skye, coffee in the kitchen. Now."

She wrinkled her still-pretty nose at my coffee. I said, "What're you up to? What's the scam?"

"Can't an Auntie take her nephew shopping?" She widened her innocent eyes at me. "'Tis the season and all that malarkey."

"We haven't seen each other in over fifteen years."

"So I missed you."

"No you didn't. How did you find me?"

"Were you hiding?" she asked. "How do you know what I missed? You're my big sister, or have you forgotten?"

"I wasn't the one who swanned off to the States."

"No, you were the one who was jealous."

"I tried to protect you."

"From what? Attention, pretty clothes, guys with nice cars?" I said nothing because I didn't know where to begin.

She stuck her elbows on the table and leant forward with her chin jutting. "It all began with Bobby Barnes, didn't it? You couldn't stand me being his little star."

"He was thirty. You were nine."

"A girl doesn't stay nine forever."

"He ended up in prison and we were sent to a home. He robbed us of our childhood, Skye."

"Some childhood." She snorted. "Stuck in that squalid little apartment — with no TV or anything."

"And how did Mr. Bo change that? Did he stop Mum drinking? Did he go out to work so that she could look after us? Okay, he brought us a flat-screen telly, but it got repossessed like everything else."

"He gave us pretty clothes and shoes …"

"He stole them. He taught us how to steal …"

"But it was fun," Skye cried. "He taught us how to dance too. You're forgetting the good stuff."

"He taught you to dance. He taught me how to be a look-out for a pickpocket and a thief. You weren't a dancer, Skye; you were there to distract the rabbits."

"Why're you two quarrelling?" Nathan said from the doorway.

"We're sisters," Skye said. "If you're good I'll tell you how a pirate came to rescue us from an evil wizard's castle and how your mom didn't want to go and nearly blew it for me."

"No you won't," I said.

"Is it true?" He was as trusting as a puppy.

"Do you really believe in wicked wizards and good pirates?" I asked. "Next you'll be telling him there's no Santa Claus or Tooth Fairy."

"I know there's no tooth fairy," he said. "I caught Mum putting a pound under my pillow and she pretended she'd just found it there, but she's a rubbish liar."

"She is, isn't she? Bet you took the cash anyway. Now let's go shopping."

"I'm coming too," I said, because I didn't know my own sister and I was afraid she might have inherited Mr. Bo's definition of buying shoes.

"You'll spoil it," my loyal son complained. "The only thing she ever takes me shopping for is school uniform."

"What a bitch ... sorry, witch." Skye dragged us both out of the house with no conscience at all.

A big black car, just a couple of feet short of being a limo, was waiting outside — plus a driver with a leather coat and no discernable neck.

* * *

Oddly, Mr. Bo was not sent down for anything serious like contributing to the delinquency of minors or his sick relationship with one of them. No, when he was caught it was for stealing booze from the back of the bar where Mum worked. Of course she was done for theft too, thus ensuring that we had no irresponsible adults in our lives, and forcing us to be taken into Care.

By the time I was fifteen and Skye was thirteen we'd been living in Care for two and a half years. Foster parents weren't keen on me because I didn't want to split up from Skye, and foster mothers didn't like Skye at all because she was precocious in so many ways.

Crockerdown House, known for obvious reasons as Crack House by the locals, was a girls' care home, and judging by the number of non-visits from social workers, doctors or advisors, and the frequency of real visits by the cops, it should've been called a No Care Home. No one checked to see if we went to school or if we came back. Self-harm and eating disorders went unnoticed. Drugs were commonplace. There was a sixty percent pregnancy rate.

I was scared rigid and spent as much time as I could at school. Teachers thought I was keen — most unusual in that part of town — and they cherished me. After a while I became keen.

Skye was the opposite.

It was only when a strange man turned up at the school gates in a car with Skye sitting smug as you please on the back seat that I realised she'd stayed in touch with Mr. Bo while he was inside.

I knew that she and some other, older, girls regularly went to the West End to boost gear from shops and I lived with my heart in my mouth, fearing she'd be caught. She was never caught and she always had plenty of money. What I hadn't been told was that she supplied an old friend of Mr. Bo's with stolen goods which he sold in the market. This friend kept Mr. Bo in tobacco and all the other consumables that could be passed between friends on visiting day.

"He's coming out today," she told me excitedly. "We're going to meet him."

I looked at her in her tight jeans and the trashy silk top which would've cost a fortune if she'd actually bought it. I burst into tears.

"We're not going back to Crack House," she said. "It's over."

"What about school?" I wept. "What about my exams?" I was taking nine subjects and my teachers said I had a good chance in all of them.

"We never have to go to bogging school again. We're free. He's taking us abroad."

"What about Mum?" Mum was still inside. She wasn't just a thief; she was a thief who drank, and she was a bad mother who drank and thieved. Three strikes against her. Only one against Mr. Bo. Classic!

"Oh, she'll join us later," Skye said vaguely, breathing mist onto the car window and drawing a heart.

* * *

"Is this your car?" Nathan asked the driver, impressed. "Huh?"

"It's mine," Skye said, "for now."

"Will you have to give it back?" Nathan was sadly familiar with the concept of giving a favoured book or computer game back to the library.

"Where are we going?" The last time she and I were in a car together was a disaster.

"Crystal City. I heard it was the newest."

"It's the best," Nathan breathed. "We don't go there."

"Why not?"

I said, "It's too expensive and too far away."

"I know, I know," Skye said, "and you got a mortgage to pay and your tuition fees at the Open University. Studying to be a psychotherapist, aren't you? And both your lives gonna stay on hold till you qualify and hang out your shingle. When's that gonna be — 2050?"

"How the hell do you know that?"

"You said 'hell'."

"You'd be surprised what I know. Some of us use technology for more than looking up difficult words."

"You've been spying on us."

"Cool," Nathan said. "I want to be a spy when I grow up."

"You can be a spy now," Skye said. "Don't look back, just use this mirror and if you see a car following us, tell Wayne. Okay?" She handed him what looked like a solid gold compact.

"What sort of car?"

"Black Jeep," no-neck, leather-clad Wayne said, "Licence plate begins Sierra, Charlie, Delta."

"That's SCD to you, kid."

"Clever," I said. "Have you got kids of your own?"

"Do I look like a mother?"

"No need to sound insulted. It's not all bad."

"Coulda fooled me. Do you do all your shopping from Salvation Army counters?"

"Bollocks," I muttered, but not quietly enough.
"You said b ..."
"Okay Nathan," I said. "Haven't you got an important job to do?"
"Of course I looked you up," Skye said. "How the hell else would I find you? You're my big sister—why wouldn't I want to? I didn't know about the kid when I started. And I must say I'm surprised you felt ready to start breeding, given the mom we had. But I guess you were always kinda idealistic— always trying to right wrongs."
"No one's ready," I said.
"Hah! Got caught, did ya?"
That was an incident in my life that I didn't want to share with Skye while Nathan's ears were out on stalks.

Crystal City is five enormous interlocking domes. It's a triumph of consumer architecture and weather-proofing. You could spend your entire life—and savings—in there without breathing one molecule of fresh air.

Wayne dropped us at the main entrance and Nathan, who can smell sports shoes from a distance of three and a half miles, led the way.

Walking with Skye through a shopping centre was strange and familiar. We both looked around in the same way as we used to. Searching for good opportunities, I suppose — only nowadays all I was looking for were half-price sales.

Skye bought football boots, flashy beyond Nathan's wildest dreams. They had ten differently coloured inserts for designer stripes, extra studs and a tool kit. She threw in an England strip for nine-year-olds and paid for everything with a credit card in the name of Skye Rosetti. She caught me looking and said, "I had to marry a Rosetti for the Green Card. But I liked the name so I kept it."

I called on all my nerve and asked, "What happened to Mr. Bo?"

"Oh look, shoes," she cried and flung herself through the door of the fanciest, most minimal shoe shop I'd ever seen.

"Do we have to?" Nathan whined. He wanted to change into his England strip.

"Ungrateful little toad," Skye said cheerfully. "Here kid, take your mom shopping." She handed him a roll of twenty pound notes.

"Wow!" he said.

"No," I said. "Absolutely, no."

"Fuck off," she said. "Have a good time. Meet me at the Food Court on the ground floor in an hour. Don't be late. And kid? I want to see at least one strictly-for-fun gift for your mom. Don't try to scoop it all — I know you guys."

"She said fu ..."

"Nathan," I warned as we walked away, "Grown-ups say stuff. And don't think we're going to spend all that money. You don't want your aunt to think you're greedy, do you?"

"I wouldn't mind."

All kids are wanty — they can't help it. But I love the way he's shocked by swearing. I melt at his piety. He wouldn't believe it if I told him what I was like at his age. And I was the goody-goody one who crawled away from a smashed-up childhood via the schoolyard.

An hour later he had the hoodie jacket he'd wanted for months. He also bought a notebook and the complete range of metallic coloured gel pens. I chose the *Best of Blondie* CD for myself because for some reason I can't listen to Blondie without wanting to dance. There was still a thick wedge of money to give back to Skye.

She was ten minutes late, and when she turned up she was followed by Wayne who was carrying enough bags to fill my spare room from floor to ceiling.

We sat in the octagon-shaped food court which had a carp pool and a fountain at its centre. Wayne took most of the bags back to the car.

Sky said, "C'mon over here, kid, I got something else for you."

"Skye." I held my hand up. "Stop. We have to talk about this. You're putting me in a very awkward position."

"I knew you'd spoil it." Nathan's mutinous lower lip began to shake.

Skye said, "Look at it this way, Sis — how many birthdays have I missed? How many ...?"

"Nine," Nathan interrupted, "and nine plus nine Christmases make, um, eighteen."

"See how smart he is? He's a good kid who goes to school and learns his times tables, and I got a lot of auntying to catch up with. Right, kid?"

"Right."

"But I understand your mom's point of view. She doesn't want me to spoil you. Your mom likes to do things the hard way, see. And I don't want to spoil you either 'cos I think you're perfect the way you are. So here's what we'll do. Do you have a cell phone?"

"We call them mobiles over here," Nathan said bossily. "Mum's got one but it's old and she says we can't afford two."

"I can't afford two sets of bills," I said. "Skye, you would not be doing me a favour if you're thinking of giving him one." I put the roll of twenties we hadn't spent into her hand. "You've been very kind, but rich relations can be too expensive."

She stared at the money in astonishment. Then she closed her hand over it and tucked it safely into her handbag. "Okay, okay. But I've got two phones and they have lots of cool applications. Want to play a game, kid?"

I watched them poring intently over the phones, two curly heads close enough to touch. Nathan's love of technology has been obvious since he first tried to feed his cheese sandwich into the VCR slot, so he didn't take long to master Skye's phone. I kept my mouth shut, but I was proud of him.

Suddenly I was content. I was drinking good coffee and eating a fresh Danish with my clever son and my unfamiliar sister. I was not counting pennies and rationing time. Worry went on holiday.

"Can I go, Mum?" Nathan was tugging my sleeve, his eyes alive with fun.

"What? Where?"

"Just down the end there." Skye pointed to the far end of the mall. "He'll have my phone and be in touch at all times. You don't need to worry."

"I'm Nathan Bond, secret agent."

"I don't know," I began, but exactly then Skye turned her face away from Nathan, towards me and I saw with dismay that she'd begun to cry. So I let him go.

"Gimme a minute." She blotted her eyes on her fur-trimmed cuff. "That's a terrific kid you got there. I guess you musta done something right."

"What happened to you, Skye?"

"Mr. Bo died a year ago. He was shot by some country cops in a convenience store raid. Stupid bastard. I wasn't with him — hadn't been for years — but we kept in touch. That's when I started to look for you. I thought if he was dead, you could forgive me."

"Oh Skye." I took her hand. Just then I heard my son's voice say, "Nathan to HQ — I'm in position. Can you hear me?"

She picked up her phone. "Loud and clear. Commence transmission. You remember how to do that?" She held the phone away from her ear and even in the crowded food court I heard the end of Nathan's indignant squawk. She gave me a watery smile but her voice was steady.

He must have started sending pictures because she forgot about me and stared intently at her little screen. Then she said, "HQ to Nathan — see that tall man in black? He's got a black and red scarf on. Yes. That's the evil doctor Proctor."

"Skye?" I put my hand on her arm but she shook me off, got up and moved a couple of steps away.

I got up too and heard her say, "... to the men's room. Wayne will be there. He'll give you the goods. Can you handle that?"

"No he can't handle that," I shouted, grabbing for the phone. "What're you doing, Skye?"

She twisted out of my grasp. "Let go, stupid, or you'll wreck everything. You'll put your kid in trouble."

I took off, sprinting down the mall, dodging families, crowds, balloons and Santas, cracking my shins on push chairs, bikes and brand new tricycles.

I arrived, out of breath and nearly sobbing with anxiety, at one of the exits. There was no Nathan, no tall man in black, no Wayne. I saw a security uniform and rushed at him. "Have you seen my son? He's wearing the England strip, red and white boots and a black hoodie. He's nine. His name's Nathan." I was jumping up and down. "I think he might've gone into the Gents with a tall man in black and a black and red scarf." Terror gripped the centre of my being. "I don't know where the Gents is."

"Kids do wander off this time of year" the security man said. "Me, I think it's the excitement and the greed. I wouldn't worry. I'll go look for him in the toilets, shall I? You stay here in case he comes back."

But I couldn't wait.

He said tiredly, "Do you know how many kids there are in England strips this season? Wait here; you aren't allowed in the men's facility."

I couldn't wait there either. I pushed in behind him, calling my son's name. There were several boys of various ages — several men too — but no Nathan, no Wayne and no man in black.

"Don't worry," the security man said, although he was himself beginning to look concerned. "I'll call this in. Natty ..."

"Nathan."

"We'll find your boy in no time. Wait here and ..."

But I was off and running back to the food court to find Skye. She had the other phone. She knew where Nathan was.

Except, of course, there was no sign of her.

I found our table. No one had cleared it. Under my seat was the carrier bag containing Nathan's old shoes, his ordinary clothes, his gel pens and my CD. I lifted his sweater to my nose as if I were a bloodhound who could track him by scent alone.

My heart was thudding like heavy metal in my throat. I couldn't swallow.

Sweat dripped off my frozen face.

The most fundamental rule in all the world is to keep your child safe — to protect him from predators. I'd failed. My family history of abuse and neglect was showing itself in my nature too. Whatever made me think I could make a better job of family life than my mother? Neglect was bred into me like brown eyes and mad hair. There could be no salvation for Nathan or me.

* * *

I was fifteen when I lost Skye.

"We'll start again in the Land of Opportunity," said ex-jailbird, Mr. Bo. "But we'll go via the Caribbean where I know a guy who can delete a prison record." Skye sat on his lap, cuddled, with her head tucked under his chin.

"But my exams," I said. "Skye, I'm going to pass in nine subjects. Then I can get a good job and look after us."

"You do that." She barely glanced at me. "I'll stay with Mr. Bo."

"Looks like it's just you and me, kid," he said to her, without even a show of regret.

I was forced to borrow money from Skye for the bus fare back to Crack House. I had a nosebleed on the way and I thought, she'll come back — she won't go without me. But I never saw her again.

* * *

I sat in a stuffy little office amongst that morning's lost property and shivered. They brought me sweet tea in a paper cup.

Skye lent Nathan her sexy phone and I'd watched him excitedly walk away with it. It looked so innocent.

She was my sister but I knew nothing about her except that childhood had so damaged her that she experienced the control and abuse of an older man as an adventure, a love story. Why would she see sending my lovely boy into a public lavatory with a strange man as anything other than expedient? She'd been trained to think that using a child for gain was not only normal but smart.

I was no heroine—I couldn't find him or save him. I was just a desperate mother who could only sit in a stuffy room, drinking tea and beating herself up. My nose started to bleed.

"Hi Mum—did someone hit you?" Nathan stood in the doorway staring at me curiously.

"Car park C, level 5," the security man said triumphantly. "I told you we'd find him. Although what he was doing in the bowels of the earth I'll never know."

"Get off," Nathan said crossly. "You're dripping blood on my England strip."

"Nathan — what happened? Where have you been?"

"Don't screech," he said. "Remember the black Jeep — Sierra, Charlie, Delta? Well, I found it."

"Safe and sound," the security man said, "no harm done, eh? Sign here."

Numbly I signed for Nathan as if he was a missing parcel and we went out into the cold windy weather to find a bus to take us home. There would be no limo this time, but Nathan didn't seem to expect it.

On the bus, in the privacy of the back seat, Nathan said, "That was awesome, Mum. It was like being inside of Xbox. I was, like, the operative except I didn't have a gun but we made him pay for his crime anyway."

"Who? What crime?"

"Doctor Proctor — he hurts boys and gives them bad injections that make them his slaves."

"Do you believe that?" I asked, terrified all over again.

"I thought you knew," he said, ignorant of terror. "Skye said you hated men who hurt children."

"I do," I began carefully. "But I didn't know she was going to put you in danger."

"There hardly wasn't any," said the nine year old superhero. "All I had to do was identify the bad doctor and then go up to him and say, 'I've got what you want. Follow me.' It was easy."

I looked out of the window and used my bed-time voice so that he wouldn't guess how close I was to hysteria. "Then what happened?"

"Then I gave him the hard-drive and he gave me the money."

"The what? Hard …"

"The important bit from the inside of computers where all your secrets go. Didn't you know either? You've got to destroy it. It was the one big mistake the bad doctor made. He thought he'd erased all his secrets by deleting them. Then he sold his computer on eBay but he forgot that deleting secrets isn't good enough if you've got enemies like me and Skye. She's a genius with hard drives."

"I'll remember to destroy mine," I said. "What happened next?"

"You haven't got any secrets, Mum," Nathan Bond said. "After that I gave the money to Skye and hid in the bookshop till she and Wayne went away. Then I followed them."

"What bookshop?" When I ran after Nathan to the end of the mall there had been shops for clothes, cosmetics, shoes and computer games. There had not been a bookshop. I explained this to him. He was thrilled.

"You didn't see me. Nobody saw me," he crowed. "I did what spies do — I went off in the wrong direction and then doubled back to make sure no one was following. You went to the wrong end of the mall."

"Is that what Skye told you to do?"

"No," he said, although his eyes said yes. He turned sulky so I shut up. I was ready to explode but I wanted to hear the full story first.

When the silence was too much for him he said enticingly, "I know about Sierra, Charlie, Delta."

"What about it?" I sounded carefully bored.

"You know I was supposed to look for it but I never saw it? That must've been a test. You know how I know?"

"How do you know?"

"'Cos Skye knew where it was all along. She and Wayne went down to level 5 in the lift, and I ran down the stairs just like they do on telly. You know, Mum, they get it right on telly. It works."

"Sometimes," I said. "Only sometimes."

"Well anyway, there they were — her and Wayne — and they got into the Jeep and the other driver drove them away. I looked everywhere for the limo, but I couldn't find it. I thought maybe it was part of the game — if I found it we could keep it. I wish we had a car."

"We couldn't keep someone else's car." I put my arm round him but he shrugged me off. He was becoming irritable and I could see he was tired. All the same I said, "Describe the man who drove the Jeep."

I was shocked and horrified when he described Mr. Bo. But I wasn't surprised.

* * *

Later that night, when Nathan had been deeply asleep for an hour, I crept into his room and laid his bulging scarlet fur-trimmed stocking at the end of the bed. Then I ran my hand gently under his mattress until I found the shiny new phone. Poor Nathan — he was unpractised in the art of deception, and when he talked about wanting to keep the limo, I saw, flickering at the back of his eyes, the notion that he'd better shut up about the limo or I might guess about the phone. I hoped it wasn't stolen the way the limo and Jeep almost certainly were.

I rang the number Skye gave him. I didn't really expect her to answer, but she did.

"Hi, kid," she said. Her voice sounded affectionate.

"It's not Nathan. Skye, how could you put him at risk? You're his only living relative apart from me."

"Did he have a good time? Did his little eyes sparkle? Yes or no?"

"If you wanted him to have fun, Skye, you could've taken him to the fun-fair. Don't tell me this was about anything other than skinning a rabbit."

"Well, as usual, you've missed the point. It was about making a stone bastard pay for what he'd done. Nathan was the perfect lure. He looked just like what the doctor ordered. And he's smart."

"If I see you anywhere near him again I'll call the cops on you —

you and Mr. Bo. You're right Nathan is smart. He followed you too." That shut her up—for a few seconds.

Then she said, "Tell me, Sis, what present did you buy yourself with my money?"

She'd probably looked in the bag when I went running after Nathan so there was no point in lying. I said, "A CD — The Best of Blondie. What's so funny?"

She stopped laughing and said, "That was Mr. Bo's favourite band. He taught us to dance to Blondie numbers."

I was struck dumb. How could I have forgotten?

"Don't worry about it, Sis," Skye said cheerfully. "On evidence like that, if you never qualify, and you never get to hang out your shingle, you can comfort yourself by knowing you'd have made a lousy psychotherapist. Oh, and Happy Holidays." She hung up.

Eventually I dried my eyes and went to the kitchen for a glass of wine. I sipped it slowly while I opened my books and turned on the computer. I will be a great psychotherapist — I can learn from the past.

Lastly I put my new CD on the hi-fi. It still made me want to dance. Mr. Bo can't spoil everything I love.

A Battlefield Reunion
by Brendan DuBois

I'm afraid I can't remember the first time I met Doug Greene, but I do remember the first time he made an impact on me. It was probably at the Bouchercon World Mystery Convention in Milwaukee in 1999, when we chatted, and I remember a smiling bear of a man, who had great enthusiasm for short stories.

As the proverbial red-headed stepchild, short stories don't really get that much respect. But Doug was an enthusiast of short fiction, and I was impressed — and even honored — to know that he had read my stories.

Then, he tossed a happy grenade in my direction: how would I like his publisher, Crippen & Landru, to put a collection of my best mystery short stories?

Um, yeah, who wouldn't?

I confess I didn't know that much about Crippen & Landru, but in talking to other authors and booksellers at Bouchercon, I quickly learned that Crippen & Landru published anthologies of high quality and caliber, and that it was quite the honor to be asked to have them collect your stories.

Over the next months, dealing with Doug was a joy, and I was also found it fun to learn that in every Crippen & Landru anthology, a hangman's noose is hidden somewhere on the cover.

So when my cover arrived in the mail, I spent a joyful number of minutes studying the cover, until it finally appeared to me. Go online and see if you can find it!

This anthology was published in 2002. As of now, I've had nearly 30 novels and collections published, but I'm still so very proud of what Doug did for me, my very first short story collection.

My potential client was waiting for me at the entrance to the MTA station in Scollay Square in Boston, pretty much fitting the description he had given me over the phone: mid-twenties, skinny, black hair, wearing a black suit, white shirt and black tie. But skinny didn't cover it, the poor guy looked like he hadn't eaten in a month. He had bulging eyes behind round-rimmed glasses, ears that looked like smooth scallop shells attached to his skull, and his black hair had streaks of white in it.

I went up to him and said, "Ronny Silver?"

He licked his lips, like I was a Boston cop, rousting him for doing something naughty in Scollay Square, where lots of naughty things were available for a cost. "Yes, yes, that's me," he said, holding out a hand. "And you're Billy Sullivan?"

"Yep," I said, giving him a shake. His hand felt like dry tree branches covered with old leather. "Want to head over to my office?"

"That'd be fine, thank you," he said.

It was a Friday night, nine months after the surrender documents were signed in Tokyo Bay aboard the U.S.S. *Missouri*, and there were still lots of guys in Army, Navy, Air Corps and Marine uniforms in the area, ready to raise healthy amounts of hell without worrying they'd get blown up or burnt or shot down in the months and years ahead. There were buses, taxis and trucks crowding the streets, and the noise of the bars and burlesque houses bounced around the brick walls of the near buildings and made talking and listening challenging.

Ronny kept track with me as we walked the block to my office, and I kept track of him as well. He seemed jumpy, eyes flickering around, head scanning, and I knew from personal experience where he had come from. As we approached the crosswalk there was a loud "bang!" as a truck up the street backfired, and Ronny nearly dove to the asphalt, with me right behind me.

I caught his eye. "Hard to shake it off, eh?"

Ronny said, "Yeah," and that was it.

At my building I opened the wooden door that led to a small foyer, and then upstairs, the stairs creaking under our footfalls. At the top of the stairs a narrow hallway led off, three doors on each side, each door with a half-frame of frosted glass. Mine said B. SULLIVAN, INVESTIGATIONS, and two of the windows down the hallway were blank. The other three announced an attorney, a piano teacher, and a press agent.

I unlocked the door and flicked on the light and walked in. There was an old oak desk in the center with my chair, a Remington typewriter on a stand, and two solid wood filing cabinets with locks. In front of the desk were two wooden chairs, and I motioned my guest to the nearest one. A single window that hadn't been washed since the Roaring Twenties overlooked the square and its flickering neon lights. It was stuffy in the office so I opened the window just a crack, to let in some of Boston's alleged fresh air.

I hung my fedora and suit jacket on a coat rack, and went around my desk and sat down. My prospective client said, "I thought all guys like you... you know, carried a gun in a shoulder holster. Or like that."

I stretched out in my chair. "A gat? Heater? Roscoe? No, had my full of weapons when I served. Don't particularly like them."

"Where did you serve, then?"

I took a pad of paper from underneath some unpaid bills, slid open the top drawer of my desk and removed a fountain pen. "Here and there. England at first, then France, Belgium... Germany eventually. I was in the Military Police."

"Oh," he said. "Snowdrops, right?"

I uncapped the pen, ignoring the nickname he just mentioned, a nickname all of us MPs hated. "And you?"

"Sicily, Italy, France... Germany. I was in the 45th Infantry Division. Typical G.I. Joe, you know?"

Holy crap. "A tough slog."

"You got it, brother."

He looked around, eyes flickering, and I felt a stab of sympathy mixed with shame. Sympathy for what he had gone through, fighting through landing beaches, mountains, trails, forests, swamps, villages, fields and across three nations... where nearly every second exposed you to a mine, a sniper's bullet, an 88-mm German artillery shell, or a strafing Luftwaffe fighter. No wonder he was one jumpy son-of-a-gun. And I felt shame as well, for while we had both worn the same uniforms, I had been one of those REMFs (real echelon mother-fill-in-the-blank), doing a cop's job in an Army uniform, where I was mostly stuck behind the front lines, rarely ever finding myself in danger.

"Let's get to it," I said. "How did you find my name?"

Sounds like a dumb question, but it's good to know where a potential client is coming from. A recommendation from a Boston cop? One of my old neighbors in Southie? A tip from a bail bondsman?

Ronny shrugged. "*Yellow Pages.* I'm not from Boston, don't really know anybody, and I thought I'd just go through the phone book."

"Good idea," I said. "But 'S' is pretty far along in the alphabet."

A ghost of a smile. "I know. I figured the guys in the front of the alphabet would get all the business. So I started at the rear. The guy named Yellen never answered his phone. A guy named Tucker was out of business. And so I came up to you."

My turn to smile. "Glad it worked out." I scribbled his name on the top of the paper pad, and said, "All right, then. What can I do for you, Mister Silver?"

He rubbed the palms of his hands on top of his pant legs. "I'm looking for someone. I want you to find him."

"Who is he?"

"Craig Ledder. He was a war correspondent with the *Chicago Tribune*. He was attached to my company and rode with us during the last couple of months of the war... A good guy."

"Okay. A good guy. Do you know where he might be?"

"Somewhere around here," Ray said. "I... saw him getting off a train at South Station. He walked right past me. I called out his name... but he moved into a crowd of folks, and that's the last I saw of him."

"Do you know what train he was on?"

"No."

"Could it have been one of the Boston Elevated trolleys?"

"I... I don't know."

I wrote some more. "When did this happen?"

"Last Wednesday." Today was Monday, so that was five days ago.

"Do you remember the time?"

"Yes... it sounds funny but I was at South Station and I was checking my watch. It always runs fast. The big clock there said it was 8:05 in the morning."

"Why do you want to find him? Does he owe you money? Did he steal your socks or Hershey bars while out on the front?"

A quick shake of the head. "No, no, nothing like that. You see, he stuck with us, for weeks on end. Other times, we had newsies drop in for a couple of days, to get a feel or taste of what was going on, and then they'd go back to the rear, get drunk and laid in Paris, and leave us be. But not Craig. He stayed with us through the shelling, the snow, the rains. He ate our rations, he got the shits and trench foot like we did... he was practically one of us."

"I see."

"He also took a lot of photos. He had this small camera... pretty pricey piece of equipment, I'm sure... and he told us, 'Boys, when this is all over, I'll make sure I send you copies of all these pix.' He even wrote down our names and addresses in his notebook."

I scribbled some more. "But you never got the photos, am I right? Is that why you're looking for him?"

"Yeah," he said. "I know it sounds crazy and all that, but it's been a year now. My memories... I still got memories. Bad and good. But I want to remember the good... the guys in my squad, my platoon, and a lot who didn't make it back. Their bodies are still over there… and I'm starting to forget what their faces looked like. You know? I don't want to forget them, not ever… and those photos…"

He paused, swallowed. "Crazy, hunh?"

"Not on your life," I said. "Look, can I get you a drink? Coffee? Tea?"

Ronny's voice was hopeful. "Anything stronger?"

I got up from my chair. "No, nothing stronger."

"Oh." The disappointment in his voice was real. "Coffee, I guess."

"Be right back," I said, ducking through a curtain off to the side of my office. Beyond the curtain was a small room with a bed, radio, easy chair, table lamp, and icebox. A closed door led to a small bathroom that most days had plenty of hot water. I filled up a kettle with water from the bathroom, set it on a hotplate, and switched it on. I rummaged around a crowded shelf and came down with some sugar packets and Nescafe instant coffee. I made two trips back to my desk, remember to bring along a small bottle of cream from my icebox.

He took the cup in both hands and gingerly sipped at it. "Thanks. Always thought the height of luxury was drinking your coffee from a cup made of china, instead of a steel mess kit, and sitting in a real chair, and not with your ass in mud."

"Sounds right to me," I said.

With the open window I heard a loud bellow of laughter, followed by some young women laughing as well. Hands shaking, Ronny put his coffee cup back down on my desk.

"Are you listening to that?" he asked.

"Hard not to," I said.

Ronny blinked his eyes, looked again at the open window. "Not even a year later, and they're forgetting, every day. All they care about is the end of rationing, getting raises at their jobs, and putting that war in their rearview mirror. All the sacrifices, all the blood, all the tortures… forgotten."

I sipped from my cup. "I don't think so, Ronny." A brief, painful thought of my older brother Paul, dead at Bastogne. "A lot of us still remember."

"But not enough," he said. "It's about the A-bomb, new electric appliances, and those V-2 rocket tests in New Mexico. The future, the future, all hail the glorious future, built on the corpses of millions."

It was starting to make sense. "That's why getting those photos are important to you, right?"

He raised his cup. "That's right. I… every month, every year that will come up, more and more folks will forget. I won't let that happen, Mister Sullivan. I won't. Can you help me?"

My first instinct was to say yes, but I wanted to know more. "You said this Craig Ledder wrote for the *Chicago Tribune*. Did you try to get in contact with him after the war?"

"Oh, yes, I certainly did," he said. "I wrote a few letters that were never answered, and once I even made a phone call. Some guy in a hurry said that Craig had quit the newspaper in the summer of 1945, and that's all he could tell me. Then he hung up."

"Unh-hunh." I put my coffee cup down, picked up my fountain pen. "Ronny, you said you're not from Boston. Where are you from, then?"

"Philadelphia."

"Long way from home."

He stiffened up and I knew I had struck him somehow.

"That's right," he said, after several seconds.

"What brings you to Boston?"

A few more seconds passed. "Does that matter?"

I was quick. "You bet it does."

He wiped his hands again on the legs of his trousers. "I... I had a hospital appointment."

"Where?" I asked. "Peter Bent Brigham? Mass General? Beth Israel? New England Deaconess?"

No reply. I stared at him for just a moment, and then it came to me.

"McLean Hospital?" I asked. "In Belmont, right?"

A quick nod, like even saying a word would push him over the edge.

"I see."

He cleared his throat. "Yeah. The looney bin, am I right?"

I spoke carefully. "A psychiatric hospital," I said. "Nothing to be ashamed about."

"Ashamed?" he said sharply. "You think I'm ashamed?"

Oops. "No, it's just that, well, there's a stigma, and if you need help..."

He leaned forward, clasping his hands together. "During the day I can get along, you know? Though I don't like loud noises, and I really, really don't like trains. But it's night.... That's the worst. The nightmares. You're not just dreaming, you're actually back there again, like you're using a damn time machine. You can feel the cold. Hear the gunfire, the shellfire. The blows hitting you, over and over again... the sheer... hopelessness, knowing you were doomed, would never get out alive. Those damn dreams... do you get dreams, Mister Sullivan, do you?"

My pen hesitated. I remember a young American soldier, brown hair, caught during the Battle of the Bulge. I had been called away from my regular duties to help empty ambulances as they growled in from the front lines, and he was on a canvas stretcher that me and three other MPs took out to bring him into a large tent marking a field hospital. The ground was a mush of snow and mud, tore up by the jeeps and ambulances, and a heavy sleet was falling. He had a bloody bandage wrapped around the top of his head, and he kept on repeating a street address in Spokane, over and over again, asking us to contact his grandmother. The first nurse to see him lifted up the bandage and said, "Sweet Mother of God, I can see his goddamn brain."

But the boy hadn't heard her. Over and over again, over and over again, he repeated the Spokane address of his grandmother...

I resumed scribbling. "No," I said. "I've been lucky. No dreams."

I looked up at him and he had a look of anticipating disappointment, and I said, "Ronny, I'll take your case. I'll find this Craig Ledder, see what he's up to, and if we're very lucky, maybe he still has the negatives of the photos he promised you."

He grinned. On his skinny and scared face, it looked pathetic. "That's great, Mister Sullivan, that's great."

"Not great until I find him," I said. "What does he look like?"

I took careful notes as Ronny went on: nearly six feet, bulky, short blond hair, blue eyes, small ears, with a short scar on his left cheek.

"Sounds good," I said.

Ronny said, "How much do I owe you?"

I waved a hand. "Vet discount. We'll settle up when we're done, all right?"

"Sure, sure," he said.

"Oh... and how can I get a hold of you?"

"At the McLean. You see... we're allowed off the campus if the doctor thinks we won't harm ourselves."

"Good," I said. "Tell me, are they helping you?"

A shy smile. "Not a goddamn bit."

About fifteen minutes after my client left, I opened my eyes, leaned forward and picked up my phone, and got the long distance operator. The call would be pricey but would be a good start to what I hoped would be a quick and simple case.

I looked over my notes when the phone rang. The operator said, "Your call is going through, sir."

"Thank you, operator."

There was static on the line and the sound of the phone ringing was faint. Nearly a thousand miles away. It was picked up on the first ring.

"*Chicago Tribune*, where can I direct your call?"

"Newsroom, please."

"Which part?"

Damn good question. "Ah, your foreign desk. Or overseas. Whichever fits."

"Hold, please," she said, and there was another, louder hiss of static, and I tried not to think of the long distance bill I would pay next month with each pricey second slipping away.

"Overseas, Cynewski," came a gravelly voice.

"Hello," I said. "This is William Sullivan, calling long distance from Boston."

"Yeah?"

"I'm trying to locate a foreign correspondent of yours, name of Craig Ledder."

"He doesn't work here no more."

"I know that, but I was hoping I could locate a family member of ---"

"Christ, pal, we've got a newspaper to run."

Click, which considerably cut my long distance bill but which otherwise didn't help me.

The next day I moved around a lot, starting with the Boston Public Library, located on Copley Square and built in 1895 in a supposedly great Italian Renaissance Style. Since the closest I've ever been to Italy was the towns and battlefields of France, Belgium, and Germany, I'd have to take their word on it.

In a reference room at the library, I spent a few minutes thumbing through a thick Chicago phone book published by Illinois Bell. The room was cool, dusty, and filled with phone books and directories from cities in all forty-eight states. In the 'L' section, I noted only six Ledders in the Chicago area. Doable. I checked the Philadelphia phone book from Bell Pennsylvania. The number of Silvers exceeded six pages. Not doable.

After putting the Chicago and Philadelphia phone books back in their places, I looked around. I was still alone. I went over to the New England Telephone book for Boston, and took down the volume for 1943. A waste of time and effort, shouldn't look at old ghosts, but my hand seemed to act by itself as I pulled down the thick and battered volume, and flipped through the thin pages, stopping at the Sullivan page. Like in Philadelphia, pages and pages of Sullivans.

My finger stopped at the tiny print marking SULLIVAN, Paul X., 52 L Street, S. Boston.

My older brother. My finger rubbed at the small print. Dead in Bastogne at about the same time I was helping bring in stretcher cases during that bitterly cold December 1944.

I closed the book, tossed it back in its place.

Armed with rows of nickels, I grab a payphone on Copley Square and start making long distance phone calls to Chicago, and strike out like last year's Red Sox pitching staff. Made call after call to Chicago, and none paid off. No one on the phone nearly a thousand miles away had ever heard of a Craig Ledder.

With my last roll of nickels gone, I flagged down a Yellow Cab.

"Newspaper Row," I said, and with a grunt, he flipped down the meter flag.

A few minutes later I exited the hackney on a crowded stretch of Washington Street, also known in this town as Newspaper Row. Within one block were the offices of the *Boston Post*, the *Boston American*, and my destination for today, *The Boston Globe*. After passing through the lobby I found my way to the newsroom, crowded with desks and chairs on a wooden slat floor. There was a low steady roar of men talking, phones ringing and the chatter of teletype machines in one corner, spewing out copies from the Associated Press, United Press, and INS. There was a haze of blue smoke up by the ceiling from cigars and cigarettes, and I weaved my way through the desks, stopping at a familiar place.

Don Burnett glanced up at me, gestured to a battered, empty chair. "Hey, look who's here," he said. "My favorite private dick, Billy from Southie. How's it hanging?"

"It does, here and there," I said, sitting down. Don was my age, but skinny with brown hair, thin Clark Gable-style moustache and thick round-rimmed glasses. Those glasses and a bad ticker kept him out of the war, and when he had been drinking some, would always bitterly complain that his 4-F status had kept him out of the greatest story of our generation.

I'd always change the subject, thinking about a lot of things, including that hospital tent that December, and the cleared area at the side of the tent where bodies of American soldiers were being stacked up like logs, wondering at the time if my older brother Paul might be there in that bloody pile.

He had on a faded white shirt, black slacks and a black necktie. "I'm looking for some information, was hoping you could help," I said.

From his messy desk, from city directories to competing newspapers and stacks of tan-colored reporter's notebooks, Don managed to pull out a slip of paper, fold it over, and said, "Okay, shoot."

"You don't want to know what it is first?" I asked.

He frowned slightly. "The beach off L Street, summer of 1940. I don't have to say any more, am I right?"

Yeah, he was right. He had been swimming when a stitch cut into his side --- dummy hadn't waited a half-hour after eating to go into the water --- and I had dragged him in before he had drowned.

So I said, "No, you don't, and I appreciate it. Okay. This one should be pretty easy, should just take a phone call or two."

"Unh-hunh," he said. "Go on."

"I'm looking for a guy named Craig Ledder," I said. "He was a foreign correspondent for the *Chicago Tribune* during the war. Looks like he quit work sometime after VE Day. I got a client who was a buddy of his overseas. This Ledder character promised him some photos that were taken during those last months."

Don wrote a few notes. "Some promise. Your client should know better than to trust reporters or photographers. Is your client in Boston?"

"Yep."

"And this Craig Ledder?"

"My guy saw him at South Station. My client tried to get his attention, but the station was crowded and he faded away."

"Unh-hunh," Don said. "Any one of you two bright boys think of calling the Trib and see what's up?"

"Gee, what a suggestion," I said. "No wonder you're a reporter, a real nose for news. Yeah, my client called and I've called as well. Pretty much got hung up on."

Don rubbed the end of his fountain pen against his brown moustache. "You want me to work some phone magic? That's going to be a bit pricey. Long distance, of course."

I shrugged. "I'll make you whole. Or get you lunch at Locke-Ober's, whichever one is cheaper."

"Yeah." He picked up his phone, dialed a single number. "Shirley, sweetie, it's Don up in the newsroom. Will you set up a person-to-person call to... Dave Wendell, *Chicago Tribune* newspaper, Chicago. Yeah, Dave Wendell. Thanks, sweetie...."

He hung up the phone with a clatter, tossed his pen on the crowded desk. "Dave Wendell used to work here until he got a hankering to see Lake Michigan. Setting up the call will take about ten minutes or so. You got anything you want to talk about?"

"Not really," I said.

On his desk he pulled out a copy of that day's *Globe*. "Here. Go find a corner and educate yourself, and then come back in ten minutes, I'll see what I have to share."

I took the newspaper, glanced at the headlines --- about an A-bomb test in the Pacific called "Operation Crossroads", a threatened national railway strike, and some mess involving Acting Mayor John Kerrigan. I put the paper down on an unoccupied desk and wandered around, noting some framed front pages hanging from the walls and pillars holding up the ceiling, including the ones marking VE Day and VJ Day. I stopped in front of one noting the Battle of the Bulge, the tens of thousands of American casualties.

Another memory popped up, like a fishing bob coming up in the harbor water. I was back at that tent, later moving bodies along, and an Army surgeon, smoking a Camel with shaking hands, wearing a bloody white smock over his fatigues, noted two infantrymen, as me and a guy named Cooke struggled to put them into canvas body bags. "See where those fellas were shot? Right in the back of the head. Close-range. Meant those goddamn Nazis took 'em as prisoners and executed them."

I went back to Don's desk and sat down. "You're early," he said.

"Got a lousy track of time."

"I guess," he said. "How's your ma?"

"Hanging in there," I said. "She still wants to think Paul's coming home... still has a shrine built to him on the mantelpiece, all his photos from the Army and his high school track ribbons. He was always... well, he was popular."

"Hard to be the not-so-popular brother," he said.

"Hey, you dating anyone?" I asked.

Don looked surprised at the change of subject. "Um, no."

"Gee, I wonder why, considering you have such a warm and inviting personality."

His face reddened. "Dick."

"Jerk."

The phone rang before we escalated, and he snapped it up. "Burnett, newsroom."

He stayed silent, "Well, hello Dave, how's things in the hog butcher capital of the world?" Don smiled, said, "Unh-hunh, unh-hunh, well, I'll bet you a sawbuck that the Red Sox are gonna be ahead of your White Sox come September... okay. Hey, this call is costing a lot of money, so here it is. Looking for info on a foreign correspondent of yours." Don glanced down at his handwriting. "Name of Craig Ledder. Seems to have quit last summer, right after the Krauts raised up the white flag. Unh-hunh. Unh-hunh. Well, any relations in the area? Any forwarding address? All right...."

Don rubbed at his eyes with his free hand. "That's good to know. Hey, want some advice then? Hunh? This year, root for the Cubs... hah! Later, Dave."

He hung up the phone. "Remember, you owe me for the call."

"Haven't forgotten it yet."

"Okay, here's the deal. Your guy Craig worked for the *Trib*, was in the ETO for nearly a year, and on May 8th --- VE Day --- he sent a telex back to Chicago. Saying 'to hell with you and to hell with the human race.' His severance pay was sent to an Army post office in occupied Munich. No other info, no relatives in the area, and that's all she wrote."

"Damn."

"Yeah."

I got up from his desk, offered my hand, which he shook. "Locke-Ober's, right?"

"How about the Union Oyster House?"

"How about go to hell? You know I hate seafood."

"Later, Don."

"Best to your mom, Billy."

The next day I got up earlier than usual and took a cab to South Station, the major railway hub for this part of the city, just above my old neighborhood of South Boston. Among the railroads it served was the Old Colony Railroad and the New York, New Haven and Hartford Railroad, and it was also a destination for the Boston Elevated. The building was huge, with three stories of windows and Roman-styled pillars. In my child's memory, the place looked odd, with the Atlantic Avenue Elevated Line having been torn down some years back.

At the top of the building was a huge clock, marking the time. It was 7:50 a.m., and commuters from the towns and cities to the south of Boston were already streaming out, and Yellow Cabs were lined up to take the well-paid to their jobs.

I waited at the main entranceway, watching the laughing men and women exit, the women wearing their finest and makeup after years of clothing rationing. It was good to see. Maybe winning the war was worth something after all. I made sure my watch was synchronized to the large clock above the entrance, and waited.

And waited.

And at 8:05 a.m., there he was. Strolling self-assuredly through the crowds, description matching just like Ronny had said. Nearly six feet tall, well-built, short blonde hair and small ears, scar on his cheek, snappily dressed in a dark gray suit, light yellow shirt and blue necktie. He walked past me and I kept my mouth shut, and I started walking behind him.

One-man tails are tough, especially if the someone you're tailing is spooky or suspicious. You have to duck in and out, learn to strip off your hat and necktie, muss up your hair, try to look like a different guy for the benefit of whoever you were following. But Craig acted like he was on the side of the angels, and he joined a stream of people going down D Street. He ducked into a diner at D Street and Fargo Street, came out with a cardboard cup of coffee and a small brown paper bag. I tailed him down Fargo Street, until he walked into a watch and jewelry store: BRONSTEIN FINE JEWELS. I hung outside for a few minutes, and then went into the store. Lots of glass cases, lots of displays, and there were window displays on one side that showed the work areas. Craig Ledder was back there, wearing a white chest-sized apron, with glasses on his face with those kind of optics that let you work on fine watches.

There was a young man who seemed to be running the show, with a thin beard and wearing a plain black yarmulke on the rear of his head. I showed him my professional identification and asked to see the owner.

Mister Bronstein came out from a rear office a couple of minutes later, a worried look on his face. He was an older version of the young man who had helped me earlier, and wore black slacks and a white shirt, rolled up on his thick arms.

"Yes?" he asked.

I smiled and said, "Purely routine, Mister Bronstein. I'm doing a background check on an employee of yours, Craig Ledder. He's in the process of purchasing a rather large life insurance policy, and there's just a few things I'm looking for."

At the mention of the word "routine," he visibly relaxed, and I had a brief and clear conversation with him. Craig Ledder had been working for him for about six months. One of his best. Quiet and kept to himself. No problems. One of the first in, and one of the last out. Hadn't even taken a sick day. Lived somewhere in Dorchester. Anything else?

He rubbed at his thick beard. "Oy, I'm sure he was in the war, though he won't talk about it. One day there was a construction accident down the street, a large cement block fell to the ground. Sounded like a bomb went off. And Craig, poor fellow, was underneath one of the counters."

I shook his hand and thanked him, and I said, "If you don't mind, can you keep this confidential?"

"Absolutely," he said. "You can rely on me. I'd hate to see him leave... in fact, I wish I had three more of him."

Back at my office, Ronny Silver was standing outside in the hallway. There was the sound of a typewriter being hammered from the press agent, and the tinkling of a piano from the music teacher. He was shifting from one leg to another, like he was looking for permission to pee.

"Well?" he demanded. "What have you found? What's going on?"

My first thought at seeing him was going to invite him back into my office, talk him out, maybe give him another cup of coffee, but I didn't like the buzz I was getting from him. He had been a bundle of nerves when we had first met; now he looked like he was ready to explode.

"It's just the beginning," I said. "I'll let you know when I'm finished."

"What? Won't you give me a... like a status report? What you've found so far?"

"Nope," I said. "That's not how I work. When I'm done, I'll write up a report, and you'll get it. Not before then."

His fists clenched and I automatically tensed up. Hard to believe, I really thought the skinny little bugger was going to throw himself on me.

"That's not fair."

I stepped around him, made sure I kept him in view as I unlocked my door. "Probably not," I said. "And if you don't like it, you can find another P.I. That won't keep me up at night."

I got into my office, made a point of shutting the door. From the hallway lights I could see his shadow on the other side of the frosted door glass, and he stood there for a bit, and then walked away.

I felt better after that.

The next day I did some surveillance work for some clown who thought his wife was cheating on him --- she was, and she was doing it with the guy's younger brother, which was going to make family get-togethers interesting later this year --- and then went back to my office. It was a cold, windy day for May, and I was getting ready to head out for my big job of the day, when something came to mind.

I picked up the Boston phone book, looked up a number, and gave it a quick dial.

"McLean Hospital," a woman's voice said.

"Admissions, please."

A click-clunk, hiss of static, and an older woman's voice. "Admissions, Miss Turner."

"Good afternoon, Miss Turner," I said, making my voice a bit deeper and more authoritative. "This is Ralph Sweeney, Boston office of the Veterans Administration."

"Hello, Mister Sweeney," she said. Not to be rude, but she sounded like a close-fisted battleaxe who liked her little bit of power and wouldn't take any pushing around.

"Miss Turner, I know how incredibly busy you must be, especially after the war's end, so I won't waste your time," I said, l laying it on pretty thick. "We have a bit of a records snafu on our end, and I just want to verify that a Mister Ronald Silver ---" and I ruffled a sheet of paper in front of the phone --- "of Philadelphia is a patient at your facility. We want to make sure that the McLean is promptly compensated for your most excellent service."

"Hold on, Mister Sweeney." Her voice had lightened just a bit, which seemed like a big goddamn victory. A clunk of the phone receiver on her desk, and I even could make out the sound of a filing cabinet drawer being opened and closed.

The receiver was picked up. "Mister Sweeney?"

"Yes?"

"That's correct," she said. "Former Private Ronald Silver, of Philadelphia. He's an out-patient here, referred from the Friends Hospital there."

"I see," I said, twirling my fountain pen in my hand. "You've been quite helpful. He served with the 45th Infantry Division, correct?"

And then it got very interesting and I stopped playing with my pen.

"No, I'm afraid not," she said. "The paperwork here says he was with the 99th Infantry Division. Not the 45th."

"Are you sure?"

A frosty tone returned. "I'm in charge of admissions, Mister Sweeney. I'm positive."

I knew I only had a few more seconds before she'd either hang up on me or ask some very embarrassing questions, and I said, "The 99th... that was in France, right?"

A labored sigh. "Oh, I don't know... it says here he was in Belgium, and then spent six months in Germany."

"In Germany? As part of the occupation forces?"

"No," she said. "As a prisoner of war."

Later that afternoon I was back near my home turf, trailing Craig Ledder as he emerged from BRONSTEIN FINE JEWELS and made his way back to South Station. At the entrance to the large terminal building, there was a row of men, holding up signs from The Brotherhood of Locomotive Engineers, warning of an upcoming national strike if their demands weren't met. Two men in front of me said something nasty and the other said, "I froze my ass off, riding in B-29s over Tokyo, so these cushy bastards can get a raise? Jesus!"

And the other said, "Truman should draft their sorry butts into the Army, make 'em keep the trains running."

I followed Craig and saw him bundle himself onto an electric trolley. A sign on the train said DORCHESTER. From my keen investigative abilities, that's where I determined he was going.

Dorchester is a neighborhood to the south of Boston, located right next to the city of Quincy, famed for being the hometown of John Adams, second president of the United States and the Fore River Shipyard, which turned out a lot of ships for the Navy during the war, including the battleship U.S.S. Massachusetts and the aircraft carrier U.S.S Hancock.

Ledder lived in a small gray apartment building about two blocks away from the station, and I kept my eye on him as he stopped at a corner grocery store and left a few minutes later with a paper sack. The apartment building was across the street and he lived on the ground floor. It looked like there were three other apartments there --- one on the first floor, and two upstairs, accessible by a set of side stairs.

I gave him a couple of minutes to get settled, and then I went across the street and knocked on the door.

He opened the door, wiping his hands on a dishtowel. He had taken off his necktie, hat and coat, and looked curious, unafraid. "Yes?"

"Mister Ledder? Craig Ledder?"

"Yep, that's me," he said. "What's going on?"

I showed him my Massachusetts private investigator license, and he gave out a low whistle. "Wow. A real private eye." He lifted his gaze from my hand and said, "What are you investigating?"

"Well… you."

That made him laugh. "Really? Why's that?"

"Look, it'll take just a few minutes," I said. "Mind if I come in?"

He shrugged. "Why not? Come on in."

The apartment was small but clean and tidy. There was a small kitchen at the rear, a large living room with couch, coffee table, two easy chairs and a large RCA radio, playing big band music. On the coffee table were carefully piled copies of *The Boston Post*, next to a pile of *Life* magazines, next to a pile of *Time* magazines. In the center of the table was a clean crystal ashtray, with a pack of Chesterfields and a Zippo lighter next to it. He took the couch and I took the chair, and removed my fedora, put it on my lap.

"Mister Ledder, I'll make this as quick as possible," I said.

"Sure," he said. "Look, do I know you?"

"No, but I've been hired by someone who does, and who's looking to find you." I said. "An Army vet who said you were with his unit during the war, back when you were a newspaper reporter."

"Yeah, right," he said, crossing his leg. "*The Trib*. A while ago. Why does he want to find me?"

"He says you promised to send him ---"

" --- photos of him and his buddies when the war was over," Ledder said, grimacing. "Yeah, yeah." He sighed and settled in the couch and suddenly looked ten years older, running a hand across his face. "You know, I did promise a bunch of dogfaces that I'd do that. Even took down their names and addresses... and, well, the end came. And I looked at the blasted cities and the dead American kids and the piles of bodies and the smoke and the death... I had too much of it. Way too much of it."

Another big sigh, and he rubbed his hands together. "Sent a nasty telex back to the Colonel, saying I no longer wanted to work for the world's greatest newspaper, and that was that. Dumped my notebooks, my camera, bummed around southern France for a while, and then came back to the States."

"Why Boston?"

"Why not? Got a cheap liner ticket from Brest to Boston, decided I liked it when I got here, and I got a job."

"At the jewelry store, right?"

His eyes widened. "My, you really have been poking around."

"Just my job, sorry," I said. "How did you end up at the jewelry store?"

"Worked at a store in Cleveland where I grew up, after school." He smiled, rubbed the armrest of his couch. "It sounds strange, but after a couple of years attached to various Army units, living in shit and mud, eating their rations, avoiding getting shot up and shelled...

I needed something relaxing, soothing." Ledder's smile grew wider. "The store is the perfect place. Everything is right at your hand. A very narrow and peaceful place. And when your day is done, you leave, feeling satisfied that you've fixed a watch, or repaired a ring."

"Don't you miss newspaper work?"

A firm shake of the head. "Nope. Damn, look at Ernie Pyle. He should have done what I did, walk out when the war in Europe was over. Instead, the damn fool went to the Pacific and got a Jap sniper bullet drilled into his head for his troubles."

Ledder leaned over, picked up the Chesterfields and the Zippo. He offered me the pack, and I declined. He took a cigarette out, quickly lit it and I stood up, catching the sign. "Mister Ledder, sorry to disturb you. I appreciate you letting me in."

He stood up, extended a free hand, which I shook. "Not a problem. Hey, what's this vet's name? Wonder if I can remember him."

"Sorry," I said. "Client confidentiality, and all that."

"Ah, I see."

He led me out and took a deep puff on his cigarette, and something odd had happened.

Something odd.

I tried to think about it when the door shut behind me, but I was distracted when I got out onto the sidewalk, meeting up with Ronny Silver.

Who stood there, a nickel-plated semi-automatic pistol in his right hand.

I swallowed. "Hey, Ronny."

"He's in there, isn't he," Ronny demanded. His face was flushed and sweaty, his white shirt soaked through, and his legs were trembling. But the hand holding the pistol was rock-steady.

"Ronny, look, what's going on here, I mean ---"

He stepped closer. "Billy, I like you, and I thank you for doing your job, but if you don't turn around and go back in there right now, I'll shoot you down without blinking."

I didn't move my head but let my eyes flick around. The sidewalk was empty, and only a few cars and buses were moving up and down the road. Ronny said, "Don't think I won't… I've shot old men, soldiers, young boys pretending to be soldiers… I once shot a boy of about 14 or 15 who was a sniper, hidden behind some trees in snow, and I had to crawl so close to him that his brain and blood got all over me."

"Okay," I said. "Let's go in… just calm down, all right?"

"Don't worry about me. Go."

I went back to the front door, gave it a hearty knock, and when Ledder opened it up, Ronny grabbed the scruff of my neck and with amazing strength, pushed me in. There was a tussle and a couple of "hey, hey" from Ledder, and in a moment, Ronny closed the apartment door and came into the room. Ledder and I were back in the same position, me on the chair, he on the couch, but this time, our hands were up in the air. Ronny stood in the room's center, grinning widely. Soft music continued to come from the radio, and the room smelled of tobacco smoke.

"Hans," Ronny said. "Hans, you son-of-a-bitch, sure has been a long time, hasn't it. What a goddamn surprise, eh?"

Ronny stepped forward, kicked Ledder's left shin, and he cried out and fell back against the couch. Ronny stepped back and said, "Hurts, don't it. But it doesn't compare to what you did to me, and what you did to so many others, right? Oh, Hans, can't tell you how long I've been dreaming about this."

It came to me, then. "Ronny, you lied about your service record. You weren't in the 45th Army Division. You were in the 99th... and you were a prisoner of war, right?"

Ronny laughed. "Oh, that sounds so innocent, so clean, so normal. Prisoner of war. Oh, no, Billy, I was much, much more than that... and this Kraut made me know that, day after day, week after week... month after month."

Ledder's face was red, fixed in a grimace. "I have no idea what you're talking about."

Ronny said, "Don't get off that couch, or you'll get it, right between the eyes."

"Mister Sullivan," Ledder said. "Please... can't you tell? That guy's gone nuts. I'm no Kraut."

"That's partially right," Ronny said. "Family was originally from Germany. You were born in Cleveland. Went back to the Fatherland when the little corporal started running things. And he ran things all right. Helped run a factory for torturing and killing people."

I was still trying to get my head around what Ronny was claiming. "Please... what are you saying? That he mistreated you when you were in a POW camp?"

Ronny whirled on me, but still kept his pistol pointed at Ledder. "I wasn't in any goddamn prisoner of war camp, don't you understand? I was captured during the Battle of the Bulge, me and my whole damn platoon, and when we were sent to the rear, I got separated from my buddies. The Krauts found out I was Jewish. So everybody else went to a regular Stalag. But not me. I went someplace special, someplace where I met this asshole, one Sturmbannführer Hans Kessler, at a very special place indeed."

He took a deep breath. "A place called Dachau."

The room seemed still after Ronny blurted out that evil-laden word. "But Dachau... that was a concentration camp," I said. "You were a soldier. How the hell did you end up there?"

Another, high-pitched laugh from Ronny. "What? You think the master race cared about my status as a soldier? All the hell they cared about was that I was Jewish. That's all. Dachau had a mix of Jews from all over Europe, and a few other Americans like me as well. And German-Americans like Hans here."

Ronny's voice suddenly broke. "Hans came up to me when I first got there... after the first beatings, after I was stripped and given those thin striped pajamas. He said he was from the States, and would look out for me... I couldn't believe it... and I shouldn't have. Because the bastard looked out for me, all right. Gave me extra beatings, extra work details, extra torture."

I stared at the man on the couch. "Is that true?"

Face still red, he said, "My name is Craig Ledder. I'm a watchmaker. I used to be a newspaper reporter for the *Tribune*. I don't know why he's saying this crap, Mister Sullivan." He started to move off the couch and said, "Look, let's call the police, let them sort it out, and—"

Damn, Ronny moved quick, standing close to the man, digging the end of the pistol into the side of his head. "No! No! You goddamn SS, so smart, so tough... they're good at escaping, at slipping away. Just like at Dachau... when the Americans finally came to liberate us, it was chaos. So many of us just broke out of the barracks... some of us cornered a couple of SS guards and beat them to death with our hands. We weren't scared anymore! And those poor troops... when they saw all the bodies piled up, all of those skeletal bodies... some troops rounded up SS guards, stood up against a wall, and machine-gunned them to death. Just like that."

Ronny swallowed, like the terrible memories of that time were threatening to crawl up from his gullet and choke him to death, and he stepped back "But me... I was looking for Hans... looking for payback for all the time he whipped me, starved me, made me stand still in the snow, hours after hours... and yeah, I saw him all right... he had slipped into prisoner garb, like a well-fed monster like him could pass as one of us. But he was smart all right... I saw him go into a building with a guy that looked like a soldier, except he had a patch on his upper arm... Official War Correspondent, something like that..."

He swallowed again. "I'm sure he had some bullshit story to get that guy's attention... I tried to follow him... but I was so damn weak... so weak..."

Ledder said, "Please... Mister Sullivan. You know he's crazy... look at him. One phone call to the police, we can clear this whole thing up."

"Shut up!" Ronny said. "Later... I heard from a couple of troops that Ledder from the Trib had gone missing... and they had found this SS officer in the commandant's office, head blown away, like he killed himself by putting his gun in his mouth... that's when I knew what had happened. You had taken on Craig Ledder's identity, put an SS uniform on him."

Ledder was staring at me with a pleading look. "Yeah, I was there, at Dachau," he said. "All that death... all those bodies... it was too much. I had seen too much, had photographed too much... I wanted out. And that's what I did. You heard me earlier, right? That's what I did. I got out. I couldn't stand it any more."

I shifted my glance to my client. "Ronny... give me the pistol. All right? I promise you, we'll settle this. I promise to track down his identity, make sure he doesn't slip away, make sure the truth comes out. All right? You're my client. I'll see it through. I promise."

Ledder kept his mouth shut, a wise choice for him, and Ronny stood there still, pistol still aiming at the man on the couch.

"Ronny," I said.

"You... you promise you'll help me?" he asked.

"Yes, I will."

"You mean it?"

"I do," I said, feeling the tension in the room ease out. Even Ledder was beginning to look relieved.

"All right," he said. "You can have my pistol."

Ledder started to smile.

Ronny said, "When I'm finished with it."

And he shot Ledder three times in the chest.

I'm very much used to the sound of gunshots, but not in an enclosed space. It was pretty damn loud. Ledder fell back against the couch and I jumped out of the chair, punched Ronny in the side of the head, and grabbed him and threw him to the floor. I got to Ledder and tore open his shirt, saw the bloody grouping right in the center. Ledder remained conscious for another few seconds, his eyes dimming out, and like those old memories --- ready to jump back into life in a moment --- his skin grayed out and he died.

I whirled around and Ronny was sitting on the floor, pistol in hand, pointing it at me.

We both stayed still.

Ronny flipped the pistol in his hand, and held it to me, butt first. "Here," he said. "I'm finished with it."

I resisted the urge to punch him out once more, and I took the pistol. I ejected the magazine, put it in my left coat pocket, and then worked the action to clear the chamber. The round --- it looked like a .32 caliber—clattered on the floor. I put the unloaded pistol in my other coat pocket.

Ronny was talking but I ignored him. I went back to Ledder's body, and after some maneuvering, removed his wallet from a rear pants pocket. I went back to Ronny and opened the dead man's wallet, and started dropping cards on Ronny's splayed out legs.

"Massachusetts driver's license," I said. "Social Security Card. Press pass from the Chicago Tribune. Correspondent pass from the U.S. Army. And the ones with his photos, they match his face."

Ronny smiled the smile of a man suddenly content with what he had just done, and with his place in the world. "Mister Sullivan... Billy... the SS were masters of torture, killing, and deceit. Hell, he even found himself a job at a Jewish business! Who would ever think of looking for a Nazi war criminal there? Don't you think a man like Sturmbannführer Hans Kessler could have false identification papers prepared?"

I didn't say a thing. Ronny coughed. "Look, please, just check one thing for me... and one thing only. And if it doesn't pan out, then, I'm yours. I'll confess to everything, say I forced you and duped you... and I'll even make sure my family in Philadelphia wires you whatever compensation you feel is fair."

The room smelled of death and burnt gunpowder. I found my voice. "What do you want?"

"Remove his shirt," he said. "Check his upper arm. You'll find a tattoo of a letter there."

"What the hell does that mean?" I asked.

"Please... just do it... and all will be well."

I don't know what I did it, but that's what I did. After my time in the ETO I'm not shy around bodies, so I went back to the dead man—Craig or Hans—and started taking off his shirt. Grabbing the back of his neck, I pulled him forward, managed to tug off one sleeve, for his right arm. I was lucky rigor hadn't set in yet. The skin was pale, smooth and unmarked.

"Sorry, Ronny," I said. "Nothing."

"Check the other one," he said, with confidence. "It'll be there."

So I did that again, with the smell rising of the man's body, the burps and gasps as his body shut down, and when the other sleeve was off, I had to stop.

There was a tattoo, just like Ronny had said.

I lowered the body back. "You're right," I said. "There's an 'AB' tattooed on his upper arm."

The content smile was still there. "Most members of the SS had their blood types tattooed on their upper arms, so if they were wounded, they would get priority medical care, no matter what. All German doctors had orders that SS personnel would go to the head of the line. Conniving bastards, weren't they."

At the mention of the word doctor, another memory spun to the surface, back in Belgium, back in 1944, back at that medical tent. Me and the other MP named Cooke, struggling with those two dead American soldiers, trying to get them into body bags, and Cooke saying to the doctor, "You're saying the Krauts executed these guys?" And the exhausted Army surgeon had said, "No, not Krauts. Their hardcore. The SS."

Masters of death, of torture, and of deceit.

Deceit.

And it came to me, what had bothered me just before I had left, when the man in this apartment had lit up his cigarette. Rather than hold the Chesterfield between his index and middle finger, the way an American does, he held it with his thumb and index finger.

Like a German.

I wiped my hands on my coat. Ronny slowly got up, weaving, and sat on a chair. "What now?" he asked.

"Earlier you said you wanted my help," I said. "You still thinking that?"

"Of course."

"Then you got my help."

Ronny looked confused. "To do what?"

I looked back at the couch. "To get rid of this bastard's body."

Murder on the Brighton Run
by Amy Myers

Once upon a time long ago I sat next to a stranger at a Malice Domestic conference and mentioned I wrote short stories as well as the Auguste Didier crime novels. 'Send some along to me,' he said, and lo and behold Doug Greene – for 'twas he – magicked them into a collection. Thank you, thank you, Crippen & Landru, for your enormous contribution to the crime-writing and crime-reading world in the past twenty-five years and for having included me on your list. I am so proud of Murder, 'Orrible Murder.

'Murder on the Brighton Run', first published in Ellery Queen's Mystery Magazine *some years later, is set on Emancipation Day in 1896, which in the UK was the first of the famous London to Brighton car rallies, still an annual and popular event.*

Auguste Didier was cold, he was wet and he was miserable. The correct place for a master chef on a November Saturday morning was adding the finishing touches to an exquisite luncheon and not struggling through thick mud in the Surrey countryside to push a contraption that frightened horses and called itself a motor carriage.

"That's done it. Hop up, old chap," called the Earl of Sattersfield encouragingly from the driver's seat as the contraption condescended to lurch forward again.

Fuming at being dubbed "old chap" (the earl was many years older than he was), Auguste once more took his place next to him on the two-seater *Panhard et Levassor* vehicle. He was all too conscious that much of the mud on the road was not due to Mother Nature but to the horses that used it.

The fourteenth of November 1896 was apparently an important step forward for the future of mankind. The Locomotives on Highways Act had come into force this very day and it was no longer necessary for a gentleman to walk before one of these horseless vehicles with a red flag to indicate that the monster was on its way. This, it seemed, was cause for great celebration amongst those of Her Majesty Queen Victoria's subjects who could afford such entertainment. One of them had seen fit to organise at short notice a run for motor cars from London to Brighton on the south coast and a gold medal would be awarded to the first to arrive. That was all very well for the earl, but for Auguste it would be an ordeal with no reprieve.

"Nearly there," His Lordship added. "They do a good luncheon at the White Hart."

The halt at the Reigate Inn about halfway to Brighton would indeed be welcome. The day had brought nothing but misery for Auguste since the celebratory breakfast at the Metropole Hotel in London's Northumberland Avenue earlier that morning. A red flag had been ceremoniously ripped in half to the cheers of most of the population of London, judging by the crowds that had gathered to see the motor cars depart. So many people jostled for this privilege that it had been hard to see the other contestants, especially through the fog.

This gloomy rainy day was dubbed Emancipation Day, although to Auguste there seemed no logic in this. Would the villagers of England see it as emancipation as they took their cattle along the lanes only to be mown down by thunderbolts hurtling towards them at anything up to 12 miles per hour? Would elderly people sitting peacefully outside their front doors enjoy coughing in steam and petrol fumes during this great step forward for mankind?

"Pity about old Pilkington," His Lordship yelled, his hands gripping the stick that apparently controlled – or otherwise – this regrettable invention. "He would have enjoyed this."

Auguste doubted that. The reason for Colonel Edward Pilkington's absence from this motor car run had been trumpeted last evening not only to his cousin the noble Earl of Sattersfield, but to an entire roomful of diners in the restaurant of Plum's Club for Gentlemen where Auguste was employed.

"You can deuced well do as you like if you're so set on winning this gold medal," he had boomed. "I shall be travelling to Brighton by railway in a civilised manner and you, Sattersfield, can look elsewhere for another damned fool to be your passenger." (A role that as Auguste had since discovered to his discomfort included pushing, engine-cranking, solving mechanical problems and navigating.)

His Lordship had therefore looked elsewhere and browbeaten Plum's secretary into loaning him Auguste's unwilling services. Auguste had begun a polite protest when the most extraordinary row had broken out at the next table.

"To the *Léon Bollée* and the glory of France!" shouted Henri, younger son of the *Comte de Montrousse*. He was a handsome young man of about twenty-five and a habitué of the private gambling houses. Auguste knew that for Henri each throw of the dice was a gamble between riches on the one hand versus disgrace and bankruptcy on the other, and he feared for the young man's future.

"Only my motor car," Henri had declared, flushed with wine and excitement, "deserves the gold medal."

His attention had been fixed not on Colonel Pilkington, however, but on his own dining companion. The Baron von Merkstein was his chief rival at the gambling tables, a correct and proper gentleman who played with cold determination against Henri's reckless bets – which were based, as far as Auguste could tell, on his whim of the moment.

The Baron raised his glass slowly and deliberately. "The Benz, *Monsieur le Comte*. To the future. The Benz alone deserves the gold medal. The *Léon Bollée* is but a French toy." He picked up his glass. "To Germany and the Benz."

Henri's face darkened. "Twenty thousand francs that you are wrong, Baron. I shall arrive in Brighton before you, and win the gold medal too."

The baron rose to his feet. For a moment Auguste thought he would whisk out a duelling pistol, but fortunately not. "Twenty thousand marks," he replied, "that my Benz arrives before the *Bollée*."

Auguste froze. This was an insult on the baron's part, as the gold standard value of the mark was considerably higher than the franc's.

Henri went white, his hand shaking on the glass. "Thirty thousand francs."

"Thirty thousand marks," the baron whipped back.

By now everyone was listening to the battle, and both men had risen to their feet the better to trade insults.

"Forty thousand," Henri had hurled back.

The baron smiled. He must have heard the tremble in Henri's voice. "Monsieur le Comte, we are in England. Shall we say two thousand pounds must be paid by the loser?"

Even the Earl of Sattersfield had gulped at that. And no wonder, Auguste thought. This sum would keep many of Plum's members in comfort for a year. He began to dread the coming Emancipation Day ordeal even more. This bitter quarrel between Henri and the Baron von Merkstein, together with the impression Auguste had gained of the chaos earlier that evening at the Holborn Skating Rink in Oxford Street, increased his foreboding. The motor cars were to be guarded there for the night and their misguided owners had been heatedly arguing as to which of them deserved the gold medal for first arrival at the designated finishing point, Preston Park on the outskirts of Brighton. From there, the motor cars would drive in a stately procession to the Metropole Hotel on the Brighton seafront, where the winning driver would be presented with his medal at dinner.

Tomorrow, Auguste had feared, would be a formidable day. He agreed with Colonel Pilkington. The civilised way to travel to Brighton was by railway train.

* * *

Perched now on the *Panhard et Levassor* with the rain seeping in through his hat and aware that his coat was miserably inadequate to fend off the weather, Auguste knew his fears had been justified. Fortunately, there was shortly to be balm in this Gilead of horror. Several public houses along the route had obligingly offered water and petrol to the contestants, but the White Hart, known to the earl whose home was nearby, was providing luncheon too. Not all contestants would wish to halt their headlong rush by motor car along the Brighton Road, as stopping at Reigate would affect their arrival time, so Auguste appreciated the earl's solicitude.

"My pleasure, dear chap," the earl assured him. "Gives me time to check one or two things on the old lady."

The old lady, Auguste presumed, was this motor car which was chugging and choking in a disconcerting way, as they drove through the cheering crowds along Reigate High Street to the White Hart.

The earl's solicitude for Auguste's welfare continued. "I'll set you down here at the main entrance, my dear chap, while I go round to the yard. Have a look for old Pilkington, will you? He said he'd break his train journey here for a spot of luncheon, then take a train on to Brighton to see me receive the gold medal."

The White Hart proved to be a large inn with coaching facilities and splendid gardens at its rear. A room had been set aside for the drivers and their passengers, and Auguste assessed the array of food, ranging from tartlets filled with foie gras mousse and crayfish salad with truffles to cream soufflés and flummeries. Excellent.

He could see Henri here but not the baron. Perhaps he had driven straight on in his desire to win the bet. No, there was a large jolly-looking man talking with a German accent who might be his passenger.

There was however no sign of Colonel Pilkington, although it was after one o'clock. He must have continued by train to Brighton because of the bad weather.

Henri was looking strained. "What are you doing here, Didier? Are you the chef?"

"No, A passenger, Monsieur le Comte."

Henri smiled. "My passenger Bella travels to Preston Park by train. She is too delicate to endure such rain. Her pretty feet would be wet."

"Bella?" Auguste queried. "Is she perhaps Miss Parker of the Galaxy theatre?"

"Indeed she is. You know her?"

Auguste did. He had once worked at the Galaxy theatre. She was one of the darlings of London, particularly of the mashers who vied at the stage door to escort her to dinner after the show. From what he knew of Bella she wouldn't have the least objection to getting her pretty feet wet. It would be Henri who wanted his lady friend to appear as a fragile beauty under a parasol and not an umbrella. Auguste was uneasily aware that his own clothing showed signs of the mud through which he had been pushing the car and looked surreptitiously around to see if others suffered from similar misfortunes.

He had no need to reply to Henri's question as the Baron von Merkstein had just arrived and Henri's attention immediately switched to him.

"You should have departed already, *Monsieur le Comte*," the baron said coldly, "if you wished to arrive before me at Preston Park. Perhaps you have forgotten our little arrangement? I did not see you on the journey here. No doubt you have already had trouble with that three-wheeled French toy."

"Pray do not concern yourself with my motor car, Baron. I saw no sign of yours passing me on the journey and your cumbrous machine must require your every care if you are ever to reach Preston Park, let alone before me."

With that Henri moved away. The Baron von Merkstein gave Auguste a disdainful look and he too moved away. The jolly-looking gentleman, who must indeed be the baron's passenger, beamed at Auguste in goodwill as they exchanged a few comments about the journey to come. It transpired that he too had a preference for horses, even though he worked as a mechanic for the Benz company.

The Earl of Sattersfield did not arrive until after Auguste had, to his great satisfaction, the pleasure of trying the warm chocolate soufflé that had been rushed from the kitchens and looked delicious. This was the most fragile of soufflés to achieve with success due to its tendency to sink so quickly after leaving the oven. He always took the precaution of preparing two in case the first fell too quickly to be presented.

"Drove up to Reigate Station to see if I could spot old Pilkington," the earl said. "No sign of him. When I reached the yard, I had to crawl under the old lady who was spluttering a bit. Deuced messy job. Ruined my coat and had to change. You can have a go at the dirty work next time, Didier. Pilkington here, is he?"

Conscious of the cause of his own ruined trousers, Auguste seethed.

"No, my lord," he muttered.

"He must have travelled straight on. Sensible enough if he took the Pullman train by mistake. That would mean changing at Red Hill Junction for Reigate." The earl cheered up at this very reasonable explanation.

Auguste agreed. It was common knowledge that the two railway companies which used Red Hill Junction had for many years clashed bitterly, not even deigning to share the same railway station. Now, at least, the Pullman trains from Victoria and London Bridge to Brighton used the same station as the trains from Charing Cross that served the Reigate line.

"Well, let's be off, Didier," the earl said briskly. "I can see you're eager to set off. The motor car's fixed now and I've cleaned her up a bit, so off we go. No time to waste on food, eh?"

At this heresy Auguste blenched. "Yes, Your Lordship," he said, with a wistful look at the cheese. The earl might take luncheon as lightly as the non-appearance of Colonel Pilkington, but the disregard of both seemed to Auguste to signal that trouble was not far away.

* * *

Never had a place looked more delightful than Preston Park. To Auguste its gates were like those of paradise itself. The earl, to Auguste's secret amusement, was not going to win his gold medal, however. The winner had been a *Léon Bollée* – but not Henri"s. So far he had seen no sign of that or of the baron's Benz.

The drive from Reigate had been easier than the first part of the journey, with no need for pushing through mud or for crawling underneath this monstrous object. Indeed the motor car looked very spic and span, although the earl looked as grim as Auguste felt. The motor car procession from Reigate had spread out over a long distance with the pilot and leading cars well out of sight. At what seemed to Auguste an outrageous speed, the earl had shot past both Henri and the baron – a dangerous movement as a horse happened to be trotting in the opposite direction. The earl had given both gentlemen a cheery wave and glared at the horse.

The earl was no longer cheery, however, and had already hurried away to make his complaints to the organiser after the terrible truth that he had not been the first to arrive had become apparent. Rejoicing that he had survived the journey, Auguste was about to descend from the motor car when Henri and the baron arrived together at the gates – literally. Henri seemed in front of the Benz and had turned to drive in, only to have the baron overtake him on the right as he did so. Henri was forced to halt to avoid a collision in the gateway and it was the Benz therefore that drove through first and joined the motor cars lined up ready for the final procession to the Metropole Hotel. Henri trundled miserably in behind the baron.

As Auguste jumped down from the motor car to commiserate with him, a vision of female beauty in a flowing white walking costume trimmed with fur and a large flowery hat ran past him on the same mission and stopped to greet him.

"What a to-do, eh? All sorts of tricks going on today," she said gleefully. "One chap just admitted he'd come straight off the boat at Newhaven, but he'd pretended to have driven the whole way from Londontown instead of a few miles. How's my Henri doing?"

"Very unhappy. He has lost a lot of money in a bet with the Baron von Merkstein. Two thousand pounds. Their bet depended on which of them arrived first and the baron ensured that he did."

Bella grimaced. "Don't worry, Auguste. I'll cheer Henri up."

She winked at him and ran over to join Henri. Even Bella Parker's presence beside him on the Léon Bollée failed to cheer him, though, and he clutched desperately at the driving stick as though it alone provided an answer to his problems.

Seeing the earl climbing up on to the Panhard et Levassor, Auguste was forced to follow suit. At least the earl seemed more cheerful.

"That's fixed that, old chap," he said gleefully. "Damned Frenchies winning – should have been a British motor car. The organiser quite agreed."

"But I understood your motor car is French?"

"Not a bit of it. It's English. Daimler engine."

Auguste decided not to point out that Herr Gottlieb Daimler was German, although it was true the Daimler Motor Company was based in England.

"So it was I who really won it." The earl chuckled. "Wait till we get to Brighton. Everything will turn out splendidly."

Auguste did not share his optimism. Henri and the baron were arguing bitterly.

* * *

"Ten to one Pilkington will be waiting for us," the earl announced cheerily as his baggage was unpacked at the Metropole Hotel. "Tip the porter, old chap."

Auguste obliged, relieved that there was still time to take the railway train back to home and sanity, thus avoiding the presentation of the medal as well as the cost of an overnight stay in Brighton. Then his dreams of home were wrecked.

Over the hubbub in the hotel foyer, a pageboy was shouting, "Telegraph for the Earl of Sattersfield!"

"What's this all about?" The earl snatched the telegraph impatiently from the salver, and Auguste saw his expression change as he read it.

"Hell and Tommy, Pilkington's dead," he roared.

Auguste's fears of trouble had been justified. "His heart, my lord?"

"Says here he's been murdered, Didier. Must be a mistake."

Auguste was aghast. "Murdered? On the railway train?" He had heard of such atrocities.

"Doesn't say," the earl snarled. "There's worse. This is from his wife. Says Scotland Yard's been brought in. What the devil for? This Inspector Rose fellow wants me to go back to Reigate now."

"I know Inspector Egbert Rose," Auguste told him. Indeed he did. When they had first met, he himself had come under suspicion of murder. "You must indeed return, my lord, and the Colonel's wife would surely welcome your presence."

The earl looked horrified. "Great Scott, man. I can't do that. I'd miss the presentation of my gold medal."

Auguste was thrown. "But you did not win it, my lord."

"I told you I'd fixed it. The organiser quite agrees we should fly the English flag, so he's getting hold of five more gold medals." The earl paused. "Tell you what, Didier. You're returning to London tonight. Drop in on this policeman fellow and tell him I'll come tomorrow."

* * *

What could have happened to the poor colonel? Auguste wondered. Had he been murdered at the railway station in Reigate or on the way to the White Hart Inn, or robbed in a cab?

This ill-fated day would soon be over, Auguste thought, and thankfully he and Egbert Rose got on well. At least the earl had given him the cab fare from Red Hill junction so that he did not have to wait for the Reigate train. And that would be spent on a proper hackney carriage with a driver and horses.

It was nine-thirty by the time he arrived at the White Hart, and the first person he saw coming down the stairs was Egbert Rose. His lean figure and somewhat morose expression (a misleading one) were unmistakable.

"You again?" Unsurprisingly, Egbert looked taken aback. "Just happened to be here, did you?"

Auguste explained. "Commitments prevented His Lordship from coming tonight. Tomorrow he will be here."

Egbert scowled. "Good of him. Sent you instead, did he?"

"He did. Is the colonel's wife here?"

"Gone back to London. We'd best get on with it then. We've got a room set aside here for us." He led the way to a small room at the rear of the inn. *Dare he ask for refreshments*, Auguste wondered. Even dinner?

Judging by the gleam in Egbert Rose's eye, he had read his thoughts, Auguste realised. Two pints of beer arrived, with a promise of pies to follow.

"Was the colonel attacked and robbed?" he asked. "And was it on the railway train or on the way to this inn? If so, he did not reach it. He dined with his cousin the earl at Plum's yesterday evening, and his plan was to come here."

"Not robbed, not on the train. Found at the back of the gardens here. There's a side entrance not used by the public; it's a rough track behind a thick line of bushes that provides a way out for garden, house and horse rubbish. No weapon around. Hit from behind on the head. Nasty job. Neither of the ticket collectors at Red Hill Junction or Reigate remembers him coming through, but so many people came down by train to look at the motor cars, they wouldn't remember if they saw the old Queen herself handing over her ticket. He wasn't dead when he was found, died almost immediately after that though."

"Did he say anything?"

"Only a few words. 'It shouldn't be there'."

"No clue to what?"

"None. Question is: if he left the train at Reigate, that being the nearest station to the White Hart, what's he doing at the back of the gardens? A cab either from Red Hill Junction or Reigate would take him to the front of the pub. It's too far for him to have walked from Red Hill and unlikely he did it from Reigate with this weather. There was a train arrived at Reigate just after one o"clock."

"Perhaps he took a cab and the driver planned to rob him but was frightened off. He'd know the area well."

Rose considered this. "Possible. The track comes out on Church Street, which leads east towards Red Hill, and a cab from Reigate might come from the north of the town to the near entrance too. If it wasn't murder for robbery though, any idea why anyone else would want to kill him? He was coming to see his cousin win a medal, so his wife said."

"The Earl of Sattersfield had intended him to be his passenger, but I took his place," Auguste told him ruefully.

Egbert Rose raised an eyebrow. "Never put you down as a motor car enthusiast, Auguste."

"I am not," he retorted savagely. "I had no choice."

Egbert frowned. "Think the murder has to do with this car race of yours?"

"It is possible. Motor car enthusiasts care very much about their vehicles and about winning medals. The earl with whom I rode was very determined to remain in Brighton tonight to receive his."

"He won?"

"No."

"He gets a medal for losing?"

"So it seems."

"Odd lot, these motor car drivers."

Auguste agreed. "When the colonel was at Plum's yesterday evening, he heard two of them agree to a bet of two thousand pounds on which of them arrived first at the end of the race. Both were at the White Hart today. That could have something to do with your case, perhaps?"

Rose looked interested. "Good idea, Auguste, but it's theory, all theory."

"Every good dish demands a recipe," Auguste replied with dignity, "even if the ingredients change as the chef proceeds."

"How about a recipe with a colonel coming by train and two mad car drivers?" Rose grunted.

"The ingredients clash, but it might be possible."

"Even if those two gamblers knew he was going by train, how could they know which station he was going to and when he'd be arriving or where they could find him? And why kill him? No, Auguste, this recipe of yours wouldn't work."

"It might," Auguste replied eagerly, warming to the idea. "These drivers go to great lengths. One joined the procession at Preston Park pretending he had driven over the entire route when he had really driven only a few miles."

"Cheating, eh? I thought this motor driving was a gentleman's sport."

"Every sport arouses passion, passion leads to desperation, desperation perhaps to cheating. Perhaps the colonel discovered that one of the two gambling drivers cheated."

"How?"

Auguste thought rapidly. "Suppose one of them only drove part of the way and the colonel discovered that. Both of them, Henri, *Comte de Montrousse* and Baron von Merkstein, were at the celebratory breakfast in London and at luncheon too, but I do not remember seeing either of them on the way from London to the White Hart. Perhaps the colonel realised one of them had not been driving that part of the race."

"Doesn't work, Auguste. How would he find that out? And how could the cheat have reached the White Hart?"

Auguste was flummoxed, but then the ingredients came together. "By train," he said triumphantly. "The cheat put his motor car on a train. The Pullman trains have carriage trucks and stop at Red Hill

Junction. If the colonel saw the car and its driver there — and recognised him as one of the two who had made that bet last evening, he could have threatened to denounce him to the organiser and to the other party to the bet. Much money depended on this bet, Egbert, and the financial cost of a charge of cheating would ruin their reputations in society."

The inspector thought this through. "Colonel Pilkington would probably have been on the Reigate train from Charing Cross, not a Pullman continental."

"But it stops at Red Hill Junction so he could have seen the cheat there. And it's possible he was on the same Pullman train as the cheat, intending to wait at Red Hill for the Reigate train. Either way he could have seen the car and its driver."

Egbert Rose was not convinced. "The body was found in the grounds here, not Red Hill."

"Perhaps the gambler offered to drive him here."

"Thought the colonel didn't like cars," Rose observed.

"He didn"t."

"Then he wouldn't want to ride in one, especially if he disapproved of the driver cheating."

Auguste was downcast. Egbert was right. "Nevertheless," he replied firmly, "there may be something to this recipe."

"What there isn't," Rose said drily, "is one shred of proof. But let's say you're right. Which of them is the more likely to be our man?" A long pause. "Fancy a day at the seaside tomorrow, Auguste?"

* * *

Brighton. The playground for London, originally patronised by royalty and the aristocracy but now for everyone to enjoy, thanks to railway trains. Despite his mission and the time of year, Auguste was enjoying the sea air and the famous pier. Outside the Metropole Hotel stood several motor cars ready for their owners to depart after the excitements of yesterday, but Henri's and the Baron von Merkstein's vehicles were not amongst them. Their owners and the baron's passenger were with Inspector Egbert Rose in a room inside the hotel.

Auguste, however, had seen Bella returning from a morning stroll with a different but even more charming hat perched on her golden hair, and had instantly stopped to talk to her in the foyer before joining the inspector.

She was looking worried. "What's all this about, Auguste? Should I be in there with Henri?"

"As you travelled here by train for the whole journey it hardly seems necessary." Then he changed his mind. "Perhaps you should be present, Bella. Did you leave the train at Red Hill to purchase refreshments or for any other reason, and if so did you see anyone that could have been Colonel Pilkington on the platform?"

"No," she replied, but she looked uneasy, to Auguste's concern. "When we boarded the train, Henri told me to go straight through to Preston Park. He is always so considerate."

"We, Bella?" Auguste's heart sank. "You both boarded the train? If so, you must be present when the inspector interviews Henri."

She realised what she had said and what it might mean. "Henri would not hurt a fly," she cried indignantly. "He's so kind."

"What about the Baron von Merkstein?"

"Nor would he," she said equally indignantly. "He is so generous."

Auguste smiled, despite his dismay. "Oh, Bella. Both gentlemen are your friends?"

She giggled. "Why not?"

It was with a heavy heart that he escorted her past two stalwart police constables into the room where Inspector Rose was about to begin. His eye went from Auguste to Bella and an eyebrow lifted slightly. Auguste ignored it, still thinking about the enormity of what Bella had revealed. Henri was attempting to look at his ease by lounging on an eighteenth-century chair — a difficult task and he avoided Bella's eye. The baron sat stiffly on another such chair, while the jolly-looking German mechanic sat comfortably on a Chesterfield sofa.

"Colonel Pilkington," Egbert Rose began formally, "was found on the path leading from the Church Street entrance to the rear of the grounds of the White Hart Inn. I'm told the official route that the motor cars took was to the west of the grounds of Reigate castle and along the High Street, which once past this inn becomes Church Street. The motor cars could either remain in the roadway outside the inn or continue to Church Street and a little way along turn into the coaching yard at the rear of the pub. That turn comes well before the path where the colonel was found."

The baron yawned. "How can this be of interest to us?"

The inspector ignored him. "With the exception of the young lady here, you all approached the inn on motor cars along the High Street. Is that so?"

"Certainly," the baron assured him.

Henri immediately agreed. "I too, monsieur."

"Neither of you alighted from a railway train?"

The baron leapt to his feet. "Do you doubt my word, Englishman?"

"Sit down if you please," the inspector said grimly.

The baron must have seen the police constables enter the room for he reluctantly obeyed.

Henri had said nothing, but was very pale.

He went even paler when Rose turned to him. "My sergeant tells me that a motor car resembling yours, with an owner resembling yourself, travelled from London Bridge to Red Hill Junction yesterday, arriving at 12.47 pm."

"Not mine——" Henri attempted to bluster.

Bella interrupted. "It's no use, Henri. I let it out that you were on the train with me and that was only as far as Red Hill. That doesn't mean you killed that old man though, does it?"

"I know nothing of him," Henri moaned.

The baron was quickly on his feet again. "You cheated, *Monsieur le Comte*. You dared to attempt to cheat me by driving your French toy only half the distance with half the risk of breakdown. Sir, you are a disgrace to the world of gentlemen. And, I would remind you that you still owe me two thousand pounds."

From the look on Henri's face it was clear that he was in no position to pay it. "I did travel with Miss Parker, but I am no cold-blooded murderer, inspector. Look elsewhere, if you please. Why should I kill a stranger?"

"Because he was no stranger," Auguste said sadly. "He overheard your bet in Plum's that evening."

The baron remained on the attack. "He murdered this colonel because he was caught cheating."

"I never saw him!" Henri shrieked. "I drove my motor car from Red Hill straight to the inn and left it in the coach yard."

"The colonel," Rose pointed out, "could have been travelling on your train or waiting for the Reigate connection at Red Hill, and you offered to drive him to the White Hart."

"*Non*. The colonel did not like cars."

"He told you that, did he?" Rose asked.

"Arrest him," the baron demanded before Henri could reply. "I shall now leave."

"Not quite yet, sir," Egbert said quietly. "When did you arrive at the inn?"

The baron gave Rose a disdainful look. "I, sir, was already at the White Hart when Colonel Pilkington arrived at Reigate Station."

Auguste stiffened and glanced at Egbert Rose, who nodded. "And how would you know what time that was," Rose asked, "if you drove from London in a motor car?"

The baron looked disconcerted, but his passenger took it upon himself to reply. "Because," he explained, "that is the time he told me to leave the motor car outside the railway station for him. Three minutes after one o"clock."

"The Benz motor car?" Rose quickly forestalled the Baron before he could shut his helpful mechanic up.

"*Ja*," the mechanic said proudly. "I leave it, then I walk to the inn where I have luncheon as the gnädiger Herr instructs me so that it will seem we are both there."

"*Dummkopf!*" yelled the baron.

Auguste saw Henri's head shoot up in hope. "You travelled by train too?" he asked the baron. "You also cheated? The Benz was taken there to meet you?"

"Oh, Wilhelm," Bella said reproachfully. "You as well. Why?"

"Cheat? *Nein*," the baron replied. "The Benz is the superior motor car. It had to win so I sent it down by train last evening in this *Dummkopf*'s care."

Egbert Rose had had enough. "It's murder, not cheating that concerns me, if you please. You, Monsieur Henri, could have unloaded your vehicle at Red Hill junction, the colonel could have seen you whether he travelled on the London Bridge train or the train for Reigate that had stopped at Red Hill a few minutes later. He would have left the train to protest because he knew about that bet. I'm thinking the Reigate train pulled out without him, so you told him you'd drive him to the White Hart. Then you killed him at a handy spot. You couldn't afford to lose that bet."

"No, no," Henri moaned.

"Yes, yes," shouted the baron.

"As for you, Baron," Rose continued, "you travelled on the same train through to Reigate as the colonel would have taken. He could have seen you climb on to your motor car outside the station, realised your little game and objected. You said you would drive him to the White Hart inn, but you drove not along the London Road and the High Street where the other vehicles in the race might have seen you, but on the road that would lead you east of the castle grounds and down to Church Street. There you saw a track that would be deserted enough to ensure he wouldn't be able to spoil your victory over the count here."

The baron was beside himself with rage, but Henri was delighted. "And now I owe you nothing, Baron. We neither of us completed the race."

"Only because both of you cheated." Bella began to laugh, then stopped when she saw Egbert Rose's stern expression.

"I demand my money," the baron shouted at Henri.

"And I demand attention," Rose roared. "Which of you killed Colonel Pilkington?"

"Not I," Henri cried.

"Nor I," said the baron. He hesitated, then added, "I did notice someone resembling the colonel at Reigate station. He refused to drive on my motor car. He did not like these vehicles, he told me. He preferred to walk."

"One of you killed him," Rose said grimly. "And, believe me, I'll find out which one."

* * *

"It shouldn't be there." Auguste reflected on the colonel's last words as he looked out over the promenade to the sea. A matter of cheating. As gamblers, both men knew how serious that was. Only five years ago, the Tranby Croft affair in which the Prince of Wales had been involved had ruined Sir William Gordon Cumming's career and social life although he was undoubtedly innocent of cheating. Now Egbert Rose had to work out which of these two men had committed the worst sin of all, murder. And for what reason? Because of an addiction to gambling or the amount of money involved or because of a need to win?

In that they were not alone. Auguste remembered the mud, the cars, the sheer dismal experience of the drive and yet many of those in the race barely noticed it, so determined were they all to win the gold medals of life. Gradually, Auguste began to see his way through the maze of information before him, and only when he was sure of his ground did he go to find Egbert Rose.

"Egbert," he began. "I have one more theory as to what happened. One for which I now believe the recipe will work."

"Go ahead. Happy to taste it."

"When Colonel Pilkington died on the pathway, he murmured the words 'it shouldn't be there'. Let us assume that the 'it' refers to a motor car. It could have been the Léon Bollée at Red Hill Junction, or the Benz at Reigate station. But he would have seen both of these cars much earlier than the time of the attack on him. Neither of them fits those words. When he spoke those words, he was near to death. He had seen something that puzzled him and was trying urgently to convey that."

"Go on."

"Suppose he saw a motor car on that track that struck him as strange even though he knew there was a gathering of motor cars nearby."

"What would that be?"

"If the baron was speaking the truth, and the colonel did walk from Reigate station rather than drive in a motor car, he could well have come through the castle grounds or down its eastern side which would bring him to Church Street. And there suppose he saw a motor car he recognised driving into that track and someone he knew driving it. He'd go over to have a word with him – especially if it was his cousin, the Earl of Sattersfield."

"Possible. Go on."

"He would have followed the motor car into the track to have a word with his cousin and –" Auguste drew a deep breath, for here lay the motive for murder – "there he saw an identical car and his cousin preparing to drive off in it, perhaps grasping the crank to start the engine. Two identical motor cars side by side, one that had driven from London bearing traces of mud and muck, the other much cleaner. The earl lives not far from Reigate so the other motor car could have been driven there by his coachman to await the earl's arrival. The colonel would have realised what was going on. His cousin was cheating. The family name was in danger."

"And he attacked him?" Rose was incredulous.

"I believe he did so in panic. His dreams of medals and glory were at stake. It was a crime of passion, Egbert. Not a passion for ladies but for gold medals."

A long pause. "It's time I met the Earl of Sattersfield," Rose said grimly. "How did you work that one out, Auguste?"

"A recipe, inspector. I thought of a chocolate soufflé. I always make two in case the first one fails."

"Rising to the occasion as usual, Auguste?"

A Run Through the Calendar
by Jon Breen

I first learned of Doug Greene's ambitious plan to establish Crippen & Landru in a letter dated November 21, 1993. Of course, I was delighted to encourage the project, but could it actually happen, even with one of the mystery field's premiere scholar-historians at the helm? Previous publishing lines had been devoted to single-author mystery short-story collections: the Ellery Queen-edited newsstand series of volumes by Dashiell Hammett and others in the 1940s; the earliest volumes from Otto Penzler's Mysterious Press; a few books under the Mycroft & Moran imprint of August Derleth's Arkham House, most by Derleth himself. But none of these was close to what Doug envisioned.

Now we all know Doug and his wife Sandi pulled it off. I was proud to be included in the list with Kill the Umpire: The Calls of Ed Gorgon, *and over the past quarter century I've reviewed nearly every Crippen & Landru title in "The Jury Box" column in* Ellery Queen's Mystery Magazine. *Since turning over the main job to Steve Steinbock in 2011, I've continued to do a column or two a year with single-author collections as a specialty. In that time, the quality control of Crippen & Landru has never faltered.*

When Curtis Evans requested a piece for a volume of original essays in celebration of Doug's 70th birthday, I thought about all the series characters whose cases had been gathered for the first time in Crippen & Landru volumes. But what about those series, some of them outstanding or historically important, that didn't have enough stories for a full book? I was able to salute at least a few of them in my contribution to Mysteries Unlocked: Essays in Honor of Douglas G. Greene *(McFarland, 2014). And when asked for a story for the present volume, I chose something from a series that does not have a book's worth of stories and quite likely never will.*

My series novels and stories have concerned amateur detectives (a baseball umpire, a racetrack announcer, a book dealer, a film critic on a college campus, a long-lived movie studio problem solver), but I had never written a mystery, apart from a couple of parodies, that was centered on official police.

While much of the detective fiction I admire is in the police procedural category, a lack of first-hand knowledge or special interest in the fine details of real police work kept me from writing one. Like many mystery writers, concocting artificial plots that have nothing to do with real life but need to seem real to the reader, I have gathered bits of authentic detail to sprinkle into the narrative, but my police characters were seldom on stage for long. Inventing Berwanger and Foley, detectives on an unspecified city force, gave me an opportunity to check off the police procedural box on my resumé.

The Berwanger and Foley stories belong to a short-story category (seldom if ever found in novels): the tall tale. Are their presentations to writers, school classes, and community members based on real cases or are they making them up? The reader must decide. Or not worry about it.

Detectives Berwanger and Foley enjoyed speaking to groups, and the Department enjoyed letting them. They put a human face on law enforcement, and they could adjust their delivery to any audience, from grade-school kids to college students, from service clubs to writers' groups. Eventually, their presentation, set up like a two-man comedy act, became so locally famous that they were in constant demand. "We'd like to schedule a police speaker for our next meeting," callers to the Department's community relations desk would say. "But only if it's Berwanger and Foley." The Chief had offered more than once to let them switch full-time to PR duties, but the longtime partners demurred, insisting that unless they continued to work cases on the street, they could no longer claim to be cops.

"Keeps the act fresh," Foley said.

Berwanger was the lead talker, Foley the designated interrupter. Their favorite kind of audience, next to the school kids, was published and prospective mystery writers who wanted the real lowdown on police procedure. On this particular evening, before an eager group of thirty such, they were in top form.

"Every cop knows there's no such thing as a whodunit in real life," Detective Berwanger pontificated. "There are cases where you don't know who did it, sure. There are cases, too many of them, where you never find out who did it, but not cases where you have four or five equal suspects to choose among like in a story."

"There was the Fitzgerald case," Foley said, poker-faced.

Berwanger looked at his partner as if annoyed by the interruption, then smiled at the audience as if to say, look what I have to put up with. "Well, that was close I'll grant you, but not really a whodunit for long. I mean, we wrapped it up pretty fast, didn't we?"

Foley shrugged, and his partner took it as permission to continue. "Now another thing you don't get in real life is the so-called dying message. I don't mean to suggest there haven't been cases where somebody gets to the victim just as he's popping off and he manages to gasp out the name of the person who killed him, or even to write something down with his last ounce of energy. Sure, that'll happen, not very often, but it stands to reason it'll happen sometimes. But in a case like that, the victim wants to make it clear, or what's the point? Cases where the victim leaves some kind of cryptic message you have to puzzle out—well, let's just say I've never known it to happen."

"Except in the Fitzgerald case," Foley said.

Berwanger paused and glared at his partner in mock irritation. "Technically, that wasn't really a dying message. The point I'm making, ladies and gentlemen, is when you write your fiction and guys like us are reading it, we can accept the conventions of the genre you're writing in—"

"What's a genre?" Foley asked.

"Please, don't embarrass me. My point is, we know you're going to have multiple suspects and esoteric clues, and we'll go along with you happily as readers, just so long as you don't make any serious errors in police procedure. That's when you'll lose us. And that's what we came to talk about tonight. Now does anybody have any questions?"

A hand shot up in the first row.

"Yes, ma'am."

"Tell us about the Fitzgerald case."

Berwanger turned to his partner, with a puzzled expression. "Why would they want to know about the Fitzgerald case?"

Foley shrugged. "It was kind of interesting."

"But not at all typical of our work." He sighed with exaggerated resignation. "Still, if that's what you want, I'll give you a rundown on the Fitzgerald case. Bernard Fitzgerald was CEO of his own software company and an extremely wealthy man. Early in the company's history, he pretty much quit coming to the office, working almost entirely from home. He managed to keep full control of every aspect of his operation by computer or telephone. The first week in July a couple of years ago, he was found murdered in his home office at about five o'clock in the afternoon. His housekeeper, who had been out shopping, found him seated at his desk in front of his computer screen. The latest company sales graph, covering the last year, was kind of lying on the computer keyboard, as if he'd been studying it when he died. There was a gaping hole in his forehead, which proved to be made by a slug from a .45-caliber handgun. The weapon was not on the scene.

"Our crime scene team were able to gather several pieces of physical evidence. When a recently fired weapon was found later in the home of our suspect, technicians were able to match the slug found in Mr. Fitzgerald with others test fired from that same weapon through markings on the slug picked up on its trip through the bore of the gun. The tech folks call these lands and grooves, sort of like stalactites and stalagmites. The suspect was also tested for GSR—that's Gun Shot Residue—and could be shown to have fired a gun. Unless you're writing a historical, never have your fictional cops do a paraffin test—that went out with rubber hoses—and whatever you do, don't have your cop pick up the weapon with a pencil stuck in the barrel. That could mess up the lands and grooves and make future ballistic testing pointless. It'd be as bad as having your cops stop for doughnuts every other chapter."

"I like doughnuts," Foley said.

Berwanger looked at his partner pityingly and continued. "While our suspect had cleaned up after committing the crime, we were able to find microscopic blood residue on the suspect's clothing that matched that of the victim. To summarize, by the time we went to trial in the Fitzgerald case, the proper suspect had been brought to book by solid routine police work. Are there any more questions?"

Several hands were in the air, and two of the audience spoke at once.

"Where was the whodunit?"

"What was the dying message?"

Berwanger sighed in comic exasperation. "That won't help you keep your police procedure authentic, and that's what we're here for."

"Better tell 'em the whole story," Foley said, "or they'll never invite us again."

"Okay, okay, if you insist. The last message his secretary got from Fitzgerald, at four in the afternoon, was that he had an appointment with a relative, and so would be out of touch for a while. He didn't name the relative but said something really strange. He said it was somebody who ran through the calendar. The secretary told us he often made funny little remarks like that, so it was nothing out of the ordinary. He liked to pull people's chains over unimportant things, though if anything was really important he'd make it crystal clear. He was a puzzle fan, she said, did the newspaper crossword every morning before he did anything else.

"Now, like I said, Fitzgerald was very, very rich, but he had no children of his own and no living siblings. He did have two nieces and two nephews who would share equally in the bulk of his estate when he kicked off. Naturally, they all had an obvious motive and were the first people we wanted to check out." Berwanger turned to his partner. "Okay, Foley, you've been standing there so smug, kibitzing and watching your partner sweat. Here's where you get to go to work." He turned back to the audience. "My partner's quite an actor. He can do good cop or bad cop with a minimum of preparation, and he does the greatest drag act you ever saw at the annual Bluecoat Follies. In the interrogations to follow, I will be me, and Foley will take the role of the person being interrogated."

Berwanger cleared his throat. "We first visited the victim's nephew Barry. No, not Barry Fitzgerald, Barry Montgomery, the son of one of Fitzgerald's sisters." He turned to Foley. "You have a very nice place here, Mr. Montgomery."

"Why, thank you, Officer. I certainly like it." Foley had transformed himself into a smiling, ingratiating go-getter bristling with nervous energy.

"When did you last speak with your uncle?"

"Oh, must have been last Christmas. We were on good terms, but we weren't often in touch."

"What sort of work do you do, Mr. Montgomery?"

"I'm in advertising. Account executive with Weedham and Reap, here in the city."

"You've been pretty successful at it?"

"I think so. Have you seen the ads for Happy Rest Funeral Park? Their slogan, 'Quality of Life, Even in Death'? That's one of mine."

"You must be doing pretty well. Is that an original Andy Warhol on your wall?"

"Yes, it is."

"Have much debt?"

"Well, some, like anybody else these days. Ex-wife, you know how that is."

"Actually, I don't. So were you at your office Thursday afternoon?"

"No, I had the day off. I was at the movies all day."

"Can you prove that?"

"Gee, I don't know."

"Did anyone see you?"

"I was alone, and I didn't see anybody I knew. I can show you my ticket stub."

Foley pantomimed passing something to Berwanger, who examined it. "This shows you went to see *Million Dollar Baby* at 12:30 p.m. Figure ten minutes for trailers. That picture runs maybe two hours. You're out well before 3 o'clock, and your uncle wasn't killed until after 4."

"I didn't leave the movie theatre until 5:30."

"But your ticket says—"

"Look, after the first movie, I went in to see another one, okay?"

"And did you buy a ticket for that one?"

"Of course not. Look, you know what these multiplexes are like. They never check which movie you bought a ticket for. It's no big deal to sneak into a second movie or even a third. They don't care. They make all their money off concessions anyway."

"I guess that's right. So you had something to eat at the movie?"

"Hell, no. I'm not paying those prices."

"Mr. Montgomery, your uncle told his secretary he had an appointment with a relative that ran through the calendar. Does that mean anything to you?"

"Well, I guess we all run through the calendar, don't we? Working our tails off from January to December? But it has no special meaning to me. You might check out my cousin Vera, though. You'll enjoy it, even if it's a dead end."

At that point, Detective Foley, without donning any drag, changed from hyperactive adman to indignant young woman very conscious of her beauty.

"Miss Willing, to begin with I have to ask: is that your real name?"

"Yes, it's my real name, Vera Willing, and I know what you're getting at. You think I'm some kind of sex pro, like a stripper or porno actress or prostitute or something. Well, I'm not. I'm really a very modest person. Taking off my clothes for a magazine layout in *Pentup* was an honor, a well-paid compliment to me and my body, but it was a one-time thing. Do you realize how many women from all walks of life have posed for *Pentup*? And I assure you it was done in extremely good taste. It was very classy."

"To get to the point, at the time your uncle died, he said he had an appointment with a relative who ran through the calendar. We've been trying to figure out what that means, and someone suggested that you were Miss January two years ago in *Pentup*."

"Who suggested that? Which one of my worthless cousins suggested that to you?"

"Does it matter which one?"

"It might. If somebody is trying to throw suspicion on other people, it could mean they're trying to throw suspicion off themselves, couldn't it? I've read a few books, you know. But let me say two things to that accusation. Number one, I didn't have to make an appointment to talk to Uncle Barney. He was crazy about me, and I could just drop in and talk to him any time I wanted. Number two, I was Miss January in *Pentup*, in the issue, yeah, and then I was Miss January again in their calendar. But I was only January and I've never done another *Pentup* Pin-up, and I've never done another calendar or another girl of the month in any other magazine. So having my toe in January isn't exactly running through the calendar, now is it?"

"Where were you Thursday afternoon?"

"Working, all right?"

"Working where?"

"At home. I'm an artist. I was painting a picture."

"Of what?"

"There's no easy answer to that. It's an abstract. I could show you."

"Wouldn't prove anything. Did anyone see you?"

"No."

"If your uncle's remark about running through the calendar didn't refer to you, who could it have referred to?"

"You might talk to my sister Esther, the judge." Detective Foley registered sibling resentment. "She runs through a court calendar every day of her life!"

Berwanger turned back to the audience. "That sent us to the chambers of Judge Esther Willing at the Superior Court building."

Changing persona again, Foley spoke before he was asked a question. "Let me tell you officers something: I believe the rights of a citizen are sacred. If you want a search warrant, you'd better have a good reason. I wasn't elected to this office so I could be a rubber stamp on a police fishing expedition. Is that clear?"

"Quite clear, Your Honor. But we're not here to request a warrant. It's about your uncle's death."

"Oh, that. I had very little to do with my uncle, but of course I shall answer your questions fully and completely."

"Where were you the afternoon he was killed?"

"In court."

"Did anyone see you?"

"Oh, the bailiff, the court reporter, twelve jurors, four alternates, a defendant, a bunch of lawyers for both sides, a few cranks who come to watch the show every day. That's about all."

Berwanger turned to the audience. "In short, Judge Willing was the only relative with an apparently solid alibi, but we weren't through with her." He turned back to Foley. "Your Honor, before your uncle died, he referred to meeting with a relative who ran through the calendar. That could refer to the court calendar, couldn't it?"

"I suppose it could, but detectives, I do not run through the calendar. Ask anyone in this building if I am known for undue haste in fulfilling my duties. They will tell you just the opposite is the case, and some of them find my tendency to deliberation rather annoying. Now, I do have to get back to the courtroom. Is there anything else?"

"Can you imagine what else your uncle might have meant?"

She shook her head. "As an officer of the court, I would help you if I could. But as a member of the family, I'm glad that I can't."

"There was one more relative to see," Berwanger said, "Jason Fitzgerald." He turned back to Detective Foley, who had cast off his feminine mannerisms. "Mr. Fitzgerald, you work in radio, is that right?"

"Yes, that's right." Foley had deepened his voice an octave to sound like a radio person.

"Does it pay well?"

"If you're Howard Stern or Rush Limbaugh maybe. For most of us, it's about on a par with being a grocery store manager."

"At least you're not at box boy level."

"Well, I was when I started out. I've done it all on radio, at every kind of station. Commercial, non-commercial. Every kind of assignment, too. News, sports, interviews, telephone talk. Mostly playing music, though—rock, country-western, jazz, classical, you name it. I enjoy it. My wants are simple."

"Ever do any TV?"

He shook his head. "Face for radio, as they say."

"Can you tell us where you were the afternoon your uncle was killed?"

"Well, let's see. My on-air shift ended at noon. I had a little lunch at a place near the station. They know me there, but I left by two o'clock. I came home and meditated."

"Can you prove that?"

"Only if you have a way of probing my quest for enlightenment. I was alone the whole time. Nobody called, or if anybody did, I'd let the answering machine take it."

"Any idea what your uncle's comment about running through the calendar meant?"

"Not a clue."

Berwanger turned back to the audience. "But it was a clue. Foley and I were sure of that. After interviewing them all, we returned to the crime scene and took another look at something that was found right smack in the middle of Fitzgerald's desk at the time he died and I noticed something—"

"I noticed it," Foley said.

"Well, maybe you noticed it, but I interpreted it."

"Once I noticed it, interpreting it was easy."

Berwanger clenched his teeth as if submerging a caustic remark. "Working in tandem as a good partnership should, we noticed Fitzgerald's sales graph. It had the dollar business levels along the side, the

A Run Through the Calendar | 85

"You guys are mystery writers," Foley said. "You should be able to get this."

"It's a challenge to the sitter," Berwanger said. "If you have something to write with and on—and as writers, you should—just put the first letter of each month beginning with J for July, A for August, and so forth, and see what you get."

Most of the writers in the room followed instructions, and most of them had the following on their pads: JASONDJFMAMJ.

"Anybody get it?"

"Yeah," said a booming voice from the front row. "His nephew Jason was a disc jockey, that is a DJ, and he worked on all kinds of radio stations, so he probably worked at both FM and AM stations. So Jason and his credits run right through the calendar!"

"That's it. He was the suspect we zeroed in on, and he was the one tried and convicted for his uncle's murder."

"But what does that last J mean?"

"Justice?" Foley suggested.

Berwanger shook his head. "In fiction, maybe you'd have to explain that last J. We didn't. Once we got a search warrant for Jason's apartment, we found the weapon and it wasn't too late to get him tested for GSR. In the end, we had more evidence than we needed, just the kind of forensic stuff juries demand these days if you expect them to convict. And we wrapped the thing up only a day after the murder was committed through good sound dogged police work. So, as you can see, that wasn't really much like a fictional murder case at all."

"Sounds like one to me," Foley said.

"No, not a bit. If it were fiction, the killer had to be the judge. She was the only one with a perfect alibi, right?"

A hand was up.

"Yes, sir."

"Detective Berwanger, did you guys make that one up?"

"Heck, no. We wouldn't think of encroaching on your territory. You guys make up the stories. We just protect and serve."

THE FLYING FIEND
by Edward D. Hoch

Edward D. Hoch, former President of the Mystery Writers of America, Edgar Winner, and Grand Master, was the most imaginative — and prolific — author of mystery short stories. He wrote almost 1000 of them, appeared in every issue of Ellery Queen's Mystery Magazine *from 1973 until his death in 2008, and wrote about many series characters — Dr. Sam Hawthorne (the New England small town doctor who specializes in impossible crimes, Nick Velvet (the crook who steals only worthless items), Simon Ark (the Coptic priest who may have lived 2000 years), Jeffery Rand (the spy who specializes in "Concealed Communications"), Michael Vlado (the Roma sleuth), Ben Snow (the cowboy detective who is often thought to be Billy the Kid) and many others. Ed was a friend of Crippen & Landru from its inception, and among our earliest publications was Ed's* Diagnosis: Impossible, *the first volume of Sam Hawthorne stories. Since then, Crippen & Landru has been privileged to publish eight more collections of Ed's stories.*

Ed wrote five stories about Sir Gideon Parrot, a gentle commentary on the tropes of the golden Age detective story. Among them is "The Lady of the Impossible."

I've been asked to record another exploit of my friend Sir Gideon Parrot, and it seems to me I must at last reveal certain aspects of the Flying Fiend affair, a case that baffled the best detective minds of two nations.
    One of my clients was a large West Coast corporation that maintained a vacation retreat for executives on a small island in the Strait of Georgia, off the northwest coast of Washington State. It was a picturesque region and I'd often wanted to return there after sitting in on a company meeting at the island a few years back. When one of the executives suggested that I might vacation there for a week in August free of charge, I seized the opportunity. I didn't even ques-

tion him when he suggested I might bring my old friend Sir Gideon Parrot along for the trip.

I'd never been off on vacation with Gideon before but he readily accepted my invitation. We flew across the country to Seattle and hired a boat to take us up through the inlets and straits to the cluster of islands that sat on the American-Canadian border at this point. Some, like San Juan Island, were large enough to have a national historical park. Others, like the company's Cracker Island, were large enough for only a few buildings and a dozen acres of wooded trails.

"I have to thank you for this," Sir Gideon Parrot said as we stepped ashore on Cracker Island. "We have nothing comparable in Britain, except perhaps the Hebrides off the western coast of Scotland. But the weather there is generally abominable."

"I think it can be pretty bad here too, in the winter month," I said. But this August day was beautiful, with a clear sky showing only the occasional vapor trails of high-flying jets bound across the pacific.

We were greeted at the Cracker Island dock by Seb Wrankler, a fiftyish man with a gray beard who walked with a little limp and was the company's caretaker on the island. "Hello there," he said, shaking our hands. "This your first visit to Cracker Island?"

I explained that I'd been there previously but hadn't really had a chance to look around. "We're looking forward to a week of peace and quiet."

"Well, you might not get much of that," Wrankler said. "Police boats been around a lot."

"How come?"

"Been some killings on the various islands. Bad for business."

"What sort of killings?" Gideon asked. I could see his curiosity was aroused.

"Madman, most likely. But you got nothing to worry about here, long as you don't go roaming about alone after dark."

"When did all this start?" I asked him. A suspicion was beginning to take shape in the back of my mind.

"Well, the first killing was around the end of June, but it didn't cause much of a stir. They thought it might have been done by a big bird of some sort." As he talked, Wrankler picked up our bags and started along the path to the guest cottage.

"A bird?" Gideon was fully piqued now. "How is that possible?"

"The victim was a young man who'd obviously been drinking too much and had fallen asleep on one of the small beaches. There were no footprints but his own leading to the spot. They thought a buzzard might have attacked him, believing he was dead."

"Are there buzzards in these parts?" I asked.

"Oh, we get some turkey vultures up this way in the summer, though not usually over the water. Could have been some big gulls for that matter. The face and head were pretty badly cut up."

"But what actually killed him?"

"Throat was cut."

"By a bird?"

"Well, stranger things have happened. And as I said, this was only the first of the killings."

The guest cottage was nicely decorated with watercolor paintings of the area. There were two big beds, along with a writing desk, a bathroom, and plenty of closet space. All the comforts of home, and not a mention of the corporation that was paying for everything.

"After you get settled in, come over to the main lodge," Seb Wrankler said. "I'll whip you up something to eat."

"He seems friendly enough," I remarked after Gideon and I were alone.

Gideon sniffed. "He'd never replace an English butler, but I suppose he'll do. We'll know better after we sample his food."

As I unpacked and hung my things in the closet I said, "You know something, Gideon, I'll bet they invited us to spend a week up here so you could investigate these local murders. It wouldn't be very good for the corporate reputation to have someone killed while vacationing here. They couldn't hire an official detective and run counter to the police investigation, but they could invite the two of us up here in hopes you could help."

"I doubt if my fame has spread this far," Gideon said, though he well knew that his recent successes had been widely reported in the press.

An hour later, as the sun was dropping low in the western sky, we strolled over to the main lodge. There was a large room with a mixed decor—everything from moose heads to model planes—and scattered tables that could be grouped for dinners and meetings. Wrankler was in the kitchen when we entered and he called out, "Make yourselves comfortable. I'm just getting supper."

Over plates of tastily prepared salmon from local waters, I asked Wrankler for more information about the local killings. "What happened after the first one?"

"Well, it all died down in a couple of weeks, as those things will. But then around the middle of July a young woman sunbather was killed in the same manner, just before dark. She was camping with her husband at one of the state parks—there are several on these islands—and suddenly he heard her screams from the beach area. He ran there and found her face cut up and her throat cut, just like the first one. There was no one else in sight and no other footprint but the victim's own."

"Did he see any birds?"

"Oh, they asked him that. There were a few gulls and some boats, but nothing close by. They talked to some bird expert at the university, you know, and he said it would have to be a bird with a very strong, sharp beak—like a parrot, I guess. But I suppose you know all about them, Mr. Parrot."

Gideon bristled, as he always did when his name was pronounced that way. "The t is silent, the accent is on the o."

"That sounds French. I thought you were English."

"William the Conqueror was both," Gideon pointed out, bringing a puzzled frown and silence from Wrankler.

"How many killings have there been so far?" I asked.

"Three. The last one was two weeks ago, on one of the Canadian islands about ten miles from here. Same thing. A man alone on the beach, this time at night again, attacked and killed. No witnesses, no footprints but the man's. The Canadian police have been working with our people ever since, but they've turned up no leads."

"What were the names of the victims?" Gideon asked.

"Is that important?" I wanted to know.

"It could be. There was a famous serial murder in Britain some time back in which the killer followed the letters of the alphabet—A, B, C."

Seb Wrankler went into his little office and returned with a bunch of newspaper clippings. I flipped quickly through them, calling out the names and other information. "First victim was Ross Farley, age 24, of Seattle. That was on June 28th. Then on July 14th, Mari Quinn, 29, of Portland, Oregon. And on July 25th, Pierre King, age 47, of Vancouver, Canada."

"No obvious connections there," Gideon admitted. "And the dates don't correspond to the full moon or anything else I can think of." He went back to his dinner.

"This salmon is awfully good," I said, finishing the last of it. "You catch it yourself?"

Wrankler nodded. "I go out in the boat, catch what I can. The corporation is generous with money, but every little bit helps."

"It must get lonely here."

"No. Most weeks someone's around. And I can always go over to one of the other islands."

We were cleaning up after dinner, talking about plans for the following day, which were to include a boat tour around the islands, when we heard a pounding on the door. Seb rose to answer it, looking concerned.

A woman stumbled in. She was dressed in jeans and a faded blouse. "Hel—help me," she stammered. "My husband's been killed!" I was on my feet at once. "What happened?" She was dazed with shock, barely able to speak. "Over on Cabot Island—"

"That's the next one," Seb told us.

"Something killed him on the shore. Just like those others!"

"You've got to show us where," Seb Wrankler said, taking her by the arms. "Did you call the police? The Coast Guard patrol?"

She shook her head. "No telephone or radio. We're staying at a friend's cottage and the phone is disconnected."

"Let's start across in my boat," Wrankler said. "I'll radio the Coast Guard on the way."

It was dark now and a breeze had come up over the water. We climbed aboard Wrankler's cabin cruiser and started across about a mile of open water, leaving the woman's little outboard beached on our shore. She was regaining her composure and told us her name was Maeva Armstrong. Her husband Frank, a Seattle engineer, had brought her along for a few days of fishing and camping. He'd gone out after supper to relax on the narrow strip of beach and when he didn't return, she went looking for him and found him dead.

Even in the darkness we had no trouble locating the body. After finding him dead, Maeva Armstrong had got a flare from the tent and lit it, hoping to attract help. When none came, she'd taken the boat across the water to Cracker Island. But the flare still sputtered and burned next to the body, bathing it in a bright orange glow.

Wrankler maneuvered his craft into the shallow water near the flare and tossed an anchor to the shore. We waded the last few feet through the cool shallow water.

Frank Armstrong lay on his back by the flare, his face and throat cut by some sharp instrument. I tried to imagine a bird's claws or beak doing such damage. It seemed possible but highly unlikely. Wrankler had radioed for help on the way across, and we saw the lights of the Coast Guard craft already turning in toward shore.

"Are these your footprints?" Gideon asked the woman.

She nodded, turning away from the body. The only prints were those of the dead man, and then the single track of her sandals coming up to the body, pausing, and running over to where the boat had been beached. "The killer certainly didn't come by foot," I said, stating the obvious.

Gideon bent to pick up something from the sand. "This was by his hand," he said, holding up a little card not much larger than a business card. On it were printed the words "The Flying Friend." A jagged line of blue ink had been drawn through the "r" in "Friend", so that the card now read "The Flying Fiend".

It was one of the Coast Guardsmen who immediately identified the strange calling card. "The Flying Friend. That's the Reverend Horace Black, an ordained minister who travels around the islands in a helicopter. He's forever giving away Bibles with this calling card stuck in them."

Gideon Parrot grunted and continued studying the card. "Was anything like this found with the other bodies?"

The Coast Guardsmen shook their heads. No one knew anything about it. "You might talk to Sergeant Monticello," Wrankler suggested. "He's coordinating the investigation for the various jurisdictions involved."

I could see that Gideon was hooked. Whether by intention or not, the corporation had invited the very person most likely to get to the bottom of these killings. In the morning, all thoughts of a leisurely week in the sun put aside for the moment, Gideon and I found ourselves in the office of Sergeant Monticello of the Bellingham police. He was a deep-voiced man with a barrel chest and big hands. He kept moving a glass paperweight around his desk nervously as he spoke.

"You realize only the first of the killings—that of Ross Farley—took place in my jurisdiction," he told us. "The county lines and national boundaries are a bit confusing out there among the islands, so for the time being I'm coordinating everything. If these killings keep up, though, somebody with higher rank will probably get the assignment. That's the way it usually goes." His flat voice carried just a trace of bitterness toward the system.

I explained how we'd happened on the body of the latest victim the previous evening, and described the card Gideon had found near the victim's hand. Sergeant Monticello nodded, picking up a typed report from his desk. "It was all here waiting for me this morning. This is the first instance where a card or signature of any sort has been left on the scene. It could mean our killer is getting more sure of himself, or a little crazier. In either case it means more murders to come. There'd be no point in leaving that card if this was to be the last of the killings."

"Do you know anything about the Reverend Horace Black?" Gideon asked.

"Oh, he's a bit of a kook, flying around in his helicopter, but he's certainly no murderer. Everyone in these parts knows him."

"I'd like to meet him," Gideon said. "Ask a few questions."

Sergeant Monticello sighed. "I know you've got quite a reputation in London and New York, Sir Gideon, but you might be out of your territory a bit here. These aren't any big-city killings, and you can't use big-city techniques to go after the murderer."

"I could hardly be accused of using big-city techniques," Gideon answered with a slight smile. "I merely want to ask the man a few questions. He may be above suspicion as a mass murderer, but the fact remains he possesses a helicopter—and we're looking for a killer who seems to drop out of the skies."

Monticello dismissed us with a wave of his hand. "Go. Talk to him if you want. Come back and see me when you've got the murderer."

Horace Black was not a hard man to find. We learned that his church, a vaguely defined Protestant denomination, was located on the largest of the area's islands, at a place called Oak Harbor. It was connected to the mainland by a bridge, and when we arrived there by rented car we saw the helicopter just settling down for a landing behind the church itself.

Gideon Parrot got out of the car and strode forward like some official greeter, welcoming Black back to his own church. The minister, wearing aviator's goggles more suited to a World War I biplane, looked very little like a man of God, but he accepted Gideon's welcome with good humor. "All are welcome at my church," he said, smoothing down his long sandy hair. He was younger than I'd expected, probably still in his early thirties, with a thin mustache that heightened the sense of someone from a past era.

We followed him inside where he quickly picked two books from a shelf and handed them to us. They were Bibles bound in imitation leather and probably costing no more than a couple of dollars apiece—the sort one found in hotel-room drawers. Inside the front cover of each was a printed card reading "The Flying Friend".

"Now what can I do for you?" Horace Black asked, sitting behind a desk piled high with unopened mail and assorted literature. "Interested in our Bible class?"

"We came about the murders," Gideon responded. I'm investigating them on an unofficial basis."

"Oh, yes. I've already been in touch with Sergeant Monticello about it. I understand one of my cards was found by the latest victim."

"That's correct. The word friend had been changed to—"

"Fiend. The killer is not without humor, despite his godless depravity. Of course I leave the cards everywhere on these islands. It's like my parish, in a sense."

"Were you recently on Cabot Island?" Gideon asked.

"Yes, I'm sure I was."

"The victim's wife was not familiar with you."

"Well, these summer people come and go. I may have visited the island's previous residents and left a Bible for them."

Gideon seemed to study the man for a moment and then said, "Of course there remains the possibility that the killer didn't leave that calling card, that the dying man struck out the letter r himself to indicate his killer."

"You are accusing me of murder?" The thought seemed to amuse the minister.

"Not at all. Just examining the possibilities."

"Sergeant Monticello already examined the same possibilities. He tells me the dead man had no pen or pencil on him. He could not have altered that card before he died."

"Then I guess I've been wasting your time," Gideon admitted.

"Not at all." Black was gracious now. "Look, I have to fly over to Glover Island. Come along with me, you two, and I'll show you a view of these islands you'll never see from the ground."

It was an offer we couldn't resist. We followed him out to the cabin of his helicopter and climbed inside. Though there were four seats we seemed a bit cramped, and when Black took off straight up, I lurched into Gideon, thrown off balance as in a suddenly rising elevator that stops and then starts again.

It was nearly noon, and the sun bathed the entire area in a soft unreal glow. The waters of the straits were unusually calm, and their mirrored surface resembled the glass in some child's diorama from this far up. Horace Black talked without stopping, pointing out and naming the various islands as we passed over them. He showed us the scenes of each of the four killings, swooping low over the rocky beaches to pinpoint these and other spots of interest.

We settled down on Glover Island and watched while he delivered a carton of Bibles to a colony of summer cottages. Then we were off and flying again, "We keep hearing there could be oil under these waters," Black told us as we glided in low over the straits. "But I guess you hear that all up and down the west coast these days. Be a shame to ruin all this beauty with a bunch of oil rigs." He turned to look at Gideon. "That's something I could kill for, to keep God's land as he intended."

"I doubt if our Flying Fiend has quite such noble motives."

"Of course there's always drugs."

I saw Gideon perk up. "Drugs?"

"Sure. A lot of it comes in from Canada this way. Cocaine, heroin, pot—you name it. I see it all the time when I work with younger people."

"Could the killings be drug-related?"

"None of the victims have been regular island residents. And you read in the papers what goes on every day in Miami. Any time there's a rash of killings along the fringes of the country you have to consider the possibility of drug traffic. I told that to Monticello."

"What did he say?"

"Just that he's looking into all possibilities."

We came in over Black's church and dropped gently onto his landing field. It had been a pleasant scenic flight, even if it hadn't gained us any new facts about the murders. We said goodbye to the Reverend Horace Black and drove back to the mainland.

"What do you think about his narcotics theory?" I asked Gideon.

"I think that a hollowed-out Bible would be a perfect way to deliver drugs without anybody noticing."

We went back to the corporation's island and tried to relax. There were no clues to the Flying Fiend except the card left with the latest victim, and that seemed to be a dead end at the moment. Seb Wrankler had one of the minister's Bibles in the main lodge, but it certainly wasn't hollowed-out.

"Oh, the minister's all right," Wrankler conceded. I'm not a religious man myself, but I don't mind him setting his helicopter down for a visit now and then. Sometimes when I'm all alone here I'm downright glad to see him."

"That helicopter seemed pretty noisy," Gideon remarked.

"Oh, sure. When he comes to call, you know it."

Toward evening Gideon managed to reach Maeva Armstrong at the funeral home, where preparations were being made for her husband's service. I heard him say, "I hate to bother you at a time like this Mrs. Armstrong, but I have just one question to ask you. It might help the investigation. Shortly before you found your husband's body, did you hear any loud noise in the sky—the sort of pulsating noise that a helicopter makes? You didn't? You heard nothing at all?"

After a bit more conversation, Gideon hung up and turned to me. "She heard nothing, and I doubt if anyone else did. If the killer is using a helicopter he must have some sort of silencing device for it."

"Is such a thing possible?"

"Not that I know of."

Wrankler was pouring our after-dinner coffee. "Maybe the killer comes in on a hang glider, towed behind a boat."

"Or in a scuba diving gear from under the water," I suggested, entering into the spirit of the thing.

"A hang glider would pass too quickly over the victims," Gideon answered seriously. "And a scuba diver would have left footprints between the water and his victims."

Our after-dinner conversation was getting us nowhere, so we soon abandoned it. The fresh salt air had tired both Gideon and myself and we retired soon thereafter, sleeping soundly through the night.

In the morning when we awakened, the sun was already high among the treetops. It was after nine o'clock, and as we made our way sleepily to a belated breakfast at the main lodge. Seb Wrankler met us with news of another murder.

The victim this time was an elderly man who'd fallen asleep while fishing off a pier on one of the larger islands. The killing had occurred soon after darkness fell, but there were witnesses to swear that no one had gone out on the pier until a couple of them walked out together to waken the elderly man and found the usual fatal wounds around his face and throat. There was no calling card from the Flying Fiend this time, or if there was perhaps it had fallen into the water or blown away. The dead man's name was Herbert Thompson and he was 67 years old.

"Always near the water," Gideon mused. "As if it was a swimming fiend rather than a flying one." This is two nights in a row. What do you think it means?"

He didn't answer, but after breakfast he went to the telephone and managed to reach Sergeant Monticello at his office. They talked for a long time, very quietly, but when he rejoined Wrankler and me at the table he seemed dejected.

"No new leads," he told us. "It seems hopeless."

"Didn't you ever have anything like this back in London?" I asked him. "Jack the Ripper and that sort of thing?"

"I'm not old enough to remember Jack the Ripper," he answered dryly. "But I do have one idea I'd like to try out on you. It involves something Horace Black told us about there being oil under these waters."

Seb Wrankler snorted. "You believe that old story? The only oil there'll be around here is if the pipeline springs a leak."

"Still," Gideon said, "I think it's worth looking into."

We spent the day exploring the island, with Gideon concentrating especially on the area near the water's edge. I couldn't imagine what he was up to. Finally, in late afternoon, he told me, "I want you to go back to the lodge now. I'm going to stay out here alone."

"Won't it be dangerous after dark? The killer—"

"Exactly! I'm setting myself up as a target and I expect the killer to come after me. Here's what I want you to do. Go back to the lodge for supper as usual and tell Seb I've got a clue and I stayed down by the water. Then, after supper, leave him and go back to our cabin alone. Tell him you're going to lie down. But whatever you do, don't drink any of the coffee."

"The coffee?"

"We were drugged last night."

"You mean that Seb——?"

"No time for talk now——do as I say. I want you to sneak out later and try to follow Seb when he leaves the lodge."

Then he was gone, moving away from me down the shoreline. I felt bewildered and a little frightened, but I did what he asked me. Under the circumstances I found it difficult to converse with Seb Wrankler, and I may have been too obvious when I declined his offer of coffee. But later I acted properly drowsy and told him I was turning in early. Maybe he'd decide the drugged coffee hadn't been needed.

I waited in our cabin for about ten minutes and then made my way through the woods to the back of the main lodge. After an uncomfortable half hour squatting behind a bush, my vigil was rewarded. Seb Wrankler came out carrying a large cardboard box carefully in both hands.

I followed him through the woods, staying under cover at all times. It was dusk now, but I could still see him as he reached the dock and went aboard the boat with his strange cargo. Gideon was nowhere in sight, and I assumed he was still on the other side of the island. After a few moments Wrankler started the boat's inboard motor and pulled away from the dock. Before long the darkness would make it impossible to see anything but the boat's running lights.

Quickly I crossed the island, seeking the area where I'd left Gideon. He was still there, sitting on the sand, staring out at the darkness which was quickly enveloping the water. I wanted to run to him and warn him, but I hung back, hidden at the edge of the trees. I thought I heard the noise of an approaching boat, but it died as quickly as it had begun.

So I waited.

After about five minutes I was impatient to tell him of my presence. I was about to yell something when I heard a low humming sound in the sky above the beach. It grew louder but not too loud, and Gideon appeared not to notice.

And then I saw it——a great winged creature circling about ten feet over Gideon's head.

I broke from the trees, unable to restrain myself any longer. But even as I ran out onto the beach, the creature dove and came in straight for Gideon's face. He started to rise, seeing it at last, but the thing was almost upon him.

Then a sudden single shot rang out and the creature seemed to come apart in midair. There were shouts from the water and two more shots.

"Gideon! Are you all right?" I asked as I reached him.

"I think so. It was a close call."

A Coast Guard boat came into view, and I recognized Sergeant Monticello standing in the bow with a high-powered rifle in his hands. "We got him!" he shouted to Gideon. "He went for a gun and we had to kill him."

I looked back at Gideon. "Wrankler?"

He nodded and walked to the water's edge where the thing I'd taken for a creature lay smashed in the shallow water. It was one of the model airplanes from the lodge. That was the murder weapon?" I asked in disbelief.

Gideon Parrot nodded. "The Flying Fiend will fly no more."

Later, back at the lodge, with Monticello and me as an avid audience, Gideon explained. "Wrankler used model airplanes with propellers sharpened to razor-thin edges. They were guided from his boat by a thin, almost invisible wire. The killings usually took place around dusk or shortly after dark, when he could still see his victims but the small model planes were almost invisible. He could guide them quite accurately with the wire, and he chose victims who were dozing or otherwise off-guard. Before they knew what hit them those razor-sharp propeller blades were slicing up their face and throat. If the plane was damaged after the attack and unable to fly back to the boat, Wrankler could jerk on the wire, flip the plane into the water, and pull it back on board. There'd be no trace on the hard wet sand between the body and the water."

"But what was his motive?" Sergeant Monticello asked.

"I suspect it was oil. Some other corporation—other than the one that employed him—wanted to drill for oil on these islands. They secretly hired Seb Wrankler to scare people away and make the area unpopular, so there'd be less opposition to their buying mineral rights to the islands. I mentioned oil to him today, figuring if that was the motive he'd probably mark me as the next victim just to get rid of me."

Gideon got to his feet. "Meanwhile, Sergeant, we'll be getting a good night's sleep and heading back in the morning." He paused at the door. "You were here right on schedule after our telephone conversation this morning. I believe I asked you something else too."

"About Frank Armstrong's funeral. It's tomorrow morning at ten."

Gideon nodded. "We'll want to stop there on our way to the airport."

"What for?" I asked.

"Simply to pay our respects to one of the victims."

By morning the newspapers had the story of the Flying Fiend's demise and were speculating as to the motive behind the series of bizarre crimes. As he drove us to Frank Armstrong's funeral, Monticello told us he'd discovered monthly payments to Wrankler by an oil company.

"It's only a matter of time before we put it all together."

Gideon waited until after the funeral to approach Mrs. Armstrong. She recognized him at once and hurried over to thank him. "You're the man who exposed the Flying Fiend, aren't you? I don't know how to thank you for avenging my husband."

"He hasn't yet been avenged," Gideon said sadly. "Your husband was not one of the victims of Seb Wrankler and his fiendish device."

"What do you mean?"

"None of the other bodies had the Flying Fiend calling card, only your husband's. That was because the killer's murder device, a model plane, could not deliver and drop such a card. It was important in your husband's murder, though, because you wanted to direct our attention toward the sky and away from the ground—which is the route by which his killer really approached."

"Are you accusing me——?"

"It was a copycat killing, something the police often encounter in serial murders. You killed your husband as he dozed on the sand, probably using a razor to make it look like the other murders. And you left that card so we'd look for an airborne killer."

"I hope you can prove these charges, because I'll sue you for every——"

"Oh, I can prove them, Mrs. Armstrong. You told us you got a flare from the tent after finding your husband's body, and lit it to summon help. The flare was by the body, all right, but there was only one set of your footprints to the body and then to the boat. You never went back for the flare, which means you had it with you all the time. And you had it with you because you knew you'd be needing it when you walked up to your husband with that razor."

Her body seemed to sag then, as she turned to look at our faces all around her. "And this is Sergeant Monticello," Gideon continued. "I'm sure you remember him, Mrs. Armstrong."

The Spare Key

by Edward Marston

I first met Doug at Malice Domestic and was struck by his passion for short stories and by his encyclopaedic knowledge of the mystery genre. At a subsequent Malice Domestic, the two of us took part in a play written in tribute to Ngaio Marsh and I remember telling him how much I'd enjoyed his biography of John Dickson Carr, a compelling read in every way.

She knew that it was coming. What she had not anticipated was the sheer force of the blow. When her literary agent, Kenneth Hooper, invited her to luncheon at the Ritz Hotel — and was excessively attentive to her throughout the meal — Elvira Coyne sensed that there was bad news in the wind, and she braced herself accordingly. Hooper had represented her for thirty years and, until recently, it had been a profitable relationship. He had always treated her with the kind of studied respect that he reserved for an elderly maiden aunt, even though he was actually the same age as his client. For the first time ever, he was now almost flirtatious with her. It was an unmistakable danger sign.

As they sipped their coffee, she could bear the suspense no longer.

"What's happened, Kenneth?" she asked.

"I'll come to that in due course."

"Come to it now, man. I'm on tenterhooks."

"Finish your coffee first," he suggested, gently.

"Right," she said, downing it in one large gulp. "I'm ready."

"Another cup, Elvira?"

"No! Put me out of my misery. They're offering me less money this time, aren't they?" Hooper shook his head. "They're demanding exclusive world rights?" He lowered his eyes. "They're going to cut back on the print run, is that it?"

He sipped his black coffee before meeting her anxious gaze.

"It's worse," he said in a funereal whisper. "They've rejected the manuscript altogether."

She was flabbergasted. "Rejected it?" she cried. "But it's the best book in the series. You said so yourself."

"I did," he agreed, loyally. "And it is. No question of that."

"Then why did they turn it down? *The Cat Who Conquered Everest* is my unchallenged masterpiece."

"The very peak of Elvira Coyne—if you'll forgive the pun."

"I'll forgive anything but those treacherous publishers," she said, grimly. "After all I've done for them, this is how they repay me!"

"It's shameful."

"Utterly disgraceful."

"I expressed my disappointment in the strongest language."

"To hell with them! We simply take the book elsewhere."

"That won't be easy," he warned.

"Why not? I have an excellent track record. And I have a name."

"Yes, Elvira. Unfortunately, it's a name that's inextricably linked with feline mysteries and your publisher feels—not to put too fine a point on it—that cats have had their nine lives."

"Fiddlesticks! Find me another publisher."

"I've tried them all—in vain."

"You mean, there's not one publisher in London who likes cats?"

"No," he replied, sadly. "As pets, they love them; but not as the protagonist in a mystery novel. One publisher went so far as to say that he finds such books more akin to cat litter than literature."

"Didn't you show them my sales figures?"

"That would have been fatal. There's been a steady decline over the past three years. Nothing to do with the quality of the writing, of course," he added with an emollient smile. "That's been consistently high. It's just that tastes change."

Elvira was shaken. After three decades as an author, she had come to take her success for granted, turning out one book a year and following the same tried-and-tested formula. Now, it seemed, she had reached the end of the line. A tall, full-bodied, handsome woman in her sixties, she had enjoyed her fame to the full. Nothing pleased her more than to be able to boast to her friends about her forthcoming book.

"What will I say to them?" she gasped.

"To whom?"

"To my fans, Kenneth. They expect their annual Elvira Coyne."

"Then they'll have to get it in another form," he argued. "It's one of the reasons I wanted us to meet today. It's time to go in a new direction. You must branch out."

"What do you mean?"

"Publishers want noir fiction nowadays."
"I gave them that in *The Cat In the Black Hat*."
"Or thrilling spy stories."
"That's why I wrote *The Cat Who Worked for the KGB*."
"Historical mysteries have also taken off."
"Have you forgotten *The Cat Who Met Abraham Lincoln?*"
"Art theft is another productive field."
"I covered that in *The Cat Who Collected Picasso*."
"Granted," he said, "but only from the point of view of a four-footed feline. Very amusing, of course, but necessarily lightweight. What a publisher would like to see you do is to tackle crime from a human perspective. More realism, Elvira," he urged. "More bite, more blood, more purpose. Give us something new."

By the time she got back to her apartment, Elvira Coyne was in a state of profound depression. Her writing life had come to an abrupt end. The book over which she had slaved for an entire year had been universally rejected. Kenneth Hooper had praised it effusively but that was typical of him. He never upset his authors by offering frank criticism. That would be too unkind, especially where a female client was concerned. Hooper was a gentleman of the old school, a balding sage with an honors degree in Politeness. He had done his best to break the bad tidings gently, but Elvira was nevertheless shattered.

How on earth could she come up with something different? The only thing she knew about was cats. Sharing her life with four of them, it was not difficult to study their habits, sense their moods and monitor their behavior. She was essentially a cat person—unlike Dorothy Fielding, for instance, who was an unrepentant dog lover. Dorothy owned the apartment block in which Elvira lived, and her dog, Pancho, was the scourge of the four cats. The vendetta between the animals had been used in *The Cat and the Mexican Bandit*, one of Elvira's earlier novels, a stirring saga in which Pancho had been transformed into the Sombrero Outlaw. Dorothy had an autographed copy on her bookshelf, along with everything else from the pen of her talented lodger.

Elvira returned home in time to see her landlady about to take her dog for a walk. A game old bird with silver hair and a kind face, Dorothy gave her a welcoming smile.

"What's the title of the next book, Miss Coyne?" she wondered.

"It's still under discussion, Mrs. Fielding."

"You come up with such whimsical stories."

"I do my best," said Elvira through gritted teeth.

"I read them aloud to Pancho, you know," confided the other, "though I have to change the central character to a dog for his benefit. His favorite was *The Dog Who Won the Battle of Waterloo*."

"It was the Cat who won the battle," corrected Elvira.

"Shush! Don't say that word. It always upsets him."

Pancho gave a low growl and turned a bulging eye on Elvira. He was a big, smelly bulldog with heavy jowls and huge teeth. Elvira loathed the animal, and not only because he terrorized her four cats. Pancho was like a Central American dictator, a creature of explosive noise and dark menace, full of waddling arrogance. When he and Dorothy moved away, he was no docile pet being taken for a stroll, but a monarch of all he surveyed, lifting a rear leg contemptuously against it at regular intervals.

Elvira hurried into her apartment and shut the door behind her before collapsing into her armchair. She felt humiliated. It had been too embarrassing to confess to Dorothy Fielding that she had been dropped by her publisher, and she had been horrified to learn that the feline heroes of her novels had been turned into dogs in order to appease Pancho, her canine monster. It was sacrilege.

Just when she needed consolation, it came in quadruplicate. The cat flap clicked four separate times and a quartet of furry cats came in from the garden to jump into Elvira's lap. They snuggled up to her and gave a collective purr. She was back among those who loved her. Still smarting from her encounter with Pancho, she caressed her four cats lovingly. They appreciated her. Secure in their company, she was able to think clearly at last. Her mind was racing.

In order to continue as an author, she had to devise something new and completely cat-free. It was an awesome task—or was it? Perhaps she could simply emulate Dorothy Fielding and turn a cat into something else. Not a dog, of course—her pen would wilt at the very thought. No, her protagonist would not be an animal of any kind. He would be a human being. The notion excited her. She could recycle the plot of her first novel—*The Cat at the President Kennedy Assassination*—and have a hero who accidentally witnessed a crime. Better still, why not turn the man into a criminal himself—Kenneth Hooper had called for noir—and have him see a murder while in the act of committing a burglary?

Elvira let out such a whoop of joy that the four cats leapt off her in fear and fled back into the garden, leaving her to congratulate herself on her brainwave. If she could bring it off, her career would be saved. Elvira Coyne would be home and dry. The trick would be to get inside the mind of a criminal, and she had already done that once. It was her most closely guarded secret. Though she looked like the epitome of a law-abiding, middle class English spinster, Elvira had, in fact, built her whole professional life on a criminal act.

She was an unredeemed plagiarist. The idea of a series about cats had not been hers at all, but that of a sick friend, Isobel Nolan, who whiled away the long months she spent in a hospital bed by dreaming up tales of feline adventure. Teachers at the same girls' school, Elvira and Isobel had lived together, without scandal, for a number of years. It was Isobel who had the creative imagination. During her illness, she wrote a series of engaging short stories featuring a cat. Elvira was so impressed with them that she promised to have them published by way of a memento. What she did not tell her dying friend was that the stories would be developed into full-length novels and that the name of Elvira Coyne would be attached to them. It was a cruel and calculated theft from a woman who was in no position to protect her work.

Fame as a writer enabled Elvira to retire from teaching and to move into a luxury apartment close to Regent's Park. She felt no sense of guilt at passing Isobel Nolan's stories off as her own. Indeed, each time she pillaged her friend's work for a new novel, she experienced a sensation of pure joy. Only when she was established as the ruling queen of the cat mystery did she deign to dedicate one of her books to the person who had actually created the series.

It was time for Elvira to commit a more daring crime, one that involved the risk of detection and gave her a real insight into the criminal psyche. The beauty of it was that she would not even have to leave the building. Elvira could steal from another woman—Dorothy Fielding—and strike back at her for the way that the landlady allowed Pancho to chase the four beloved cats. Dorothy had other properties in London and they brought in a substantial income. Her penthouse apartment was larger and more lavish than anything else in the block. Elvira had always coveted its Turkish carpets and its array of antiques.

What she had particularly envied was Dorothy's collection of jewelry. Kept in three mahogany boxes, it was shown off to selected friends, and Elvira had been one of them. It had been a mouth-watering experience. There were so many different items of jewelry that Dorothy would not possibly miss a few of them. Because the theft would go unnoticed, it would be the perfect crime. The burglar would have additional insurance. Elvira would not even have to break into the apartment.

There was a spare key.

Friday was the ideal time. Dorothy Fielding and Pancho always went to visit friends in Golders Green that afternoon. The trip would take a minimum of three hours and all that Elvira required was three minutes. From the moment she woke up that morning, her heart was pounding with excitement at the prospect of what lay ahead. To add more spice, Elvira listened to an audio tape of *The Cat Who Stole the Crown Jewels*, the favorite of her novels and, coincidentally, the one that Isobel Nolan had liked most when she first conceived the story.

It put Elvira in the right mood. When the taxi arrived that afternoon, she was at her window to watch landlady and bulldog climb into it. Allowing it a quarter of an hour to get well clear of the apartment block, Elvira then went into action. She took the elevator to the top floor and stepped out onto the landing. Elvira knew exactly where the spare key was hidden because she had been asked to feed the tropical fish while Dorothy Fielding was in France the previous summer. After using the key to unlock the door, she replaced it behind the fire extinguisher. Elvira then stepped into her landlady's apartment.

She felt such a thrill that her whole body seemed to be alight and her eyes misted over momentarily. It was quite unlike the feeling she had had when coming to feed the tropical fish in their illuminated tank. That was a case of sanctioned entry. Elvira had now broken the law of trespass and that filled her with elation. She looked around the living room, admiring the exquisite taste of its furniture and fittings. She even permitted herself a look at the wonderful view of Regent's Park through the massive plate glass window. Then she remembered the jewelry.

Tingling all over, Elvira hurried into the bedroom. Dominating the room was the king-sized four poster bed with elaborate hangings. Against the opposite wall was a television set with a vast screen. The burglar did not spare it a glance. All that interested her were the three jewelry boxes, standing on a Regency table like the caskets in Shakespeare's *The Merchant of Venice*. Which one would Elvira choose first?

She began with the central box, marveling at its contents and letting her fingers play with the strings of pearls, the diamond necklaces and the emerald brooches. Elvira then inspected the other boxes and found them equally well stocked. At the most cautious estimate, the jewelry was worth hundreds of thousands of pounds. Envy flared up inside her but she resisted the urge to purloin too much. Instead, she took one item from each box—a ruby ring, an opal pendant and a gold watch. Small pickings from such a treasure trove, but enough to give her the most extraordinary sense of elation as she slipped them into the pocket of her cardigan.

The feeling did not last. Before she could escape with her booty,

Elvira heard the sound of the apartment door opening. She froze instantly. Was her landlady returning unexpectedly? If so, what possible excuse could Elvira give her? She could hardly pretend that she had popped in to feed the tropical fish. When she heard a man's voice, she was at first relieved, spared the horror of confronting Dorothy Fielding. A woman then laughed in the living room. Elvita guessed the awful truth. She was not the only person who knew about the spare key.

Diving into the fitted wardrobe, she closed the doors behind her only a split second before two people hurried into the bedroom. Elvira recognized the man's voice as belonging to Robert Waller, a City analyst, who rented the apartment immediately opposite hers. Staid and solemn, the middle-aged Waller was always immaculately dressed. Not any more. When she peeped though a crack between the wardrobe doors, Elvira saw, to her amazement, that he was now being divested of his smart suit by a giggling woman in a desperate hurry. His jacket and trousers went sailing across the room.

Elvira was even more stunned when she realized that the female was none other than Janice Mead, another resident of the block, a graphic artist in her thirties, whose husband was a contract lawyer. Robert Waller was also married. Elvira throbbed with righteous fury. What she was witnessing was an act of Adultery. Thanks to the spare key, the lustful couple had arranged a rendezvous.

And it was clearly not the first time they had done so. When they flung themselves naked onto the bed, they made love with such passion and invention that Elvira was both shocked and mesmerized. She would not have believed that two human beings could get into such a variety of positions, or take such outrageous liberties with each other's bodies. It was scandalous. It was also highly alarming to a virginal spinster whose only physical contact with the opposite sex had been to submit to a guzzling kiss under the mistletoe once a year, from a panting uncle with a glass eye. The experience had put her off men forever.

Sexual intercourse was a closed book to her—until now. The pages suddenly fluttered open and, unable to look away, Elvira read every licentious line. It was not just the thrusting buttocks of the City analyst and the bouncing breasts of the graphic artist that offended her delicate sensibilities. It was the coarse language with which the pulsating lovers accompanied their sinful copulation. Elvira shuddered. In her view, stealing a few items from the jewelry boxes of a wealthy woman was a permissible lapse. Soiling her sheets with such debauchery, and polluting the air with such filthy words, was a crime of unforgivable magnitude. The miscreants should be burned at the stake.

Elvira fought hard to achieve a degree of objectivity, to view the performance through the neutral eyes of a writer instead of sitting in judgement on the pair. A mere ten feet away from her was an example of what Kenneth Hooper had urged his client to embrace. It was realism, red in tooth and claw. Elvira had never seen more bite, more (hot) blood, more purpose. Against her will, she was actually doing valuable research. There had to be a way of incorporating what she saw in a novel, though she doubted if she would have the courage to describe the exact location of the mole on Robert Waller's anatomy.

With an effort, she exerted some control over her feelings. She tried to look at the lovers as characters in a book rather than as rampant adulterers. She let professional detachment take over. Covered with sweat and sated with carnality, the couple eventually rolled apart. Janice Mead was gasping for breath.

"It gets better and better," she said.

Waller grinned. "Practice makes perfect."

"You've obviously had plenty of practice at it."

"I have to thank Elvira Coyne for that."

"What—that old bag in number two?"

"She's a nymphomaniac," he teased. "Beneath that gracious exterior there beats a lecherous heart. Elvira taught me all I know."

"You're joking," she said. "No man in his right mind would fancy a woman like that. As soon as you got her into bed, you'd have those four dreadful cats of hers jumping up and down on your bum."

Elvira's ears were burning. Her professional detachment vanished in a flash. Not only was she compelled to observe the mating of two wild animals, she now had to listen to them mocking her. When they went on to snigger at her books, she felt that she would explode. Insult followed insult. Elvira had always assumed that everyone in the block admired her work. For two of her fellow residents at least, however, she was a figure of fun. It was excruciating.

The couple eventually dressed and, to Elvira's eternal relief, left the apartment. She burst out of the wardrobe like a rhino breaking free of its cage. Standing in the middle of the room, she breathed loudly through flared nostrils. Well-mannered neighbors with whom she always exchanged a pleasant word had been exposed as sneering enemies of hers. It was a hideous revelation. Elvira needed the comfort of her four cats in order to get over it.

But somebody else knew where the spare key was concealed.

Hearing it turn in the lock, she almost fainted. It took all of Elvira's strength to stagger back to her hiding place. She prayed that she would not have to bear witness to another bout of sexual athleticism. This time, only one person arrived but he entered the bedroom with such an air of familiarity that he had obviously been there before. Kicking off his shoes, he lay propped up on the bed so that he could watch the

TV screen. Elvira saw him using the remote control to flick through the channels in search of the cricket match he wanted to see. When he found it, he reached out for the bottle of gin on the bedside table and poured himself a generous amount, adding a little tonic to it.

Elvira was mortified. The person who was treating his landlady's property as if it were his own was Victor Villiers, another denizen of the block. A thin, ascetic weasel of a man, Villiers was the Religious Correspondent for a national newspaper. Elvira had always found him dull, pious and pedantic. She had never suspected that Villiers' idea of heaven had no theological basis. It consisted of lying on a magnificent four poster bed, drinking someone else's gin and watching a test match on a massive TV screen. The Religious Correspondent, it appeared, had forsaken the twelve apostles for the England Cricket XI.

Imprisoned in the wardrobe, Elvira wanted to leap out to challenge the man like an avenging angel, but she saw the folly of such an action. How could she explain away her own presence in the apartment? In castigating Villiers, she would be admitting her guilt. All that she could do was to watch and pray. The problem was that the cricket match went on and on. When she added the time taken up by the secret lovers, Elvira worked out that her confinement amid the designer dresses in the wardrobe had lasted for all of three hours. It would not be long before Dorothy Fielding returned.

Elvira made another discovery. Villiers had an accomplice. The telephone rang three times by way of a signal. Switching off the TV, the cricket lover drained his last gin and tonic then went into the bathroom to wash out the glass. It was soon replaced beside the bed. Villiers took care to rearrange everything as it had been on his arrival then he ambled out of the apartment. Elvira erupted from the wardrobe and rushed into the living room. This time, she even got as far as the door. Then she heard the elevator clanking to a halt and saw that there was no hope of escape. Villiers had obviously gone down the stairs to avoid his landlady. Elvira was trapped once more.

The ordeal continued. Back in the wardrobe, she had to watch while Dorothy Fielding came into the room and absent-mindedly poured herself a gin and tonic. The only consolation was that Pancho was not with her. He had been left in the portion of the garden that was his private kingdom. Elvira had to listen to a lengthy monologue as the other woman padded into the living room to feed the tropical fish. She was chastened. Did she talk as stupidly to her pets as the landlady did to hers? In their own way, the sentimental banalities were almost as bad as the crude esperanto of love that Elvira had eavesdropped on earlier—not to mention the sustained boredom of the cricket commentary.

It was another hour before Dorothy came back into the bedroom to replenish her glass. She then took it into the bathroom and closed the door behind her. The moment she heard the sound of running water, Elvira came out of the wardrobe with the speed of an Olympic sprinter and raced out of the apartment, spurning the elevator and descending the stairs two at a time. Reaching her own door at last, she opened it with her key and went gratefully into the safety zone. She dropped into her armchair with a thud. Once again, her trusty friends came hurtling through the cat flap to jump into her lap, but she had no breath left to utter any of the ridiculous endearments that Dorothy had lavished on her tropical fish.

Elvira was thoroughly jangled. Yet she had accomplished her task. Three pieces of Cartier jewelry were in her pocket. Alone and unaided, she had committed the perfect crime.

Dorothy Fielding delayed her visit until mid-evening. By that time, Elvira had made a remarkable recovery. When her landlady called on her, she was able to face her with complete equanimity.

"I wonder if I might have a word with you, Miss Coyne?" asked the other woman. "It's about our rental agreement."

"In that case, you'd better come in, Mrs Fielding," said Elvira, stepping back to admit her. She shut the door and waved her visitor to a seat. "Do sit down. Can I get you anything?"

"Not for me," replied Dorothy as she lowered herself on to the sofa, "but you might care to have a glass of brandy at hand."

"Why?"

"It might help you to absorb the shock."

"Shock?"

"Yes, Miss Coyne," said Dorothy, sweetly. "I'm afraid that I'm going to ask for double the rent from now on."

"Double!" echoed Elvira. "That's quite impossible."

"Oh, I don't think so. Which would you prefer, Miss Coyne—to pay me twice as much or to acquire a criminal conviction?"

"What on earth are you talking about?"

"The three items of jewelry you stole from my apartment."

"I did nothing of the kind!" insisted Elvira, summoning up all of the indignation she could find. "I strongly resent that accusation."

"Not as strongly as I resent the theft. That ruby ring was a present from my first husband. The opal pendant was a wedding gift from my second. And that gold watch you took was a cherished souvenir of an admirer I once had." She glanced round. "Where have you hidden them?"

Elvira's cheeks were like ripe tomatoes but she still tried to brazen it out. Crossing to the door, she opened it dramatically.

"Good day to you, Miss Fielding," she said. "I can see that there's been a breakdown of trust between us. Since I refuse your exorbitant demand for additional rent, I've no option but to give you notice. I'll leave at the end of the month."

"You'll leave as soon as the police get here," warned Dorothy. "Now close that door and sit down before I lose my temper."

Elvira obeyed with reluctance. There was a steely quality about her landlady that she had never seen before, and an authority in her voice that was unsettling. Elvira had been caught, after all.

"How do you know?" she asked, slumping into a chair.

"Because I watched everything when I'd taken my bath," explained the other. "My television set has a security camera fitted to it, you see. It records all that happens in that bedroom while I'm away."

Elvira gulped. "All of it?"

"Yes, Miss Coyne. After I'd watched you stealing my jewelry, I saw Mr Waller and Mrs Mead taking advantage of my spare key as well. They've been doing it for weeks, you know. I have to admire their stamina," she said with a twinkle in her eye. "It revived so many happy memories for me."

"And Mr. Villiers?"

"He was the first to discover where I concealed the key. Every Friday afternoon, he watches my television and drinks my gin. It was an expensive hobby for him," she went on. "I'm trebling his rent."

"What about the others?"

"Their rent has been trebled as well, Miss Coyne. After a spate of blustering denials, Mr. Waller and Mrs. Mead eventually saw sense. They had no wish for me to pass on the video tape to Mrs. Waller or Mr. Mead." She gave a laugh. "I don't think that either of the spouses would be quite as entertained by the bedroom gymnastics as I was. But," she said, "enough is enough. I'm calling a halt to their antics. They abused my hospitality in the most blatant way and they must pay for it. So must Mr. Villiers." She pointed a skeletal finger. "And so, Miss Coyne, must you."

Elvira was in despair. The three minutes she intended to spend in Dorothy's apartment had turned into three grueling hours, and there had been unforeseen consequences. After being forced to return the stolen jewelry to its owner, she had to sign a punitive rental agreement and was condemned to remain in an apartment block with an adulterous City analyst and an unfaithful wife, both of whom treated Elvira as a laughing stock. The alcoholic Religious Correspondent would also bump into her from time to time, another victim of the landlady's security camera. Life in the block was going to be like residing in the seventh circle of hell.

"There's one compensation," said Dorothy, cheerily. "At least, you now have a title for your next book."

"Do I?" asked Elvira, wondering if she would ever write again.

"Yes, Miss Coyne. You can call it *The Cat Burglar Confounded*." She got up and walked to the door. "Oh, by the way," she said with a saccharine smile, "the spare key is no longer behind the fire extinguisher. I've attached it to Pancho's collar. Nobody would dare to borrow it from there."

Dorothy Fielding made a graceful exit from the room and left her lodger distraught. Elvira's bold venture into the criminal world had been a disaster. She had lost her nerve and her respectability. Nothing had been gained in return. It was enough to make a cat laugh. One thing was certain. Somewhere up in heaven, Isobel Nolan was shaking with mirth.

Change The Ending
by Terrence Faherty

I believe I was introduced to Doug Greene by Janet Hutchings, editor of Ellery Queen's Mystery Magazine, *at an Edgar dinner. That would have been back in the late nineties. Shortly after that, Michael Lewin, who had published a short story collection with Crippen & Landru and who had helped me get my first Owen Keane novel,* Deadstick, *published, suggested that I approach Doug about doing a book of Keane stories. I think Mike actually dragged me over to pitch the collection to Doug in person at a Bouchercon somewhere. I remember that Doug was very gracious about it, and we ended up doing* The Confessions of Owen Keane *in 2005. As was always the case with Crippen & Landru books,* The Confessions *was a handsome volume, and I'm still very proud of it.*

ONE

Sandra Magerum knew she was not a danger to herself. Dr. Naismith was mistaken about that. There was nothing at all wrong with her mentally. She'd experienced a period of mourning, deep mourning, which was a condition of the soul, not the mind, and as far outside Dr. Naismith's purview as particle physics. In any case, that period, that episode, was now closed.

Certainly no one with lingering mental problems could have organized this trip so efficiently. And Sandra was a woman who knew and prized efficiency. She'd selected the ferry operator on whose dock she now stood not because it was the company she and her husband had used ten years earlier but because on that occasion it had performed like the Swiss Guard.

Today was no different. She'd left her car at the valet parking sign and within five minutes a team of young men and women—so like her students at the college—had taken her bag from the trunk and checked her in for the short trip to Mackinac Island. By the time she'd joined a group of passengers huddling under the gangway's bright blue awning to escape a light rain, their ferry had been entering the little harbor.

Sandra remembered a larger boat and wondered if that could be a trick of her memory. Perhaps the ferry had simply seemed larger and safer because James had been along, his hand on her back as they'd descended the aluminum gangway and holding her elbow as they'd stepped through the opening in the ship's rail. Theirs had been more than a marriage. It had also been a long friendship. That was the point she'd tried to impress upon Dr. Naismith, though without success. She'd lost a soul mate, not merely a spouse.

Once she was on board the ferry and it had started out into the straits, Sandra was sure she had been wrong. This was certainly the type of boat they'd taken ten years earlier if not the very craft. She clearly remembered the long rows of bench seats—so like church pews—in the main cabin, remembered that every seat in that moving chapel had been occupied on their July trip, at the height of the island's season. Now, in September, Sandra had a long seat to herself.

Almost to herself. Just as a young crewmember began addressing the passengers, a woman moved forward from the rear of the cabin and sat beside her. From old habit, Sandra made a rapid inventory of the newcomer: medium height, stout, short hair uniformly white, black eyeglasses sequined. Sandra turned away from the woman's opening smile and saw her own reflection in the cabin window. She made another inventory: small, dark, prematurely stooped, haunted eyes.

The crewman's welcome was really a sales pitch for a guidebook to Mackinac. The woman in the sequined glasses bought a copy so quickly that Sandra toyed with the idea she might be a shill, planted in the audience to jumpstart sales, a conceit the woman fell in with by holding up her copy for Sandra to examine.

"Don't need one," Sandra said. "I've been here before."

"By yourself?"

"No, with my husband. My late husband."

"I'm sorry."

Sandra nodded, pleased with the matter-of-fact way she'd said the words "late husband." Her friends had questioned the wisdom of choosing for this trial vacation a place where she and James had been together. But Sandra had been insistent, not because they'd traveled so much that she had had few alternatives, though that was true, and not because it was easier to plan a trip to a familiar place. She wanted this to be a real test. She wanted to prove to Dr. Naismith what she believed in her heart: James and all he represented were now part of the past.

"My name is Lola Mae," the woman beside her said.

Her voice reminded Sarah of that irritating woman on the cooking channel who pronounced "oil" as though it had three syllables. Sandra gave her own first name, reluctantly.

"Is it true there aren't any cars or trucks on Mackinac?"

"No private cars," Sandra said. "I believe there are fire trucks and an ambulance, though I never saw them."

"So everyone travels by bicycle?"

"Or by horse and buggy. And all the businesses use horse-drawn wagons."

Lola Mae was beaming. "It's just like stepping into the past."

"Stepping into the past" was an innocent enough expression, but it still rankled. Sandra had been a professional historian for thirty years and she detested the modern tendency to see the past as something living or, worse, something pliable, something to be reshaped to fit the latest political or ideological whim. It could be reinterpreted, certainly, or illuminated by some new discovery, but its basic landscape was as fixed as any painting. And one could no more step into it than into an old master.

Sandra realized that she had drifted off and looked to see if Lola Mae had noticed. Luckily, the other woman was trying to photograph, through the rain-spattered windows of the cabin, the giant suspension bridge that connected Michigan's upper and lower peninsulas.

Sandra was free to return to her mental essay on the immutability of the past. Perhaps inevitably, she thought of her theory's greatest critic, James. To be fair, James had been no great believer in the immutability of anything. A professor of English literature, he had delighted in every new theory in his own field that called for the deconstruction and reshaping of books and poems.

He'd had a favorite game he would play with his freshman students, which he'd called "Change the Ending." He'd maintained that any work of literature could be completely transformed simply by changing the ending. If Hamlet doesn't end with the death of the prince, it ceases to be a tragedy and becomes a coming-of-age story. If Huckleberry Finn ends with Jim, the runaway slave, being condemned to a plantation, it ceases to be a coming-of-age story and becomes a tragedy. James had even predicted that future "artists" would rewrite the last few pages of classic books and reissue the complete texts as their own work.

Sandra considered that hypothetical "art form" vandalism and the discussion of it a waste of good classroom time. She had often told James—

"There it is," Lola Mae broke in. "There's Mackinac."

TWO

The little island was more crowded than Sandra remembered. And a more homogenous green, though even at a distance she could clearly see the long white walls of the fort that stood guard above the little harbor. They'd be within cannon range in a very few minutes. She could make out individual cottages now and, to the left of the fort and more hidden in the trees, the colonnade of the Grand Hotel.

Lola Mae asked her to point out the hotel, and she did so, though with a feeling of dread. It was a large establishment, but was it large enough to share with Lola Mae?

To her relief, the other said, "Too expensive for me. I'm staying at the Harborside Bed and Breakfast. But I'd love to be a guest at the Grand Hotel. It's where they filmed my favorite movie, *Somewhere in Time*."

Sandra knew the name, knew she'd seen the film, though at that moment she couldn't recall the plot. She put it from her mind as they entered the harbor.

The two women parted in a shelter open on one end to the ferry dock and on the other to the island's main street. The people on that street were still wearing rain jackets, though those with umbrellas carried them furled under their arms. Even so, Sandra was grateful that the hotel's omnibus—you could hardly call something built of gleaming wood and drawn by a pair horses a shuttle—was covered. By the time it reached the hotel, which, with its many columns and its shingled roof complete with crowning pavilion, looked to Sandra like a racetrack grandstand monstrously grown, the sun had broken through.

Hotel guests were starting out with golf clubs and tennis rackets, people James would have talked up in the hopes of finding a partner and a game. Sandra didn't even nod hello to those she passed as she and her bag were escorted into the lobby, where the many irregularities of the floor were almost hidden by the plush wine carpet. She intended to explore the island's history, something she'd been denied on her last stay. And it was an interesting history, sited as Mackinac was at a choke point for Great Lakes shipping and at the center of what had once been a thriving fur industry. There'd been two wartime invasions of the island and one pitched battle. They would be more than enough to fill the two days of her visit.

She unpacked quickly in her small room, strapped on her camera, and headed out. In the lobby, her eye was caught by a framed movie poster, by the name on that poster: *Somewhere in Time*. She crossed to it. The poster showed a full length drawing—or a photo massaged to look like a drawing—of a young man in contemporary dress. From behind him peeked the face of a beautiful woman, done in a much larger scale. On either side of the poster were framed photographs of the cast taken all around the hotel, making the wall a little shrine to the film.

She remembered it now. It had starred the unfortunate Christopher Reeve and Jane Seymour. The hotel had been showing the film during her previous visit, and James had insisted they see it. Then he'd laughed up his sleeve at the whole thing. Sandra remembered being mortified at first but soon giving up and laughing herself. The plot had been that absurd: A man on a visit to Mackinac sees an old photograph of a turn-of-the-century beauty and falls in love. More than that, through self-hypnosis he sends himself back into the past so he can consummate that love. Kitsch, James had called it. He could always—

Sandra started as though caught at something illicit. She wasn't there to think about James. On the contrary, the point of the exercise was to be where he had been without thinking of him every minute of every day.

She set out from the hotel at a brisk pace, descending into the town proper and crossing it on the high street, Weldon Street, which ended at the park-like grounds of Fort Mackinac. Sandra paid for her admission and for a guidebook, though she was sure she could have written a more comprehensive one herself based on her recent research.

The fort had been built by the British in 1780 and it had passed to the United States by treaty after the War of Independence. Unfortunately, the fort had been incorrectly sited, a problem the British knew all about, having created it themselves. There was higher land directly behind the fort and commanding it. During the War of 1812, the British had landed at night on the far side of the island and approached the fort overland. When the Americans had awakened the next morning, they'd found the guns of the British looking down at them from the heights. Exit the Americans, for a time.

Sandra spent a happy hour examining the foundations of the outer wall and touring the restored buildings behind it, the barracks and infirmary and the officers' quarters, judging the reconstructions to be too pristine but otherwise accurate. Then she attended a demonstration cannon firing, standing apart from the tourists but jumping as they did when the gun went off.

Afterward, she treated herself to a pot of tea and a piece of blueberry pie at the fort's café, which overlooked the harbor. The café had been the only part of the grounds James would enter, though he'd loved their table's view of the yacht basin and had pronounced the pie the best he'd ever eaten.

Sitting in the warm sunlight, Sandra was overcome by a choking sense of injustice. She shouldn't have been there alone. She shouldn't have been facing the rest of her life alone. She wouldn't have been, but for a dangerous hill and a bit of wet pavement and a hairpin turn. But for James being James.

"How could you have—" she began before she realized she was addressing the empty chair beside her. She dropped some bills on the table and hurried away.

THREE

The fine weather continued the next day. After breakfast, Sandra went down into the town and rented a bicycle whose basket and balloon tires reminded her of the Schwinn that had been the centerpiece of her happiest Christmas morning. After stopping to buy her lunch at a grocery with a deli counter in back, she set out, heading east.

The island was circled by a fairly flat coast road, which offered impressive views of Lake Huron at almost every point. Sandra knew the eight-mile circuit, having ridden it with James. She knew she would have to be on her guard for memories of him, as she'd been the night before, when she dined at the Grand Hotel's formal restaurant. She'd been seated next to a couple from Cleveland—a dentist (tall, crew-cut) and his wife (buxom, freckled)—and had managed to have a long conversation without mentioning James once. Today she lacked the distraction of strangers, but she had a specific plan in mind for losing her unwelcome shadow.

The water to her right was an almost Caribbean blue. Sandra could still see the rocky bottom a hundred feet from shore. She enjoyed the novelty of riding down the road without a thought to traffic, though the constant calls of "On your left!" as one bicycle after another whizzed past her grew irritating. Once out of town, she entered one of the island's many nature preserves, land protected from development. It would have been impossible to build in any case, the narrow road being the only flat land between the shingle beach and great cliffs of stone.

At one point, she saw a lone picnic table, remembered it is a place where she and James had lunched, and pedaled on resolutely. "You don't ambush me that easily, James Magerum," she muttered between breaths. "You'll never ambush me again."

Mackinac, Sandra knew, was shaped like an irregular arrowhead, with the harbor and the town at its base. Just beyond the arrowhead's point, opposite the town, was the site of the successful British invasion of 1812 and the unsuccessful American one from two years later. It was now the home of a picnic ground, where, with a few other bicyclists, Sandra ate her lunch. Then, with one glance back at the tourists pedaling along Lakeshore Drive, she struck off inland on British Landing Road.

That parting glance had contained a mental wave of her hand to James. She pictured him surprised and disconcerted by her change of tactics. Like the British, she was using this overland route, on which James had never tread, to defeat her enemy. Though in her case, rather than approaching that enemy stealthily, she was leaving him behind.

The road was steeply inclined, and Sandra quickly ran through her bicycle's handful of gears. On either side of the narrow pavement was a forest where trees competed for space with scattered boulders. Sandra felt a tremendous sense of isolation, wonderful after the crowds in the town and at the hotel, off-season though it was.

Eventually, she had to give up riding and walk her bike. She marveled at the discipline and determination it must have taken to drag cannon and shot and powder up that hill. And to do it in the dark. That was where the real battle for the island had been fought, on that hill, and with ropes and hand spikes. The subsequent taking of the fort had been a mere epilogue.

Sandra was so pleased with that thought that she stopped to write it down in her notebook for use in a future article. At the same time, she took photographs of the tangled forest on either hand. Then she trudged onward.

And upward, the road growing steeper, it seemed, with every step. Finally, she reached a comparative plateau, and breaks appeared in the trees to her right. Sandra saw a tiny red flag fluttering on a grassy mound and knew that she'd reached the golf course. Not the newer one on the hotel grounds—that someone she wouldn't name had played—but the original 1901 course, the site of a battle in 1814.

Sandra pictured the Americans, after the humiliation of losing the fort and the island, sneaking back using the Britishers' landing place and dragging their own cannon up that same steep slope. Their plan had been to capture the same heights the British had used to threaten the fort. Unfortunately that high ground had been garrisoned and ready for them. Sandra could see the redcoats marching out to meet the invaders in that sunlit, buzzing pasture, where golfers now wandered in twos and threes. Meeting them and driving them off the island.

To reinforce these images in her memory, Sandra took a series of photographs. There then remained one stop on her program, the high ground that had served the British so well and on which they'd thrown up an earthwork fort, Fort Holmes. According to her map, the earthworks were reached by a turning to the left. She found it clearly marked, a sharply rising lane overhung by a canopy of trees.

At its foot, Sandra paused to catch her breath but discovered instead that her breathing was growing more and more shallow and that her heart was racing. She knew the reason at once. The little lane was an almost the exact duplicate of the one on which James had lost control of his car. The place where she stood, breathless and trembling, was the very double of the spot where he'd died.

And where the woman had died. Ambushed and defenseless now, Sandra could not prevent the name from entering her head: Peggy Asbery. She even pictured the graduate student against her will. Not beautiful, but pretty certainly and young. So very young.

When Asbery had been found dead in the car beside James, the college gossips had all claimed prior knowledge of the affair—and it had been an affair, the police had found ample evidence of that. But Sandra herself had not known, had not had any idea that her comfortable, well-ordered life was a house of cards and that she would go overnight from a figure of respect to one of derision and—after her breakdown—of pity.

The only thing missing to make this lonely spot identical to the one where her real life had ended was a steady rain. Sandra found that she was supplying that deficiency with her own tears.

"James," she said aloud. "How could you have done this to me? How could you have done it to yourself?"

Change the ending! He'd certainly rewritten his own life by changing the ending everyone had expected for him. And rewritten her life as well.

She was aware again of her complete isolation on that lonely road, but this time the awareness frightened her. She was cut off from other people, cut off even from the safe past of dates and battles by a more recent past she couldn't control.

At once she gave up the climb to Fort Holmes—who knew what trap awaited her there?—and hurried down the road that led to town.

FOUR

Sandra's only thought as she descended into the back streets of the town was to find people, living people who didn't know her story, and to lose herself among them. At the first block of shops, she leaned her bicycle against a lamppost and forgot it. She moved from one store to another, scanning shelves and counters, filling her mind with an avalanche of bright and empty images and with the faces of strangers.

Eventually, she was calm enough to walk along the brick sidewalk, examining the windows of the shops but not going in. Toward the end of the block, she came to a store that had photographs in its window. They were from that awful movie, *Somewhere in Time*. The shop was featured in all the photos, and Sandra realized that it must have been a location for the film. Of all the ridiculous things to be proud of! Though, she conceded, the association might attract a certain class of customer. The Lola Maes of the world.

Just thinking of the woman from the ferry was like an unlucky charm, for there she was, crossing the street and calling out, her white hair tucked beneath a ball cap and a plastic shopping bag in each hand.

"Hello, Sandra! Hello! I was hoping I'd run into you. I wanted to show you those photos. And here you are, right in front of them."

"You wanted to show me these?" Sandra asked, so surprised that she didn't even think of getting away. "Why?"

"Because it's you. It's your story. I don't know why I didn't think of *Somewhere in Time* on the boat, when you told me you're a widow and that you'd been here to Mackinac with your husband. But when I was on this street yesterday and I saw that display, it came to me in a flash: What you're doing is exactly what Christopher Reeve does in the movie. He wills himself into the past so he can be with Jane Seymour. And you're revisiting the past so you can be with your husband again. What was his name?"

"James. But——"

"So you can be with James. It's so romantic. Even the ending is the same. I mean, it will be the same. In the movie, the young man from the present can't really be reunited with his love from the past until he dies. That's the same as you and James, too. Not that I'm rushing you along, darlin'. I'm just saying that everything will work out in the end. You two will be together again!

"Oh, wow, is that the time? I'm supposed to be on a sunset cocktail cruise. You want to go with? No? Well, I'll run into you again."

FIVE

As she watched the retreating Lola Mae, Sandra tried to feel anger, tried to get herself to call the other woman back so she could repeat the arguments she'd made to Dr. Naismith and to her friends. She'd not come to Mackinac to relive the dead past. She'd come to prove to herself and to everyone else that it was truly dead.

Sandra didn't call out to Lola Mae or follow her. She knew she would never convince her, not when Lola Mae was armed with an unshakable faith in a silly movie. Not when Sandra herself secretly feared that Lola Mae was right. James had been a presence for her ever since she'd boarded the ferry. She'd pushed him away again and again for form's sake but she'd always known that he remained somewhere nearby, as she had in the lost days when she'd heard the drone of his mower on a summer afternoon or some piece by Fauré coming through the wall of his study or when she'd listened to his steady breathing in the last hour before dawn. For all her show of independence, the only time she'd really been free of him was on that lonely road above the fort when she'd been forced to accept that he was gone forever. And her reaction had been panic.

Sandra started out for her hotel, but took turnings at random and found herself instead at a little park next to the marina. It was a place for the very wealthy who came to Mackinac by yacht to picnic and to walk their dogs. The afternoon was giving way to evening, and the park was deserted. Sandra sat down on a bench that overlooked the harbor.

So she'd come to Mackinac to relive the past. Pitiful. Lola Mae ,the remorseless romantic, was right about that. But she was wrong about something else. Sandra would never be reunited with James in any afterlife. His mistress, the eternally youthful Peggy, was there already. Sandra would be as unwanted beyond the grave as she had been in life. Twice pitiful.

For the first time since the days just after the accident, Sandra began to think of taking her own life. She'd been stopped then by Dr. Naismith—not by any of his talk or nostrums but by her own stubborn determination to deny his concerns. Nor had she wanted to give the campus wags one last reason to wink and nod their heads.

None of that mattered to her now. She only had to think of a way. She could climb to the pavilion atop the Grand Hotel and jump. But she might only cripple herself. Worse, Lola Mae might tell her story and Sandra's photograph might end up as part of the lobby shrine to Somewhere in Time. She could wait until dark and slip into the water at the end of one of the floating docks. The cold of that water would finish her soon enough. But to drown. . .

If only she hadn't stubbornly refused all of Dr. Naismith's pills. If only there was some way to change the immutable past, to erase the embarrassment of these last days on the island and of every day since the accident.

Then Sandra felt James' presence one last time, and her eyes welled up with tears. And she heard him quite plainly whisper the answer in her ear.

SIX

The next morning, Sandra stood with a small group of early risers, awaiting the arrival of the day's first ferry. The water of the harbor was glittering almost painfully, but Sandra couldn't get enough of the view. On a nearby piling, a cormorant was drying its wings. Sandra removed her camera from its belt pack and focused on the bird, which turned its long beak at the last second, giving her a beautiful profile shot.

Beside her, a woman said, "They think she was drunk."

The cormorant hopped around on its perch, presenting its brown back. Sandra's camera snapped again.

"Drunk?" a second woman asked. "Why do they think that?"

"She'd just come off a sunset cocktail cruise. I guess there were more cocktails than sunsets."

"She was young then."

"Oh no, honey. Our age. White hair and everything. Old enough to know how to say when."

"Old enough to know how to swim."

"They say she hit her head when she fell in. She could've been Esther Williams after that, and it wouldn't have done her any good."

"Maybe somebody hit her on the head and pushed her in."

"Bite your tongue, honey. If they decide it was murder, they'll keep us here for a week."

"Like women our age go around killing strangers."

"We don't go around blowing up airplanes, either, honey, but that doesn't save me from being frisked in airports."

The cormorant flew off, and Sandra moved a little way apart from the other passengers. Again, her eye was drawn to the glittering water. Always so mesmerizing, the sun on water. Like a fire or a roiling thunderhead.

James had been right after all. One could change a story, however long, simply by changing its ending. One could change history. She would never again think of Mackinac Island as a place where she'd been with James, never remember it as a place where she'd gone in weakness and distress to hide herself away in the past. Those memories were completely overlaid now. Redacted with a broad black stroke.

In a sense, James had sacrificed himself for her, since, in giving her this relief, he'd ended his career as a living force in her life. At least on this one island.

The little ferry boat rounded the breakwater, and at that moment, Sandra had an epiphany. She could use the same method to erase the memory of James from every place they'd ever visited, to expunge him from the world.

Her heart, already buoyant, rose higher at the prospect. Where to go next?

Reader, I Buried Them
by Peter Lovesey

Little did the notorious murderers Crippen and Landru realise when they faced execution that their names would grace a prestigious American publishing imprint in the next century. I sometimes wonder how Douglas and Sandi Greene settled on these two as their brand identity when they started up in 1994. Why not a pair of killers closer to home, like Sacco and Vanzetti or Leopold and Loeb? Whatever the reason, their choices worked. Crippen & Landru have become bywords for single author collections of short stories published to the highest standard. Enlightened readers of mystery fiction rejoice each time a fresh set of killings is announced.

For 25 years a steady supply of elegant books has appeared from this small but distinguished press in Norfolk, Virginia. The care that goes into the process of publication never ceases to delight. A note appears in each volume about the typeface and the paper used, the cover artist and designer and the number of copies printed in hardback, sewn in cloth and signed and numbered by the author (if the author hasn't long since written the last chapter and gone to the reading room in the sky), for these are collectors' items. Devotees look for the gallows trademark always hidden somewhere in the cover illustration. Often, as an extra treat, there is an insert, a specially printed pamphlet with a contribution from the author.

More than most, I have reason to celebrate the first 25 years, for I'm lucky enough to have been reader, author, editor, and subject matter of books with the Crippen & Landru imprint. My friendship with Doug Greene goes back a long way, certainly longer than the quarter of a century of Crippen & Landru. His authoritative biography, John Dickson Carr: The Man Who Explained Miracles, is one of the most frequently consulted books on my shelves. While researching Carr, Doug became an authority on the early history of the Detection Club, of which Carr was secretary at a critical time in its existence. Doug's speech at the annual dinner at the Ritz in 2006 was a revelation to all present, for it was stunningly clear that he knew more about the history of the club than any of the members. That same evening we managed to surprise the club president, H.R.F.Keating, with The Verdict of us All, a collection of stories I had edited in a secret collaboration with Doug to mark Harry's eightieth birthday and published by Crippen & Landru.

The club honoured me when I got to eighty with a *festschrift* entitled Motives for Murder, edited by Martin Edwards, and the US edition was published by Crippen & Landru – who else? I was particularly touched that Doug travelled to London again for the presentation. He has now handed over the reins as publisher to Jeff Marks, while retaining an active interest as Series Editor.

The story that follows is about a small, well-established community with pride in doing everything to the highest possible standard, even when faced with a change.

Yes, I was the gravedigger, but my main job was overseeing the wildflower meadow. I'd better correct that. My main reason for being there was to worship the Lord and most of my hours were spent in prayer and study. However, we monks all had tasks that contributed to the running of the place and I was fortunate enough to have been chosen long ago to be the meadow man. If that sounds a soft number, I must tell you it isn't. Wildflower meadows need as much care as any garden, and this was a famous meadow, being situated at the back of a Georgian crescent in the centre of London. The monastery had once been three private houses. The gardens had been combined to make the two acres people came from far and wide to admire. My meadow had been photographed, filmed and celebrated in magazines. Often they wanted to include me in their reports and I had to be cautious of self-aggrandisement. I had no desire for celebrity. It would have been counter to the vows I took when I joined the brotherhood.

Closest to the monastery I grew rows of vegetables, but nobody except Brother Barry, the cook, was interested in them. My spectacular meadow stretched away beyond, dissected by a winding, mown-grass path. In the month of May we were treated to a medieval jousting tournament, the spring breezes sending the flagged wild irises towards the spikes of purple helmeted monkshood, cheered on by lilies of the valley and banks of primroses. Summer was the season of carnival, poppies in profusion, tufted vetch, ox-eye daisies, field scabious and foxgloves along the borders. Even as we approached September, the white campion, teazle, borage and wild carrot were still dancing for me. At the far end was the shed where my tools were kept and where, occasionally, I allowed myself a break from meadow management and did some contemplation instead. To the left of the shed was the apiary.

If you have a wildflower meadow you really ought to keep bees as well. And to the right were the graves where I buried our brothers who had crossed the River Jordan. When their time had come I dug the graves and after our Father Superior had led us in prayer, I filled them in and marked each one with a simple wooden cross. You couldn't wish for a more peaceful place to be interred.

And that was my way of glorifying God. The others all had their own tasks. Barry, I have mentioned, was our cook, and had only learned the skill after taking his vows. A straight-speaking man, easy to take offence (and therefore easy to tease), he had done some time in prison before seeing the light. Between ourselves, the meals he served were unadventurous, to put it mildly, heavily based on stew, sardines, baked beans and boiled potatoes, with curry once a week. Although my stomach complained, I got on better with Barry than any of the others.

A far more scholarly and serious man, Brother Alfred, was known as the procurer, ordering all our provisions by phone or the internet, including my seed and tools. Being computer-literate, he also communicated with the outside world when it became necessary.

Brother Luke was the physician, having been in practice as a doctor before he took holy orders. A socialist by conviction, he combined this responsibility with humbly washing the dishes and sweeping the floors.

Then there was Brother Vincent, a commercial artist in the secular life, who was painstakingly restoring a fourteenth century psalter much damaged by the years. Between sessions with the quills and brushes, he also looked after the library.

Our Father Superior was Ambrose, a remote, dignified man in his seventies who had been a senior civil servant before he received the call.

You may be wondering why I'm using the past tense. I still live the spiritual life and manage a garden, but it is no longer at our beloved monastery in London. One morning after matins, Father Ambrose asked us all to remain in our pews (for your information, the chapel had been created out of two living rooms by knocking down a wall and installing an RSJ. Not everyone knew this was a rolled steel joist and we had fun telling Barry we were expecting a Religious Sister of St Joseph). "I want to speak to you about our situation," our Father Superior said. "It must be obvious to you all that our numbers have been declining in recent years. Three brothers were called to higher service last year and two the year before. I won't say our little cemetery is becoming crowded, but the dead almost outnumber the living now. None of us are in the first flush of youth any more. Tasks that were manageable ten years ago are becoming harder now. I watched Jeffrey cropping the meadow at the end of last summer and it looked extremely demanding work."

As my name had been singled out, I felt I had a right to reply. "Father, I'm not complaining," I said, "but if I had a ride-on mower instead of the strimmer, it would ease the burden considerably."

"Jeffrey," he said, "I am discussing much more than your situation. I might just as well have used Barry and his catering as an example."

"What's wrong with my cooking?" Barry asked.

"The curry," Luke muttered. "Oh, for an Indian takeout."

"Did you say something?" Father Ambrose asked.

"Trying to think what could be done, Father," Luke said.

Ambrose moved on with his announcement. "In short, the Lord in His infinite wisdom has put the thought into my head that we should move to somewhere more in keeping with our numbers. This beautiful building and grounds can be used for another purpose."

He couldn't have shocked us more if he had ripped off his habit and revealed he was wearing pink spandex knickers.

"What purpose might that be?" Luke asked eventually.

"I know of a school in Notting Hill in unsuitable accommodation, much smaller than this, and in a poor state of repair."

"A school?"

"A convent school."

"You're suggesting they move here?"

"It's not my suggestion, Luke. As I was at pains to explain, it came to me from a Higher Source."

"Our monastery converted into a school? How is that possible?"

"It's eminently possible. This chapel would double as the assembly hall. The spare dormitories would become classrooms, the refectory the canteen, and so on."

"What about my meadow?" I asked.

Ambrose spread his hands as if it was obvious. "The playing field."

I was too shocked to speak. I had this mental picture of a pack of shrieking schoolgirls with hockey sticks.

"And my studio would become the art room, I suppose?" Vincent said with an impatient sigh.

"I see that you share the vision already," Ambrose said. "Isn't it wonderfully in keeping with our vows of sacrifice and self-denial?"

"Where would we go?"

"I'm sure the Lord will provide."

"Do we have any say?" Barry asked.

"Say whatever you wish, but say it to Our Father in Heaven."

This is one of the difficulties with the monastic life. There isn't a lot of consultation at shop floor level. Decisions tend to be announced and they have the authority of One who can't be defied.

We filed out of the pew dazed and shaken. If this was, indeed, the Lord's will, we would have to come to terms with it.

I returned to my beautiful meadow and tried to think about self-denial. Difficult. I vented my frustration on a patch of brambles that had begun invading the wild strawberries. After an hour of heavy work, I remembered I had recently put in an order for seed for next year's vegetable crop. If Father Ambrose's proposal became a reality, there wouldn't be any need for vegetables. So I went to see Alfred, the procurer. He has a large storage room with racks to the ceiling for all our provisions. There's a special section for all my gardening needs and beekeeping equipment.

I said what was on my mind.

"Good thinking," he said, looking up from his computer screen. Eye contact with Alfred was always disconcerting because he had one blue eye and one brown. "I'll see if it isn't too late to cancel the order."

"Did you know what Father Ambrose was going to say this morning?"

"Not at all," he said. "Has it upset you?"

I knew better than to admit to personal discontent. "I don't like to think about our departed brothers lying under a hockey pitch."

He shook his head. "Those are only mortal remains. Their souls have already gone to a Better Place."

He was right. I wished I hadn't spoken. "Are you in favour of this?"

"It's ordained," he said. As the second most senior monk, he probably felt compelled to show support.

I heard the slap of sandals on the floorboards behind me. We had been joined by Vincent, the scribe. He was a more worldly character than Alfred, always ready with a quip. "What's this – a union meeting?" he asked. "Are we going on strike, or what?"

"Brother Jeffrey is here to cancel his order for next year's seeds," Alfred said. "We have to look to the future."

"A future without a meadow? That's going to leave Jeffrey without a garden shed for his afternoon nap."

"We don't know where we'll be," I said, ignoring the slur about my contemplation sessions. "Wherever it is, I expect we'll have a garden."

"No problem for me," Vincent said. "All I need is a small room, a desk and a chair. And my art materials, of course. Do we have some more orpiment in stock?"

"Plenty," Alfred said.

"What's orpiment?" I asked.

"A gorgeous yellow," Vincent said. "The old scribes used it and so do I, but modern artists prefer gamboge."

"If it's so gorgeous, why isn't it used more?"

"Because it's the devil – if you'll pardon the expression – to grind the natural rock into a pigment. In fact, the variety I use is man-made, but based on the same constituents. I'll take some with me, Alfred. Chin up, Jeffrey. I'm sure there'll be a little patch of ground for you at the new place. If we leave London altogether, you could find yourself with acres more to grow things on."

But you never know what the Lord has in store. The concerns we had over moving from the monastery were overtaken by a shocking development. Our Father Superior reported to the infirmary with stomach pains, vomiting and diarrhoea. Some of us suspected Brother Barry's cooking was responsible, but Brother Luke diagnosed an attack of gastro-enteritis brought on by a virus infection. All that could be done at this stage was to make sure the patient drank plenty of fluids. Normally the infection will subside. But poor Father Ambrose didn't rally. His condition worsened so quickly that we barely had time to administer the last rites.

Was it a virus, we asked each other, or food poisoning? The latter seemed unlikely considering all of us had eaten the same food and no one else had been ill. A post mortem would have settled the matter, but, as Luke remarked, it wouldn't have altered anything. Being a qualified doctor, he issued the death certificate and nothing was said to the local coroner. I dug a grave and we buried Father Ambrose the following Monday.

After a period of mourning, we resumed our worship and work. Life has to go on for the survivors. Vincent returned to his restoration work. Barry got on with the cooking, and assured us all that he was using fresh ingredients and regularly washing his hands. Luke, with no patients to tend, scrubbed the infirmary. And I made a wooden cross for Ambrose, carved his initials on it, placed it in position and then went back to caring for my wildflowers. The ever changing, ever beautiful meadow was a source of solace. Already the bee orchids were appearing.

There was no debate about installing our next Father Superior. Alfred, through seniority, was the obvious choice. And he had gravitas. We held a token election and he was the only candidate. A well-organised monk I haven't mentioned, called Brother Michael, took on the mantle of procurer and computer operator.

One afternoon I was in my shed having a few minutes' contemplation when I was startled by someone tapping on the window. It was Michael.

"Did I wake you?" he asked when I invited him in.

"I was fully awake," I said. "Meditating."

"I've been doing some thinking myself," he said.

"What about?"

"Father Ambrose's sad death."

"He was getting on in years," I said. "It comes to us all eventually."

"But not so suddenly. He was gone in a matter of hours. I was wondering whether he was poisoned."

I was aghast. "Food poisoning was mentioned, but we all eat the same and no one else was ill, so the virus seems more likely."

"I don't mean food poisoning. I'm speaking of murder by poison – as in arsenic."

"Oh, my word! You can't mean that."

"I'm sorry," Michael said, "but I have some information that I feel bound to share with somebody. When I took over the store I decided to do an inventory and there was one item that was new in my experience, called orpiment."

"It's paint," I told him. "Brother Vincent needs it in his work. It's a shade of yellow the medieval scribes used."

"So I understand. But have you seen the packet it comes in? There's a warning on the side that it contains poison. I checked on the internet and it's produced by fusing one part of sulphur with two parts of arsenic."

Shocked by this revelation, I tried to answer in a level voice, not wishing to turn our peaceful monastery into a hornets' nest. "I didn't know that," I said. "Presumably Brother Vincent is aware of it."

"I also looked up the symptoms of arsenic poisoning," Michael said. "Nausea, vomiting, abdominal pain, diarrhoea – easily confused with acute gastro-enteritis."

"What exactly are you suggesting, Michael?" I said, still trying to stay calm. "None of us had any reason to poison Father Ambrose."

"The motive may not have been there, but the means was."

"Let's not get carried away," I said.

"It's tasteless," he said.

"You took the words out of my mouth."

"No. I'm saying that arsenic has no taste. And if you remember, it was a Friday – curry night – when Father Ambrose died. The orpiment wouldn't show up in curry."

"But no one else was ill. We all had the curry."

"If someone meant to poison Father Ambrose, they could have added some of the stuff to his bowl."

"But when?"

"As you know, Barry spoons the curry into the bowls with some rice and then one of us carries the tray to the table. Then we bow our heads and close our eyes for the grace. The opportunity was there."

Clearly, he'd thought this through in detail and believed it.

"Are you accusing Brother Barry of murder?" I asked.

"Or whoever carried the tray. Or whoever was seated beside Father Ambrose, or whoever was opposite him."

"Any of us, in fact?"

"Well, yes." His eyes widened. "And when I said just now that there was no motive, I was trying to be charitable. If one thinks the worst, there is a motive – Father Ambrose's master plan to remove us all to another monastery. No one likes change. Let's face it, we were all shocked and distressed when he announced it. By getting rid of Ambrose, we would save the monastery."

I shook my head sadly. "Michael, if this were not so silly, it would be a wicked slander. Do I need to remind you of the vow of obedience we all took? It's unthinkable for any of us to question our Father Superior, let alone cause him harm."

He appeared to see sense. "I hadn't thought of it like that."

"Then I suggest you put it out of your head and don't mention it to anyone else. I'm going to forget you ever spoke of it."

Months passed. I cropped my meadow late in August after the seeds had spread and Michael's alarming theory was as weathered as the bronzed hay. I'm bound to admit I had been unsettled by it. Despite my promise to forget about the conversation, I couldn't stop myself casting my brother monks in the role of poisoner. Once the seeds of suspicion are sown and growing, they are as difficult to root out as ground elder. Take Alfred, for example. He had attained the highest position in our community through Ambrose's death and as the procurer he had easy access to the orpiment. Equally, Vincent was in possession of the deadly stuff and although he professed to be indifferent to a move, he'd reacted strongly when it was first mentioned. Luke, with his doctor's training, probably knew more about the dangers of poisoning than any of us. Barry, as the cook, was best placed to administer the poison, and had been deeply upset by the criticism of his culinary skills. And Michael had benefited from Ambrose's death and risen to the position of procurer. What was his reason for spreading suspicion of everyone else? Uncharitable thoughts come all too readily when you're gardening and most of them are best ignored.

Late in October, when the last butterflies had gone and autumn mists were appearing over the meadow, the harmony of our community received another jolt. Arnold, our new Father Superior, had made almost no significant changes to our routine since being called to lead us. Then he announced he would be leaving the monastery for a week on a small mission. From time to time, the calls of family disturb the even tenor of our existence, so we thought nothing of it. In Arnold's absence, our services were led by Brother Luke. But when Father Arnold returned, he addressed us in chapel and my heart sank, for he stood to one side of the altar, just where Father Ambrose had been when he announced his ill-omened plan.

Arnold cleared his throat before saying anything. "You may not all appreciate what I have to say, but hear me out and when you have had time to absorb it, you will be better able to consider the matter without personal feelings intruding. Six months have gone by since our dear departed Father Ambrose raised the question of vacating this building so that the school could move in. As his successor, I feel bound to give consideration to his last great idea. It had been revealed to him, as he made clear, in the nature of a divine vision. After much prayer, I was moved this week to take the process a step further and I am pleased to tell you I have been to see a building, that with the Lord's help, we can transform into a monastery better suited to our numbers."

After a moment's uneasy silence, Luke asked, "What is it, a private house?"

"No, a lighthouse."

"God save us," Barry said in a stage whisper.

"These days, the warning lamps are automatic, using solar powered batteries, so there's no need for a keeper, but the living space is still there," Arnold said. "The rooms are wedge-shaped, most of them, smaller than the dormitory you're used to, but they will actually provide more privacy."

"I don't think I'm hearing this," Vincent said in a low voice.

"There are kitchen facilities," Arnold went on, warming to his theme and sounding awfully like an estate agent, "and a telegraph room that we can convert to the chapel. The building isn't just a glorified cylinder, you see. There's a keeper's house attached and most of our communal activities would take place in there."

"Where exactly is it?" I asked.

"Off the north-west coast of Scotland."

"Off the coast?"

"It's a lighthouse, Jeffrey."

"Some lighthouses are on land."

"This is an island a mile out to sea, a crop of rocks known as the devil's teeth."

He wasn't doing much of a selling job to a bunch of London monks.

"So it's built on solid rock?" I said. "Isn't there a garden?"

"That's one thing it does lack," Arnold admitted.

I was speechless.

"When you say 'kitchen facilities'," Barry said, "can I run a double oven and two hobs, as I have at present?"

"I believe there's a Primus stove."

"I don't believe this."

"Where will I do my restoration work?" Vincent asked. "I need a north-facing light."

"Top floor, in the lamp room," Barry unkindly said.

But there was no question that Father Arnold was serious. "Brothers, we must be flexible in our thinking. It can only do us good to adjust to a new environment. Try to come to terms with the concept before we discuss your individual needs."

We had curry as usual on Friday. Brother Barry's curries were notable more for their intensity than their flavour, so nothing was unusual when Father Arnold gasped and reached for the water jug. We always drank more on curry night. We smiled and nodded fraternally when he complained of a severe burning sensation in the mouth and throat, extending to his stomach. There was more concern when he retched and ran from the table.

Four hours later our Father Superior was dead.

Brother Luke, who was with him to the end, could do nothing to reverse his rapid decline. The patient vomited repeatedly, but brought up little. Severe stomach cramps, diarrhoea and convulsions set in. He complained of prickling of the skin and visual impairment. Before the end he became intensely cold and was talking of his veins turning to ice. A sort of paralysis took over. His facial muscles tightened and his pulse weakened, but his brain remained active until the moment of death.

You will have gathered from my description that Luke gave us a full account next morning of Arnold's last hours. A chastened group of us discussed the tragedy after morning prayers.

Barry insisted it couldn't have been the curry. "It must have been the same virus that killed poor Father Ambrose."

"Again?" Michael said. "I don't think so."

"Why not?" I said. "The symptoms were similar."

Michael gave me the sort of look you get from a dentist when you insist you brush after every meal.

Then Luke said, "I must admit, my confidence is shaken. I've never come across a viral condition quite like this. In fact, I'm thinking I should report it to the Department of Health in case it's a new strain."

"Before you do," Michael said, "Let's consider the other option — that he was poisoned."

I raised my hand to dissuade him. "Michael, you and I went over this before. Speculation such as that will damage our community."

"It's damaged already," he said. "Aren't two violent deaths in six months serious damage? I was silent before, at your suggestion, but this has altered everything. We know for a fact that a poisonous substance is stored here."

"What's that?" Barry said.

"Orpiment. The pigment Vincent uses is two-thirds pure arsenic."

"Vincent?"

All eyes turned to our scribe.

Michael added, "It doesn't mean Vincent administered the stuff. Any one of us could have collected some from his studio or my shelves. I don't keep the store locked."

"And used it to murder Ambrose and Arnold? That's unthinkable," Barry said.

"Well, maybe you can think of some other way it got added to the curry you serve," Michael said, well aware how the words would wound Barry. He wasn't blessed with much tact.

While Barry struggled with that, Luke asked, "What possible reason could anyone have for murdering Father Arnold?"

"Come on," Michael said. "Just like Ambrose, he was about to uproot us. None of us wants to see out his days on a lump of rock in the Atlantic Ocean."

"So there was motive, means and opportunity, the three preconditions for murder." A look of profound relief dawned on Luke's features. As our physician, he was no longer personally responsible for failing to contain a deadly virus. "You must be right. I'm beginning to think we can deal with this among ourselves."

"What — a double murder?" Michael piped up in disbelief.

"We don't want a police investigation and the press all over us."

I added in support, "They'll want to dig up Father Ambrose for sure. Let him rest in peace."

Barry agreed. "No one wants that."

Michael, in a minority of one, was horrified. "We'd be shielding a killer. We're men of God."

"And He is our Judge," Luke said. "If we are making a mistake, He will tell us. Shall we say a prayer?"

This was the moment when we all became aware that Luke, as the senior monk, was the obvious choice to be elected our new Father Superior. Even Michael bit his lip and bowed his head.

I dug another grave and we buried poor Father Arnold with the others at the edge of the meadow next morning. None of us asked what Luke had written on the death certificate. He was now our spiritual leader and it wasn't appropriate to enquire. I constructed the cross and positioned it at the head of the grave.

The lighthouse wasn't mentioned again. Father Luke had more sense. He wasn't quite as paternalistic as some of his predecessors. He believed in consulting us as well as the Lord and we left him in no doubt that we wanted to remain where we were, in our beloved monastery in the heart of London. Life returned to normal. I managed my meadow and kept the graves tidy. Vincent worked on his psalter. Barry kept us fed. Michael ran the store with efficiency and ordered our supplies online.

It came as a surprise to me one afternoon in January when I was in my shed wrapped in a quilt, indulging in my post-prandial contemplation, to be disturbed by a rapping at the door. Michael was there, hood up, arms folded, looking anything but fraternal.

"Is something up?" I asked, rubbing my eyes.

"You could put it that way," he said. "The Father Superior wants to see you in his office."

"Now?"

"He's waiting."

The office was in the attic at the top of our building. Michael escorted me and said not another word as we went up the three flights of stairs.

Father Luke's door stood open. He really was waiting, seated behind his desk, hands clasped, but more in an attitude of power than prayer. "Come in, both of you," he said.

There wasn't room for chairs, so we stood like schoolboys up before the head.

"This won't be easy," Father Luke said. "It's about the deaths of Father Ambrose and Father Alfred. Michael has informed me, Jeffrey, that he spoke to you after Ambrose died, about the possibility that he was poisoned with arsenic."

I said, "I think we all agree that he was."

Michael said, "But at the time you told me to keep my suspicions to myself."

Now I understood what this was about: a blame session. I'd never felt comfortable with Michael, but I hadn't taken him for a sneak. "That's true," I said. "It was the first time anyone had suggested such a thing and it was certain to cause friction and alarm in our community."

"Go on," Father Luke said to Michael. "Tell Jeffrey what you told me."

Michael seemed to be driving this and enjoying it, too. "When I took over as procurer, I gained access to the computer and this enabled me to confirm my theory about the orpiment. It is, indeed, a pigment made of sulphide of arsenic that was used by monks in medieval and Renaissance times to illuminate manuscripts."

I couldn't resist saying, "Clever old you!"

Father Luke raised his hand. "Listen to this, Jeffrey."

Michael went on, "However, when I searched the internet for information about the effects of acute arsenic poisoning, some of the symptoms Father Luke reported didn't seem to fit. Typically, there's burning in the mouth and severe gastroenteritis, vomiting and diarrhoea — all of which were present — but the second phase of symptoms, the prickling of the skin and visual impairment, the signs of paralysis in the face and body, aren't associated with arsenic."

Father Luke said, "Symptoms very evident in Ambrose and Arnold."

Michael said, "It made me ask myself if some other poison had been used, something that induces paralysis. I made another search and was directed away from mineral poisons to poisonous plants."

I was silent. Already I could see where this was going.

"And eventually," Michael continued in his self-congratulatory way, "I settled on a tall, elegant, purple plant known, rather unkindly, as monkshood, the source of the poison aconite. Every part from leaf to root is deadly. After the first violent effects of gastroenteritis, a numbing effect spreads through the body, producing a feeling of extreme cold, and paralysis sets in. The breathing quickens and then slows dramatically and all the time the victim is in severe pain, but conscious to the end."

"Precisely what I observed," Luke said, "and twice over."

"This proved nothing without the presence of aconite in the monastery," Michael said. "There are photos and diagrams of the monkshood plant on the internet, so I knew what to look for and where best to search. It prefers shady, moist places. I spent several afternoons while you were taking your nap and checked along the edges of the meadow where the water drains, close to the wall. Of course you hacked the tall stems down, so the plants weren't easy to locate, but eventually I found your little crop. The spiky, hand-shaped leaves are very distinctive. Some of the ripe follicles still contained seeds. Are you going to admit to using it, adding it to the curry?"

Father Luke said, "The Lord is listening, Jeffrey."

I didn't hesitate long. I'm not a good liar. I hope I'm not a liar at all. If you read this account of what happened, you'll see that I always spoke the truth, even if I didn't always volunteer it. "Yes," I said. "I used some root, chopped small. I made sure I was sitting beside our Father Superior when he spoke the grace. Then I sprinkled the bits over the curry. I couldn't face life without my beautiful meadow."

"So you took the lives of two good men," Michael said to shame me.

Our Father Superior shook his head sadly. "Now I'll have to notify the police."

I said, "I'll save you the trouble." I walked to the window, unfastened it and started to climb out.

"No, Jeffrey!" Father Luke shouted to me. "That's a mortal sin."

But he was too slow to stop me.

I was indifferent to his plea. I'd already committed one of the mortal sins twice over. Here on the roof I was at least fifty feet above ground. Below me was a paved area. When I jumped, I was unlikely to survive. If I had the courage to dive, I would surely succeed in killing myself.

With my feet on the steep-pitched tiles, I edged around the dormer to a place where no one could lean out and grab me. Then I climbed higher, intending to launch myself off the gable end.

Father Luke was at the open window, shouting that this wasn't the way, but I begged to differ.

Up there under an azure sky, on the highest point of the roof, I was treated to a bird's-eye view of my meadow, and if it was the last thing I ever saw I would be content. Glittering from the overnight frost, the patterns of my August cut were clearly visible like fish scales, revealing a beauty I hadn't ever observed from ground level. This, I thought, is worth dying for.

I reached the gable end and sat astride the ridge without much dignity, collecting my breath and getting up courage. A controlled dive would definitely be best. I needed to stand with my arms above my head and pitch forward.

I grasped the lightning conductor at the end and raised myself to a standing position.

And then I heard a voice saying, "Jeffrey, don't do it."

For a moment, teetering there on the rooftop, I thought the Lord had spoken to me. Then I realised the voice had not come from above. It was from way below, on the ground. Brother Barry was standing in the vegetable patch with his hands cupped to his mouth.

I called back to him. "I'm a wicked sinner, a double murderer."

"That's not good," he called back, "but killing yourself will only make things worse."

I told Barry, "I don't want to live. The police are coming and I can't bear to be parted from my meadow."

He shouted, "You'll get a life sentence. It's not as bad as you think, believe me. You'll share a cell with someone, but what's different about that? The food is better, even if I say it myself. And with good behaviour you'll be sent to a Category C prison where they'll be really glad of your gardening experience."

I was wavering. "Do you think so?"

"I know it."

What a brother he was to me. I'd never considered the prison option, but Barry had personal experience of it. And he was right. I could pay my debt to society and make myself useful as well. Persuaded, I bent my knees, felt for the lightning conductor and began to climb down.

In the prison where I have been writing this account of my experiences, I am proud of my "trusty" status. Barry was right. I can still lead the spiritual life and I always remember him in my prayers. The governor has put me in charge of the vegetable garden and I have persuaded him to allow me a wildflower section. No monkshood or other poisonous plants, of course. But by May we'll have an explosion . . . of colour. And I built my own tool-shed. Every afternoon I go in for an hour or so. Even the governor knows better than to disturb me when I'm contemplating.

THE CHATELAINE BAG
by Bill Pronzini and Marcia Muller

We're fortunate to have known Doug and Sandi for more than twenty-five years. In addition to enjoying their company at various conventions, we've exchanged scores of emails with Doug on a variety of topics, and added numerous volumes to each of our respective libraries of vintage crime fiction. We couldn't ask for more engaging and supportive friends in the writing and publishing community.

As he has done for so many others, Doug honored and showcased several of our contributions to the mystery/detective short-story pantheon. We're proud to have had ten volumes published by Crippen & Landru from 1996 to 2010: two collections of Sharon McCone stories by Marcia, three collections of Bill's stories (one in partnership with Barry Malzberg), and five "Lost Classics" edited by Bill.

"The Chatelaine Bag" was our first Carpenter & Quincannon collaboration; all of the previous C&Q stories were written by Bill alone, most of them collected in Carpenter and Quincannon, Professional Detective Services *(C&L, 1998). "Chatelaine" was an experiment to determine how well we could work together on the series — plotted jointly, with Marcia writing the scenes from Sabina's viewpoint, Bill those from Quincannon's. Satisfied with how the story turned out, we continued the C&Q collaborations in novel form, five having been published by Tor/Forge. Doug's enthusiasm for the series was also a contributing factor in our decision.*

Handbags. Reticules. Bah!
     Perhaps he was "a man of low tastes," as Sabina had accused him of being, but the appeal of such fancy antique gewgaws escaped him. He could understand why well-to-do women from Rincon Hill and Nob Hill might find Reticules Through the Ages of some interest. A certain type of thief, too, given the declared value of the exhibition's centerpiece, a bejeweled chatelaine bag that had once belonged to Marie Antionette; the remote possibility of theft was the reason he and Sabina had been hired to protect the confounded

collection. But men in general? Why would a respectable gent worth the name give two hoots about carryalls that had belonged to ladies a hundred and two hundred years ago? And yet, fully one-third of the visitors to the Rayburn Art Gallery over the past two days had been men. Some dragged there by their wives, no doubt, but the rest were a puzzle he had no interest in solving.

From his vantage point between the front entrance and the wine and liquor buffet, Quincannon again scanned the dwindling crowd before the long exhibit table at the inner wall. It was nearly seven o'clock of a dark February night—closing time for this second day of the three-day exhibition. Electric light from old gasoliers fitted with incandescent bulbs made the large room bright as day and his observations that much easier.

The only familiar faces other than Sabina's belonged to Marcel LeBeaux, assistant curator of the Louvre Museum in Paris, the man in charge of the collection and their client; Andrew Rayburn, the gallery owner; and his two clerks, Holloway and Eldridge. Quincannon had recognized only a few visitors since yesterday's opening, none of those suspicious. Every professional thief, yegg, and miscreant in San Francisco and environs was known to him and none had dared show his or her face. Not that this was a surprise. Any Barbary Coast or East Bay scruff caught snaffling reticules, even one bristling with small diamonds and rubies, would be the butt of jokes by his fellows for the rest of his days.

Besides which, what chance did even the cleverest of them have of managing such a swipe? The exhibition was well watched by Sabina and himself, as well as by Rayburn and the two clerks, during the hours it was open; and after closing, LeBeaux and Rayburn carefully locked the collection away in the gallery vault, which was not only as close to being burglarproof as any manufactured safe but was under guard by an armed night watchman.

Day watchmen were what he and Sabina were. Necessary, he supposed, but nonetheless mere window dressing. The job paid moderately well and Carpenter and Quincannon, Professional Detective Services, was otherwise between clients, but by Godfrey it offered no challenge whatsoever to a sleuth of John Quincannon's considerable talents. Dull, stand-about work of the sort any average or even sub-average fly cop could handle.

Sabina felt differently, of course. The two dozen or so ancient items on display fascinated her, by her own admission, and she seemed to find guard duty in a Post Street gallery stimulating because it allowed her to mingle with some of the city's elite. Women. Marvelous creatures, but he would never understand them. Sabina was a constant mystery to him. So was her infuriating and inexplicable refusal to have anything to do with him of a romantic nature, despite his persistance and what he considered to be honorable intentions.

Quincannon looked across at where she was standing next to the food buffet. If you could call cheese, crackers, nuts, skewered pieces of fruit, and strange-looking canapés food. She wore a Nile green embroidered silk frock that accented her handsome figure; the rather large, plain handbag she carried had a .22-caliber pistol tucked inside. He sighed and fluffed his freebooter's beard. He wouldn't have admitted it, but he was feeling a touch sorry for himself and not a little jealous of the smiles she kept bestowing on the well-dressed gents who stopped to speak to her. The person her smile was favoring at the moment was a corpulent middle-aged man whose expression—at least to Quincannon's jaundiced eye—was one of ill-concealed lust.

Reticules Through the Ages. Bah and double bah!

Sabina

Sabina smiled at a man whose large corporation strained the buttons of his lacy white shirt. That one's never missed a meal, she thought—words her late mother had been prone to utter in embarrassingly loud tones. And every one of those meals seemed to have expanded his stomach while leaving the rest of him of more or less normal size. Then she chided herself for being unkind. After all, the man had yet to partake of the buffet since his arrival a few minutes earlier. Perhaps he was on a diet.

Nonetheless, smiling in return, he chose to compliment the table. "A sumptuous buffet, is it not?"

"Very nice."

The corpulent man persisted. "Allow me to introduce myself: Thaddeus Bakker, of the Sacramento Bakkers. Perhaps you've heard of me?"

"Of course," she said, although she had not. "Sabina Carpenter."

"A most excellent exhibit, too," he added.

"Yes. Are you a connoisseur, Mr. Bakker?"

"Of handbags and reticules? No, no, merely an art lover and a student of history in all its forms. And you, Miss Carpenter? A connoisseur?"

"Mrs. Carpenter. Yes, you might say that."

Bakker bowed, rather clumsily given his bulging midsection. "If you'll excuse me, I believe I'll have another look at the exhibition." He favored her with another smile and moved ponderously toward the display table.

Behind Sabina at the food buffet stood a gentleman with a tortoiseshell pince-nez, squinting through its lens at a brick of Stilton cheese as if he found it suspect. "Harrumph!" he exclaimed repeatedly, as though something were lodged in his throat. At the other end of the long table, a group of ladies clad in the slimmed-down dresses of the nineties—bustles, thank the Lord, were no longer in fashion—milled about nibbling canapés and talking. She looked away from the well-dressed crowd and again let her gaze wander over the bags on display.

Her favorites were the chatelaine bags: reticules that in olden times had hung from an ornamental hook on the jeweled girdles of ladies of high station and contained useful household items. Made of beadwork or silver or gold mesh, many were set with semiprecious or precious gems, such as the diamond-and-ruby encrusted bag that Marie Antoinette had worn at Versailles. The Antoinette bag was wide and long, six by ten inches, with a rigid gold frame and clasp. It was the jewel of this exhibition, valued at several thousand dollars.

Across the room she spied her partner near the wine and liquor buffet, something of an irony because he had renounced Demon Rum after a tragic accident during his days with the United States Secret Service. With his luxuriant freebooter's beard and in his gray sack coat, matching waistcoat, and striped trousers he cut a handsome figure. The red four-in-hand was a bit garish, but then he could be flamboyant when the mood struck him.

Still, he was finely turned out—not that Sabina would flatter him by telling him so. Any such praise would only encourage him in his pursuit of her, set him to spouting the poetry he so loved and importuning for opportunities to dine together. She had been a widow too long for such romantic nonsense—her husband, like she, had worked as a Pinkerton agent in Denver, and had been foully murdered several years ago in the line of duty. Besides, she valued John too much as a friend and business partner to welcome any sort of dalliance.

Although at times, being well aware of the pleasures of the flesh, she wondered—

None of that now! You are here to observe and protect, not woolgather.

She moved closer to the display to once more marvel at the Antoinette chatelaine bag. It was suspended from a hook in its blue velvet display case, jewels winking in the soft electric light. Such a history it had: seized by French revolutionists and paraded through the streets of Paris as an example of the monarchy's excesses. Lost for two decades, it had resurfaced in the possession of a descendant of a minor revolutionary, who donated it to the Louvre Museum. And there it had been permanently displayed until Bernard La Follette, curator, joined with curators from museums in Florence and Venice to organize this exhibition and bring it to selected American cities under the guidance of Marcel LeBeaux.

The gallery venue was especially favorable: small, secure, and most of the visitors were known to Andrew Rayburn, the owner. Far better here than a large exhibition hall with many entrances and exits, or even the local museums with their dark nooks and crannies. Yes, the reticules should be quite safe here. Mr. LeBeaux's hiring of the Carpenter and Quincannon agency had been an unnecessary precaution, perhaps, but Sabina was glad of it even if John groused at a job he considered beneath his talents. The opportunity to view such a splendid collection was a pleasure, and the fee was excellent.

She looked over the crowd again, then crossed the room to speak with John.

"All seems well," she said in low tones. "Another day without incident or suspicious characters among the viewers."

He nodded and then said in tones that bore an undercurrent of jealousy, "You and that fat gent appeared to find each other amusing."

"Amusing?"

"All smiles, both of you. Who is he?"

"Mr. Thaddeus Bakker, of the Sacramento Bakkers."

"Whoever they are. What did he want?"

"Why, I assume what men always want."

John narrowed his eyes at her. "And that is?"

"A pleasant conversation, of course," she said serenely, and went back to her station near the food buffet.

Quincannon

The number of visitors had thinned to less than a dozen men and women, all of them grouped in the middle of the room between the two buffets. Quincannon consulted his stemwinder. Six minutes until closing. And seven o'clock would arrive not a moment too soon. He was weary of the day's long, standing vigil, and in need of a genuine meal such as the unparalleled seafood fare at the Cobweb Palace at Meig's Wharf. Perhaps Sabina—

"Excuse me, young man."

A rather overdressed, middle-aged matron had sidled up next to him. "Yes, madam?" he said through an artificial smile.

"Are you an employee of this establishment?"

"Why do you ask?"

"You have been standing in this same place the entire time I've been here, looking at everything except the exhibition. Are you an employee?"

"After a fashion."

"That is not an answer. I don't believe you are. I have been a patron of Rayburn's for many years and I've never seen you before." She waved a lorgnette at him as if it were a miniature sword. "I find you suspicious."

Quincannon managed to maintain his professional smile; "Do you, indeed."

"Just who are you?"

"A gentleman of industry."

"A what? Bosh. You look like a thief."

And you look like a bulldog, he thought. "Have you ever seen a thief, madam?"

"Yes, and he looked exactly like you. Though I must say his attire was of much better quality."

This altered his smile into a ferocious glower. "Madam, if you—" And all the lights went out.

The sudden darkness was nearly absolute. There were no street lamps in the immediate vicinity outside the gallery; the only light that penetrated, and only faintly, came from the lamps of hansoms, carriages, and one of those infernal horse-frightening motorized contraptions passing on Post Street. The bulldog emitted a startled sound that was more bark than shriek. Voices rose querulously; there was a confused milling about.

Quincannon's reaction was immediate. Three long strides took him to the front entrance; he barred it with his body and outflung arms, and shouted in stentorian tones, "Stand clear of the doors! No one is allowed to leave!"

Sabina had moved just as quickly and instinctively. Her voice rose out of the darkness: "Rear doorway secure!"

Andrew Rayburn's came next: "Remain calm, ladies and gentlemen, remain calm. I'll soon have the lights back on."

The others in the room quieted and grew still. Someone brushed up against Quincannon, either by accident or in an attempt to exit; a none-too-gentle shove brought instant retreat. A lucifer scratched and flared, then a brighter flame that came from a flint lighter. In the flickering glow the faces of the dozen or so people appeared like masks of shadow. Quincannon squinted toward the Reticules Through the Ages display. No one was in close proximity to it except

George Eldridge, one of Rayburn's clerks.

The sudden extinguishing of the lights might have been accidental; such blackouts were not uncommon in this new age of electricity. But Quincannon distrusted coincidence whenever the possibility of nefarious activity was afoot—the more so when something like this happened at such a convenient time. He pressed his back more tightly against the doors, the fingers of his right hand touching the butt of the Navy Colt concealed inside his coat.

No one made any effort to push past him while the blackout lasted, a period of no more than two minutes. But when the lights came on again—

"The Marie Antoinette bag! It's gone!"

The outcry came from Eldridge, who stood pointing at the Reticules Through the Ages display. Even from a distance, Quincannon could see that the blue velvet centerpiece case was empty. He bit back a richly inventive and sulphurous oath, settled instead for a muttered, "Hell and damn!" His scowl was one of malignant ferocity.

Another babble of voices had followed the clerk's pronouncement. Most of the people were grouped together in the center of the room, all except for Holloway and the corpulent gent who stood off by himself, looking frightened and twitching his fingers across the front of his corporation. Marcel LeBeaux and Andrew Rayburn stood next to Sabina at the rear doorway, both men gesticulating wildly. She said something to LeBeaux that resulted in a violent head shake, after which the Frenchman turned, spied Quincannon, and came rushing over to him with Rayburn at his heels.

The Frenchman was a tall, spare gent with elegantly tonsured silver hair; the gallery owner, by contrast, was a fussy little man with a fussy little black moustache. LeBeaux still waved his arms, his saturnine face mottled with a mixture of outrage and anxiety. "The chatelaine bag is missing! Stolen!"

"So I understand."

"Diable! Do something, m'sieur! You were hired to prevent such a thing from happening—"

"Which neither Mrs. Carpenter nor I could very well do in a blacked-out room full of people."

"Yes, yes, but the Marie Antoinette, the Marie Antoinette—" One of LeBeaux's flailing hands narrowly missed Quincannon's nose. "The gendarmes, the police—we must summon them immediately."

The police. Faugh! The present regime was as corrupt and incompetent as any in the city's history. Should the bluecoats be brought in and one happen to stumble across the missing bag, like as not he would steal it himself.

"There's no need for the police," Quincannon said, "when you have the finest detective west of the Mississippi River, if not in the entire nation, already on the premises."

"Eh? Who?"

Quincannon's glower grew even more malignant. "John Quincannon, naturally. At your service."

Rayburn said, "Yes, well, then do something, for heaven's sake!"

"I have been doing something—guarding this door."

"No one slipped past you before you took up your position? You're sure?"

"Positive. Nor did anyone slip past Mrs. Carpenter, I take it?"

"Only me. I went into the storeroom just after she took up her position, to find out what happened to the lights."

"Could you tell if anyone else was in the storeroom?"

"I didn't see anyone when the lights were restored."

"What caused them to go out?"

"A fuse had come loose. I screwed it back in."

Come loose by itself? Not likely.

"Is the rear entrance locked?"

"Yes. I made sure of it before I returned to the gallery."

"Who else has a key besides you?"

"No one. It's in my vest pocket."

"Bully," Quincannon said.

"What? Bully? What the devil's the matter with you, Quincannon? Don't you understand that someone has made off with the most valuable chatelaine bag in the collection?"

"Calm yourself, Mr. Rayburn. No one has made off with it."

"Eh?" LeBeaux said. "What's that you say?"

"Everyone who was in the gallery before the lights went out is still here, Quincannon said. "Ergo, both the thief and the missing reticule are still here. We'll soon have both in hand."

Sabina

After Andrew Rayburn locked the front doors, he and M'sieur LeBeaux gathered all the guests and the two clerks together in the middle of the gallery and revealed her and John's identities. There were exclamations of surprise. The man with the pince-nez still seemed to be trying to dislodge an obstruction in his throat; a series of "Harrumphs!" overrode the other voices. A dowager with great sausage-shaped curls topped by a feather-strewn hat said in a disbelieving voice, "Detectives? A woman and this ... this man?"

John glowered at her. "And why not, madam?"

"You still look like a thief to me. Mr. Rayburn, are you sure he isn't the one who pinched the missing bag?"

Mutters and grumbles followed this. John, who had little patience at the best of times, looked as if he would like to strangle the woman; Sabina put her restraining hand on his arm as he took a step forward. The gallery owner sought to reassure everyone that not only was John innocent of the theft, but that Carpenter and Quincannon, Professional Detective Services, was the city's most reputable detective agency. His words were met with more mutters and dubious expressions, none more sceptical than the sausage-curled dowager's.

It was John who restored order by taking control of the situation. He did this in typical John Quincannon fashion, by expanding his chest and shouting in a voice loud enough to rattle window glass. "Quiet! Quiet, I say!" The words brooked no argument, and there was none. "Whoever took the confounded bag is still in this room. So is the bag itself. A careful search will turn it up."

A gentleman in a derby hat said meekly, "Do you intend to search each of us?"

"If necessary."

"Outrageous!" This from the dowager. "I refuse to be treated like a common thief—"

"Whether or not you're a thief, madam, common or otherwise, remains to be seen."

"What? How dare you!"

Tact was sometimes as lacking in John as patience. Sabina hurriedly interceded. "If a search of your person is necessary, it will be done privately and with the utmost prudence. No one will be unduly inconvenienced."

"I, for one, have no objection to being searched," Thaddeus Bakker said. "No innocent person should have."

"Just so, Mr. Bakker."

John ordered everyone to move over to the wall behind the food buffet and to stay there in a group. When this was done, he, Sabina, LeBeaux, and Rayburn held a brief conference on the opposite side of the gallery.

"I don't see how searching everyone will turn up the bag," Rayburn said. "Surely the thief wouldn't have it on his person."

"And why not?"

Sabina answered John's question. "You didn't pay much attention to it, but it's too large to be hidden in men's or women's clothing." She held out her hands in an approximation of the chatelaine's size. "The clasp alone would make it virtually impossible to conceal."

The Frenchman concurred. "Mais oui. Quite impossible."

"Everyone will have to be searched nonetheless."

"Perhaps the thief has hidden it somewhere in this room, with the idea of returning for it later."

"Or in the storeroom or my office," the gallery owner added.

"Not likely in either of those places, Mr. Rayburn," John said. "It's a certainty no one left this room while the lights were out, nor has left it since you put them on again."

'Yes, that's right."

John fluffed his beard and smacked his hands together. "We'll search the lot of them now," he said, "and have done with that first. Sooner or later, in one place or another, we'll find your Marie Antoinette."

"We had better find it, M'sieur Quincannon," LeBeaux said portentously. "We had better!"

Quincannon

While Sabina watched over the women, Quincannon searched each of the four male guests and the two gallery employees in Rayburn's private office. LeBeaux then insisted that his and Rayburn's persons be searched, and when that was done, that Quincannon submit to a search as well. The Frenchman's pat-down technique was more thorough than Quincannon felt was necessary, but he offered no complaint. The chatelaine bag remained missing.

Sabina took her turn with the five women guests, the blasted bulldog still outraged and making dire threats of a lawsuit against all parties concerned. If a muzzle had been close at hand, Quincannon would cheerfully have used it to still her yapping.

None of the women possessed the bag, either.

So it must be hidden somewhere in the gallery. Either by design, in which case the thief believed himself to be more clever than he was; or because he had realized he couldn't get away with his crime and stashed the bag to avert detection. He would be unmasked and snaffled in any case. No thief had yet outwitted John Quincannon and no thief ever would.

Guests and employees were herded into the storeroom, with Sabina again on guard, after which the three men commenced a careful exploration of the gallery. Every possible hiding place was examined—nooks and crannies, the undersides of the display table, chairs, and pedestals used to exhibit sculptures, the backs of paintings mounted on the walls, and the food, bottles, plates, and glassware on the two buffets. Quincannon even went so far as to test the walls and floor for possible hidey holes, of which he found none.

The bag was not there.

"Zut alors!" LeBeaux said in exasperation when they were finished. "C'est incroyable. You are certain, M'sieur Quincannon, that the thief could not have left this room during the blackout?"

"Unless he or she has the power to walk through solid walls, I am."

"Then where is the Marie Antoinette?"

Quincannon had no idea where the blasted bag was, not that he would ever have admitted it to the Frenchman or anyone else. "No one will leave these premises until we find it," he said with more conviction than he felt. He went to the storeroom door and gestured to Sabina to come out.

"Mrs. Carpenter," he said formally when she joined them, "do you agree that there are two people involved in the theft?"

LeBeaux and Rayburn both seemed surprised at the question. But only until Sabina answered it.

"I do," she said. "One to loosen the fuse at a prearranged time, the other to lift the bag from the display table."

"Is it likely one of the guests would know where the fuse box is located and be able to find it by matchlight in a dark room?"

"Not likely at all."

Rayburn's thin moustache twitched. "Are you saying the accomplice, if there is one, is one of my employees?"

"Holloway or Eldridge, yes. How long have they worked for you?"

"Eldridge for four years, Holloway for just under one. But—"

Sabina said, "I kept a watchful eye on the storage room door, of course, but not every second. One or the other could easily have slipped through."

"And hidden and then returned after Mr. Rayburn," Quincannon said.

"Yes. Not before."

"Did you notice where Holloway and Eldridge were standing prior to the blackout? My attention was diverted by that dowager bulldog."

"They were both near the display table, on the side nearest the storeroom door. When the lights came on, Eldridge was in front of the table—apparently the first to notice the Antoinette bag was missing."

"And Holloway?"

Sabina didn't answer immediately. She seemed to be cogitating, as if something had just occurred to her. Whatever it was, she chose not to share it. After a few seconds she said, "Holloway? I don't know. I didn't see him."

"I did," Rayburn said. "He was at my side just after I came in from the storeroom. I remember because he spoke my name."

The Frenchman confirmed this. "Oui, I heard him as well."

"Could he have followed you in?" Quincannon asked Rayburn.

"… I suppose he could have, if he'd been hiding somewhere near the door."

Elias Holloway was summoned to join them. He was about Rayburn's size, with delicate features and fair hair. He had a habit of clasping his long-fingered hands at his waist; now he stood rubbing them together in a nervous fashion. But his gaze was steady and his posture one of defensive innocence.

He vehemently denied having been in the storeroom. "I was at the wall behind the display table," he said, "from just before the blackout until light was restored."

"Who else was near the table before?" Quincannon demanded.

"George Eldridge. Moving about in front."

"Just him?"

"In the immediate vicinity, yes."

"And you have no idea who snatched the bag?"

"None. None at all."

Quincannon had a sharp eye for facial expressions and body movements, a sharp ear for nuances of speech; it was the rare miscreant, male or female, who could dupe him successfully. He drew himself up and loomed over the small man, fixing him with a basilic glare.

"You lie, Holloway," he said. "I know you're guilty. We all know it. Confess and identify your confederate and perhaps Monsieur LeBeaux will be inclined to be lenient with you."

"But yes, I will," the Frenchman said. "My only concern is the recovery of the Marie Antoinette."

But the clerk foolishly maintained a misguided faith in his partner and the hope for his share of the spoils. "You can't intimidate me," he said. "I had nothing to do with the theft. Nothing, do you understand? And you can't prove I did."

Quincannon resisted an impulse to hoist up the little man and shake him until his bones rattled. Such action might have the desired effect, but he had built his reputation as a premier sleuth on his mental prowess, not on the use of force in front of witnesses. If Holloway refused to cooperate, so be it. The truth of the matter would be discovered in other ways, and soon. Failure was not a word in Quincannon's lexicon.

He sent Holloway back to wait with the others and summoned George Eldridge, a few years older and several pounds heavier. Eldridge was cooperative, but had nothing of importance to relate. He had stopped near the far corner of the table when the room went dark, he said, and remained there until it was lighted again. He couldn't recall if Holloway had been in the room or not when he spied the empty blue velvet case; his attention had been riveted on that. Nor could he say who else might have been close enough to the table to snag the chatelaine bag in the darkness."

"What now, M'sieur Quincannon?" LeBeaux asked when Eldridge had left their company. "What now, eh?"

Quincannon, despite his silent bluster, was nonplussed for one of the few times in his life. He was still struggling for a suitable response when Sabina stirred and put a hand on his arm. She had remained quiet the entire time Holloway and Eldridge were being questioned, evidently lost in thought. Now she seemed more animated than ever, her dark blue eyes bright.

"John," she said, "there's another person to be questioned, and without delay."

"Yes? Who would that be?"

"Mr. Thaddeus Bakker, of the Sacramento Bakkers."

"Why? Do you think he knows something useful?"

"Fetch him, please."

"I repeat, why?"

"Because he ate nothing from the food buffet prior to the blackout. Because his neck is slender and so are his arms and legs. And because of his frilly white shirt. Now will you please fetch him?"

For a moment Quincannon wondered if she had gone daft. But Sabina's tone was commanding, and when she spoke in such a fashion it was usually for a well-considered reason. Without further comment he went and fetched the corpulent gent, who seemed as puzzled as he was by the summons.

"I don't know what I can tell you," he said. "I know nothing at all about the theft."

Sabina studied him for several seconds, then nodded crisply as if in confirmation of what she was thinking. "Don't you, Mr. Bakker?"

"I've just said so, haven't I?"

"Where were you when the blackout ended?"

"Why … I don't recall exactly. By the liquor buffet, I believe."

"No, you were standing near the wall beyond the Reticules Through the Ages display."

"Was I?"

"You were," Quincannon said. "I saw you there myself when the lights came on, just turning around and fussing with your shirtfront."

"Not exactly fussing," Sabina said. "What he was actually doing was refastening one of the buttons."

"What of it?" Bakker drew himself up. "Are you suggesting I stole the Marie Antoinette reticule and hid it inside my shirt?"

"Stole it, yes. Hid it, yes. But not inside your shirt."

"The accusation is preposterous. Mr. Quincannon here searched me himself. If, the bag was in my clothing, he would have found it."

"It wasn't and isn't in your clothing, Mr. Bakker."

"Then what do you——"

To Quincannon's open-mouthed astonishment, Sabina suddenly punched Thaddeus Bakker in the stomach with all her might.

Sabina

Her closed fist must have sunk two inches into Bakker's midriff, yet the man's only reaction was a small startled grunt. Thus confirming her suspicion and justifying her bold action. No genuinely fat man could have absorbed such a violent blow without indications of hurt.

Rayburn gasped and LeBeaux exclaimed, "Mon Dieu!" But John understood immediately.

"False, by Godfrey! A false corporation!"

Bakker realized the game was up and made a clumsy attempt to flee. John tripped him, pounced on top, and tore open the man's shirt to reveal a padded convex mound wrapped in an elasticized garment resembling a woman's corset—a false corporation cunningly made so it would look and feel genuine when the clothing that covered it was searched. The corsetlike garment fit tightly, but not so tightly it couldn't be pulled up along one side. Which John quickly proceeded to do. A moment later he removed the chatelaine bag from among wads of cotton padding inside and held it up for all to see.

A good deal of confusion followed. Monsieur LeBeaux seized the bag, examined it, and then, with a Gallic flourish, he threw his arms around Sabina and bestowed a kiss on each cheek. John glowered at this but said nothing; he and Rayburn were busy lifting a weakly struggling Thaddeus Bakker to his feet. Some of the guests had spilled out of the storeroom to look on, chattering in excited voices. Holloway, realizing his partner had been caught, made a foolish attempt to escape through the rear door; Eldridge and the man with the pince-nez halted and held him until he could be locked away in Rayburn's office with Bakker. Eldridge was then sent to summon the police.

It was two hours before the bluecoats finished their officious duties and allowed everyone to leave. Two facts resulted from their interrogation of the culprits. Thaddeus Bakker's real name was Horace Bean and he was indeed from Sacramento, where he had twice been arrested on suspicion of jewel theft. And Elias Holloway was his brother-in-law.

John remained uncharacteristically silent the entire time, speaking only when spoken to and avoiding Sabina's eye. She knew why, of course. He was pouting because she had upstaged him by solving the puzzle before he could.

Sometimes working with him was akin to walking a tightwire. His pride and his conceit were considerable, and often justified, but also easily bruised; he was far more vulnerable and insecure than he would ever admit. He would also never admit she was his equal as a detective, which of course she was, and on the occasions when she out-sleuthed him he found ways to rationalize her success. As he did in the hansom cab on the way from Post Street to her flat on Russian Hill, when he finally broke his brooding silence.

"A woman's eye," he said.

"Pardon?"

"A woman has an eye for such details as whether or not a man eats from a buffet and the size of his neck and if one of his shirt buttons has been opened. That's why you were able to deduce the hiding place of the bag before I did."

"I'm sure that's so." She tried not to smile.

"I would have come to the same conclusion eventually."

"I'm sure you would have."

"As a matter of fact, my mind had already begun to work along those lines."

"And such a nimble mind it is. We both know there is no better detective west of the Mississippi than John Quincannon."

He said nothing, but in the glow from the side lamp she could see that he was his old preening self again.

A woman's work is never done, she thought. And smiled her secret smile.

THE TEST
by HRF Keating

What writer would not want to be associated with a publishing house with the inspirational name of Crippen & Landru? Certainly HRF (Harry) Keating was no exception and was delighted to work, on many occasions, with Douglas Greene.

Contributions to anthologies were made, over the years, before C & L undertook to do the American edition of Harry's own collection, published in the UK by Flambard Press, of In Kensington Gardens Once.

Subsequent to that Doug was asked by Malice Domestic to do an in-depth interview when Harry was being honoured at their convention and such was the obvious rapport between them that Sheila (Harry's wife) asked Doug if he would be prepared to publish a book in conjunction with The Detection Club to commemorate Harry's fairly imminent 80th birthday. The result was The Verdict of Us All, *an astonishing collection of short stories and tributes edited by Peter Lovesey.*

As always it was not only the content that was superlative but the whole arresting presentation. The sheer pleasure of holding a Crippen & Landru publication in the hand make them the standard bearers in any crusade to keep the printed word alive.

From the very beginning Inspector Ghote had doubts about Anil Divekar and the Test Match. Cricket and Divekar did not really mix. Divekar's sport was something quite different: he was a daylight entry ace. Excitement for him lay not in perfectly timing a stroke with the bat that would send the ball skimming along the grass to the boundary, but in the patient sizing up of a big Bombay house, the layout of its rooms, the routine of its servants, and then choosing the right moment to slip in and out carrying away the best of the portable loot.

But here Divekar was, as Ghote on a free day stood with his little son Ved outside the high walls of Brabourne Stadium, ticketless and enviously watching the crowds pouring in for the start of the day's play. He even came up to them, smiling broadly.

"Inspector, you would like seats?"

At Ghote's side, clutching his hand, little Ved's face lit up as from a sudden inward glow. And Ghote nearly accepted the offer. Ved deserved the treat. He was well-behaved and already working hard at school—and it was only a question of a pair of tickets. Some of his own colleagues would have taken them as a right.

But Ghote knew all along that he could not do it. Whatever the others did, he had always kept his integrity. No criminal could ever reproach him with past favours.

Angrily he tugged Ved off. But, marching away from the stadium, he could not help speculating as to why Divekar should have been there at all. Of course, when every two years or so a team from England or Australia or the West Indies came to Bombay, Test Match fever suddenly gripped the most unexpected people. But all the same ...

The crowd outside the stadium had not been all college students and the excited schoolboys you might expect. Smart business executives had jostled with simple shopkeepers and grain merchants. The film stars' huge cars had nosed their way past anxious, basket-clutching housewives, their best saris already looking crumpled and dusty.

Fifty thousand people, ready to roast all day in the sun to watch a sedate game that most of them hardly understood. Waiting for someone to "hit a sixer" so that they could launch into frenzied clapping, or for someone to drop a catch and give them a chance to indulge in some vigorous booing, or—the height of heights—for a home player to get a century and permit them to invade the pitch with garlands held high to drape their hero.

Where did they all get the entrance money, Ghote wondered. With even eighteen-rupee seats selling for a hundred, getting in was way beyond his own means. Little Ved's treat would have to be, once more, a visit to the Hanging Gardens.

But when they reached this mildly pleasurable—and free—spot, everywhere they went transistor radios were tuned teasingly to the Test Match commentary. Nothing Ghote offered his son was in the least successful.

He bought coconuts, but Ved would not even watch the squatting naralwallah dexterously chop off the tops of the dark fruit. He held out the gruesome spectacle of the vultures that hovered over the Towers of Silence where the Parsis laid out their dead, but Ved just shrugged. He purchased various bottled drinks, each more hectically coloured and more expensive than the previous one, but Ved drank them with increasing apathy.

He even attempted to enliven things by starting a game of hide-and-seek. Disastrously. After he had twice prolonged finding Ved—whose idea of hiding did not seem to stretch beyond standing sideways behind rather too narrow trees—as long as he possibly could, he decided that the game might go better if he himself were to be the one to go into hiding. So while Ved was temporarily absorbed in examining a cicada which, in a moment of aberration, had mistaken day for night and emitted its shrill squeak, he dropped to the ground behind a nicely sturdy bush and crouched there, keeping a paternal eye on his small son through the leaves.

For some time Ved stayed deeply engaged with the cicada, squatting beside it and turning it over with one delicate finger in an effort to see how such a small stick of a creature could produce that single extraordinarily loud squeak. But then he looked up, as if he were going to consult the parental oracle. For an instant he looked round merely puzzled. But then …

Then it was plain that the end of the world had come, the end of his small safe world. He lifted up his head and gave vent to a howl of pure, desolate anguish.

In a flash Ghote was beside him, hugging, patting, reassuring. But nothing seemed to restore that confidence there had been before. Not another offer of a cold drink. Not pointing out half a dozen "funny men", though none of them was in fact particularly odd. Not promises of future treats, not stern injunctions to "be a little man". Ved's face remained tear-stained and immovable.

At last Ghote gave up in a spasm of irritation.

"If that is all you care, we will go home."

Ved made no reply.

They set off, Ghote walking fast and getting unnecessarily hot. And still, going down Malabar Hill with its huge garden-surrounded mansions and great shady trees, there were passers-by with transistors and the unwearying commentator's voice. "What a pity for India. A glorious captain's knock by the Rajah of Bolkpur ends in a doubtful decision by Umpire Khan."

Ved swung round on him with an outraged glare. Whether this was because of the umpire's perfidy or because of simply not being there it was hard to tell.

And at that moment Ghote saw him. Anil Divekar. At least the figure that he half glimpsed ahead, sneaking out of a narrow gate and cradling in his arms a heavy-looking sack looked remarkably like Divekar. Ghote launched himself into the chase.

But the sound of running steps alerted the distant figure and in moments the fellow had disappeared altogether.

Ghote went quickly back to the house from whose side entrance he had seen the suspicious figure emerge. And there things began to add up. The big house had been rented temporarily to none other than the Rajah of Bolkpur himself, and a few minutes' search revealed that all the Rajah's silver trophies and personal jewellery had just been neatly spirited away.

Ghote got through to CID Headquarters on the telephone and reported. Then he and Ved endured a long wait till a squad arrived to take over. But they did get away in time to go down to the stadium again to see if Ved could catch a glimpse of the departing players.

And no sooner had they arrived at the stadium, just as the crowds were beginning to stream out, when there was Anil Divekar right in front of them. He made no attempt to run. On the contrary, he came pushing his way through the throng, smiling broadly.

No doubt he thought he had fixed himself a neat alibi. But Ghote saw in an instant how he could trap Divekar if he had slipped away from the game just long enough to commit the robbery. Because it so happened that he himself knew exactly what had been occurring in the stadium at the moment the thief had slipped out of that house on Malabar Hill.

"A bad day's play, I hear," he said to Divekar. "What did you think about Bolkpur?"

Divekar shook his head sadly.

"A damn wrong decision, Inspectorji," he said. "I was sitting right behind the bat, and I could see. Damn wrong."

He looked at them both with an expression of radiant guiltlessness. "That was where you also would have been sitting," he added.

You win, Ghote thought and turned grimly away. But on his way home he stopped for a moment at Headquarters to see if anything had turned up. His Deputy Superintendent was there.

"Well, Inspector, they tell me you spotted Anil Divekar leaving the house."

"I am sorry, sir, but I do not think it was him now."

He recounted his meeting with the man at the stadium a few minutes earlier; but the Deputy Superintendent was unimpressed.

"Nonsense, man, whatever the fellow says, this is Divekar's type of crime, one hundred per cent. You just identify him as running off from the scene and we've got him."

For a moment Ghote was tempted. After all, Divekar was an inveterate thief: it would be justice of a sort. But then he knew that he had not really been sure who the running man had been.

"No, sir," he said. "I am sorry, but no."

The Deputy Superintendent's eyes blazed, and it was only the insistent ringing of the telephone by his side that postponed his moment of wrath.

"Yes? Yes? What is it? Oh, you, Inspector. Well? What? The gardener? But . . . Oh, on him? Every missing item? Very good then, charge him at once."

He replaced the receiver and looked at Ghote.

"Yes, Inspector," he said blandly, "that chap Divekar. As I was saying, he wants watching, you know. Close watching. I'll swear he is up to something. Now, he's bound to be at the Test Match tomorrow, so you had better be there too."

"'Yes, sir," Ghote said.

A notion darted into his head.

"And, sir, for cover for the operation should I take this boy of mine also?"

"First-rate idea. Carry on, Inspector Ghote."

WHAT THE DORMOUSE SAID
by Carolyn Wheat

When Doug Greene asked me about publishing a book of my short stories, I was elated. That my stories could join a roster that contained Ed Hoch, mystery short story maven, was nothing short of amazing.

Crippen and Landru has done the mystery community a tremendous service in collecting, preserving, and disseminating mysterydom's most ephemeral form, the short story. Yes, we could find stories in crumbling EQMMs and in out-of-print anthologies, but with C & L, we can savor the delights of one author's short-form output in a binge-reading orgy. I'm honored to be a small part of that legacy.

August 1970: The Freaks

I wish I were dead.
    Sweat pours from Bobbie Tate's face onto her tie-dyed tank top as she climbs, positioning one exhausted booted foot after another up Slide Mountain and thinks long, hard thoughts about death.
    How could love go so wrong so quickly? It's like that song by Janis Joplin, whom Bobbie never used to like all that much, but now it's as if she and Janis are soul sisters in pain and grief. Joplin's raw-liver voice cuts through the haze of sweat and pain, searing itself into Bobbie's brain as she climbs ever closer to the white angels of death.
    "Take another little piece of my heart, why don't you? You know you got it, if it makes you feel good."
    Enid takes pieces of her heart any time she wants them, and Bobbie, like Janis, dares her to take more, to chew bits of her heart between her even little teeth, and spit them on the ground. The meadow behind the commune, which was once known as the Thompson place, is littered with pieces of Bobbie's sixteen-year-old heart.
    One day she and Enid were like two vines intertwining. They couldn't leave the house to go to the barn without holding hands and halfway there starting to kiss and then fondle one another and by the time they were in the barn, the fragrant hay called to them and they

gave in. She couldn't get enough of Enid, not the taste of her kisses or her green apple breasts, and she was sure Enid felt the same, the way Enid's slender fingers always went to the zipper of her jeans, the way Enid's soft hand explored under Bobbie's blue cambric work shirt.

Oh, God, she'd never felt like that before, and it was like being in heaven only better, and now—

Now Quinn is here, and all Enid does is follow him around, her hand in the back pocket of his jeans, her naked body draped across his clothed one like a stole, her teasing little smile telling Bobbie how wonderful she thinks Quinn is, and how having sex with Bobbie was just another phase in her development as a woman.

Thinking about it makes Bobbie want to scream.

So she does. Long, howling screams like a dog in pain, punctuated by sobs so gusty they could sink small boats. She has never felt so much pain in her whole life, not even the day Pop told her that Mom was gone for good.

Thinking of Pop only makes it worse. She sinks to her knees halfway up the last rise to the top of the mountain, crouches down like a child, and lets her hair trail in the dust. Moans emanate from her throat, moans so deep, so anguished, she doesn't even notice she's inhaling dirt from the trail.

She's a lost child, lost and alone. First Mom, then Pop, and now Enid—will no one ever love her completely? Will no one ever not leave her?

She is consumed by pain, eaten through with it the way Grandma was eaten through with cancer, and the pain she feels is no less than what Grandma suffered in those last skeleton days.

Pain and hate. Don't forget the hate. It is, she thinks, all that keeps her alive, all that keeps her from going to Kaaterskill Falls and throwing herself off the highest rock into the stream below. Indians did that, according to local legend. Indian maidens died for love, and perhaps Bobbie Tate will, too.

Then Enid will be sorry. Bobbie sees her own corpse in her mind's eye, as she plods steadily, sweatily up the mountain toward the white death waiting to be picked and used in the final ceremony. Her face will be serene, waxen, beautiful at last. She will wear white gauze, Mandy's Mexican wedding dress, and her hands will be folded on her breast like an angel's, and candles will flank her head and feet. Enid will sob and beg forgiveness; Pop will throw himself on her coffin and tell her he's sorry for all the things he said when he found out about Enid.

She stops suddenly, as if she'd heard a rattle in the lush growth, but it isn't that. It's another thought, another vision.

Why should hers be the dead body? Why should Quinn remain alive to be with Enid?

She straightens her shoulders and pushes farther up the trail with renewed purpose, visions of little white mushroom caps dancing in her head.

"If it wasn't Quinn, it would be someone else," Mandy tells Bobbie, but that doesn't help at all. Not at all. She needs to hear that Enid is temporarily brainwashed, that this thing with Quinn is a passing phase, and Enid will wake up tomorrow and realize that Bobbie is her true love, that Quinn will leave the commune and go back to Taos without Enid.

Is it worse because Quinn's a man?

She isn't sure. Picturing Enid with Patrice doesn't feel any better—worse, maybe, because after all, Quinn does have one thing that she, Bobbie, doesn't have, whereas if it were Patrice or Mandy, then Bobbie would feel even more inadequate, more certain that something wrong within herself is what pushed Enid away.

"Go home," Warren tells her. Behind the barn, where she's feeding chickens, he walks up and says the words bluntly, no frills: "Go home. You don't belong here."

As if she didn't know that. As if she had no clue how much Warren resents her—not that he's in charge or anything. It's a commune; nobody's in charge, but somehow Warren always acts as if he is, as if he has the right to give orders.

He thinks she doesn't contribute because she doesn't make anything the way the others do. Enid with her stained glass, sharp cutting edges with bright, stabbing colors, whirls and triangles and wavy glass and little round gems that glitter like bug eyes. Leo's wooden bowls, hand-turned, polished to gleaming perfection, the touch of them as soft as silk; Mandy's patchwork quilts, like stained glass you can sleep under; Scott's pottery, so thin, so delicate, they might be made of paper instead of clay. Patrice makes big copper bracelets and brass earrings, just the slightest trace of Africa in their shape and bulk. Warren—Warren isn't the creative one; he manages the money and places the crafts at the consignment shop off Route 28A near the Ashokan Reservoir.

So if Warren contributes because he handles money, why can't she contribute by feeding chickens, cleaning the house, tending Joachim, and minding Katie?

She doesn't say this to Warren, any more than she tells him she has no home to go to. She hasn't told anyone her father threw her out. She's afraid to say the words because if she does, she'll cry forever.

And maybe it won't matter. Maybe no one will care that she has no place else to go.

Mandy sits in the rocker, her long, patchwork skirt catching the firelight. She smiles at the baby suckling her breast with loud smacking noises. She moves her leg, and one patch glares iridescent green. John's old tie. That square is flanked on one side by plum-colored velvet, on the ocher by a piece of the aqua dress she wore to be invested into Eastern Star.

So long ago, that dress, that life. She and her mother, two peas in a Methodist pod, hair identically teased and sprayed into bouffants as stiff as meringue. Long, pastel formal gowns, stiletto heels, matching clutch purses. Pat Nixon clones in suburban Chicago.

She fingers the black wool, cut from the suit she wore to her mother's tasteful funeral. No tears; Mom wouldn't have wanted them. But oh, the ache, the gaping hole where her mother had been.

Tears clog her throat; tears that even now her WASP upbringing won't let her shed. She longs to show Joachim to her mother, to point out how Katie has grown, to introduce her to the miracle that is Scott.

Truth: Mom would be horrified at the leaky old farmhouse, at Mandy's black-soled bare feet, her home-sewn clothes, the baby born out of wedlock, Scott. She'd wonder how Mandy could ever have left a man like John, a solid man with a future, for an unemployed hippie who threw pots for a living. More, she'd hate that Mandy dragged Katie into this nomadic life, commune to commune, pad to pad, rundown funky area of town to tie-dyed, psychedelic-painted section of some other town. Milwaukee to Denver to the Haight to Dupont Circle in D.C. to the East Village, and now, at last, to this little farm in the Catskills, the first place she can see herself and her little family growing old.

She smiles at the vision of herself with long white hair, of Scott a white-bearded Merlin, of Joachim grown to manhood in the image of his father, of Katie strong and beautiful in her womanhood, a baby at her own breast.

Joey's fist falls away from her breast and the hungry, milky lips still. She bends down to kiss the top of his downy head, then places him slowly, lovingly, into the cradle Leo made when he was born.

They are so lucky. Home at last, home in the cooperative with friends and comrades, safe at last.

Katie runs into the house, all flying hair and barefoot smiling excitement. "He's putting up a tepee! Like an Indian! Come and see, Mommy."

Mandy rises gracefully from the rocker and follows Katie outside to where Quinn, naked from the waist up, his tanned back oily with sweat, raises the poles for his tent.

Quinn's long, lean, sinewy body is like Dylan's voice made flesh, and a shiver of hunger, deep animal wanting, thrills through Mandy's breasts, sensitive from baby sucking.

"Come on without, come on within, you'll not see nothing like the mighty Quinn."

Quinn's sexuality is like the electrically charged air of the summer Catskills. Always there, always threatening a storm. He looks at Mandy with his avid, promising eyes even as Enid rubs her barely covered breast against his chest. He slides appreciative glances at Patrice's nut-brown skin and talks, talks, talks about open sex and throwing off the shackles of middle-class monogamy, pointedly aiming his remarks at Scott, whom he'd known back in San Francisco.

Will Quinn get to Scott, fan the flames of discontent just under the placid surface of their lives, remind Scott that once he was free?

That she will be the one to succumb to Quinn's siren song doesn't enter her mind.

"Remember that girl, what the hell was her name? The one you were balling back then?"

"Moonstar. She called herself Moonstar." The weight of Joachim in the body sling pulls down on him, weighs more than a baby should.

"Yeah. What a chick. What a free spirit. I saw her in Taos, man. Still zooming out there, still exploring. We did some peyote together, man, it was like the old days in the Haight. Next day she split for California, and I headed east. No baggage, man."

Joachim is baggage. Mandy is baggage. Katie of the blue eyes and dirty little toes, Katie is baggage. Even the tools of his trade, his art, pottery wheel and kiln, root him.

With Moonstar he was air, he was fire. Now he is earth, solid, packed down, heavy with responsibility for three other people, when once he'd refused to accept responsibility even for himself.

Through Quinn's eyes he sees at once what he has unknowingly become: his own father.

They make their own ceremonies, no longer tied to Hallmark cards and ribbons made in Taiwan. The Mushroom Feast becomes a hallowed eve, to be celebrated in song and story. Best clothes are put on, velvet skirts and silk blouses, embroidered shawls with long tendrils of fringe. Leo wears a sarape from Mexico, tinkling Indian earrings dangle from Enid's shapely ears, Patrice is adorned like an African princess, and even Bobbie, who has few clothes of her own, sports borrowed finery in the form of an Indian gauze shirt that shows her braless chest.

The priest, the shaman, Quinn the Eskimo, wears his ceremonial robes in the form of a long-fringed leather vest, a belt with silver conchas, a leather headband with an eagle feather dangling from it. Bare feet and a leather thong around his neck, with Enid's handmade glass beads and a cowrie shell from the Bahamas, Patrice's contribution.

They smoke a little grass first. Before that, they eat a fine chickpea and wild mushroom stew Mandy made with Bobbie's help. Bobbie the mushroom expert, who picked the wild fungus on the slopes of the mountains where she trekked herself to exhaustion, trying to forget Enid.

Katie is upstairs in bed; Joachim sleeping in his cradle in the corner, near the black wood stove.

At first, Bobbie feels nothing, just full and content and for once accepted by the circle sitting on the floor around Leo's low maple table. The smell of sandalwood incense romances her nose, and she rocks back with the power of it, the pungency, the taste of exotic lands, the vision of Marrakesh or Ceylon. Faraway places, gold shot through fabric, the light from the fire catching Mandy's hair, her incredible hair. The colors like wood, like Leo's work, like brass and bronze and leaves in the autumn and maple syrup. She wants to taste Mandy's hair, which looks as rich as the sandalwood smells.

The connection is like a silver thread powered by thousands of watts of electricity. It shoots from Enid to Bobbie, then from Bobbie to Mandy, Mandy to Leo, and so on around the circle, binding them forever in a state of perfect love. Bobbie sees clearly now how silly, how juvenile her passion for Enid was. The love she felt for Enid isn't special at all; it's just one tiny piece of the global love that fills her now, has her eyes streaming tears of joy, her hand clutching Mandy's with the simple faith of a child. The tears choke her and then dissolve in laughter as spontaneous as butterflies drunk on nectar.

They are all drunk, not with alcohol, not even with magic mushrooms, but with Life Itself. The love of one another, of the human race, of the earth and all living creatures, overwhelms them, and they laugh and laugh at how absurd their old lives used to be and how free they are now. Free to hold anyone's hand, free to look anyone in the eye and hold the glance until true human connection is made, free to take off their clothes if they want to—and suddenly everyone wants to.

Tasting and touching skin soft as powder, tasting of peat and curry, of roses and musk, Scott settles down to a feast of skin and hair, lips and breasts, no longer aware of identity, just knowing this woman, this amazing woman with skin the color of amber, is inside him and enveloping him at the same time. He thrusts and she parries, he kisses and she kisses back, both swept away into a world of sensory pleasure he'd never before dreamed existed.

"Patrice," he says, and the name sounds like an incantation. Her hair, luxurious and oiled, seems to melt in his hands.

Did the baby cry?
Does he have a baby?
Where's Mandy?
Does he care?

Mandy can't keep the voice of Bob Dylan out of her head. That raspy, knowing voice is the way Quinn looks, rough and male and sinewy, eager and detached at the same time, way beyond cool and hot as the devil himself.

"When Quinn the Eskimo gets here, everybody's going to jump for joy."

She wants him so much. Scott is wonderful, a tender lover and a good man, a father to both her children, and the man in whose arms she wants to die someday, but right now she has to have Quinn inside her. She sees herself as a giant black jaguar, a female animal in heat, eager for a male to enter and possess her, then walk away without looking back.

Mushrooms give Quinn to her. Mushrooms take her where she wants to go.

But once it's over, will Scott still be there? Will she still die in his arms?

Touching naked skin is the most beautiful thing Bobbie has ever done. Like velvet—no, velvet is too coarse, silk too earthbound. Like a baby, like Joachim's soft fuzzy head, and now everyone feels babysoft, baby-innocent. First she strokes Mandy's long hair, lets the hair flow over her face, drinks in the scent of rosemary from her herbal rinse, then allows her lips to wander downward until Mandy's breast is in her mouth.

Everyone tastes everyone until languor and slumber set in.

Screams bring her out of a long, velvet funk, a meditation on skin and hair, lips and—

But whose screams? And why? High-pitched, but male or female?

The crash is inevitable. Bobbie wakes in a tangle of sodden blankets, wet and sticky, smelling of sweet wine. Her head throbs and her hands shake, her stomach feels tender and raw.

Can she move? Is she alive or dead, and whose hands, whose lips, touched her last? Why does she remember blood and screaming?

The sound of retching comes from the bathroom upstairs. Bobbie wonders whether the commune's single toilet will be enough.

Earth into airy, light, shiny forms, useful things as old as mankind. Shaping wet clay with his fingers, the sensuous feel of it like making love, the hot flame hardening, setting, glazing, taking it to another dimension of existence. All this Scott loves about his work.

The ancient Japanese technique of raku separates his pottery from the clumsy chalices and honey pots turned out by most hippie potters. He creates works of art, delicate yet strong, powerfully shaped yet thin as glass, iridescent colors swirling in metal-based glazes whose formulas were intricate and tricky to produce.

Timing is all. Baking just long enough, cooling just at the right moment in a water bath of the right temperature. Some cracked, some hardened too quickly, some just didn't sing when they were finished, lay there like the mud they were, soulless and dead.

Getting rid of Quinn, saving his family from evil, will take the same attention to detail, the same precision, the same dispassionate, artistic eye.

One week later, alone in his tepee, Quinn dies.

Everyone got sick, but while most of them just felt dizzy, Quinn was still seeing visions, ranting about the earth melting and giant spiders coming after us, all kinds of weird shit. Mandy was scared for Katie, listening to all that craziness, so she asked Leo and Warren to get Quinn back into his tepee.

What were they supposed to do? Call the pigs, tell them there was a guy out here stoned out of his gourd and please send an ambulance? Get them all locked up and it was his fucking shit in the first place; none of them would have taken the mushrooms if he hadn't turned it into a fucking ceremony.

The thing is, he really seemed to be getting better. He stopped throwing up—but then he'd stopped eating, so there wasn't anything left to throw up. He slept a lot, and he did seem to have nightmares, but it wasn't until the last day of his life that everyone realized Quinn wasn't going to make it.

It was awful. Convulsions, retching horribly and blood coming out of his mouth, sweating like hell, as if every single drop of fluid in his body had to come out one way or another. The tepee smelled terrible, and Patrice sat outside in lotus position, rocking and sobbing.

The only person who seemed more upset about Quinn than Patrice was Bobbie Tate. Which was weird because if anybody hated the guy, Bobbie did.

Melting golden coins fluttering in the air, the sound like baby hands clapping. Hot sun boiling her skin, big huge blisters going to pop, flood her with water, skin so hot, so hot, hot like Enid, hot like Quinn with his crazy fever: Quinn dead and gone, could she die out here? Float away like a dry leaf, like the dry leaf suddenly in her hand, the essence of dry, no life, no softness, only decay and brittle falling apart into fragments like the fragments of her heart.

"Take another little piece of my heart, now, baby. You know you got it, if it makes you feel good."

Her heart hurts, she can feel it beating, hear blood whooshing through like water down a flume, like the Esopus when you float in an inner tube and your butt gets cold and your knees gets sunburned. Blood rushes through her veins like the Esopus, loud as a sunset, powerful as a summer storm, red life keeping her from blowing away.

Blowing in the wind, the golden coins hanging from the white birch tree, birchbark like paper, like the dead leaf, peeling like the paint on the outside of the farmhouse. Golden leaf coins from a living tree, bending and swaying. Staying alive. Sap rising in the trunk like the blood in her veins; cut the tree, and it would bleed her own red blood.

She is the tree; the tree is her secret soul made flesh.

She asks the tree for a single leaf and it says yes, bending over her like a mother, like the mother who'd left when she was eight. She cries, soft spring rain tears of relief and joy, and rubs the golden leaf against her cheek and prays to the tree for forgiveness, and when sanity returns, only partly welcome, she is Birch. Birch who bends and does not break, no matter how fierce the pain.

No longer Bobbie, Roberta Susanne, Bobbie Sue Tate—she is Birch, and she will be Birch forever.

August 1970: The Pigs

It was a hot summer, hot as any Ulster County could remember. Corn all but roasted itself on the stalk and tomatoes burst on the vine. Flowers withered unless they were watered daily, and most people knew better than to waste water that way. Some said better to waste it here than send it down to New York City, but they were in the minority.

A storm was needed. The kind of Catskill thunderstorm old Washington Irving used to write about, the kind where the gods vented their fury on a world gone mad—which it had ever since the rock festival. Lightning and thunder fit to scare the worst sinner back to church, splitting the sky with light so powerful you could read by it. Gully-washing rain, ripping whole sides of mountains, pushing boulders down the hillside for the county to plow off the roads in the fall. Maybe a storm like that would send the hippies back where they came from.

The storm was overdue by a long two weeks when the call came in. Sam Tate, Woodstock's chief of police, took it himself.

"A dead body? You sure, Al? Yeah, of course you are, I just mean, well, hell, we don't get a whole lot of dead bodies around here, so—"

"A hippie. A dead hippie out by Wittenburg Pond." Sam wasn't surprised. Ever since the festival, the whole Hudson Valley had become a magnet for dropout kids wearing fringe and headbands. Not to mention that Bobbie was one of them, living in that goddamn commune.

He couldn't think about that now. He turned his attention back to his caller.

"Just off the pond road, mile or so out of Bearsville." He nodded and jotted a note on the pad in front of him. "You're calling from where? The firehouse? You gonna wait there?"

A mental picture of the scene rose in his mind: August foliage, deep, dense, green, shading and blocking the pond from the view of passing drivers on State Route 40. So how had Al—oh, yeah, Al had a prostate the size of a grapefruit, probably stepped out of his pickup to take a piss and stumbled over a dead body.

"Well, yeah, I can see where you need to—but, Al, it would really be a big help if you'd just wait there and take me to the body, okay?"

"Al, I owe you one, buddy."

Thorsten Magnussen, the only detective on Woodstock's tiny police force, grabbed his notebook and walked to the black and white with a heavy heart. A dead body outdoors in August wasn't going to be pretty, and a dead hippie was going to make Sam madder than any other kind of dead body. The whole town wondered why Sam didn't just drive up to that commune and drag Bobbie home, but Thor didn't wonder. If Sam did that, Bobbie would run away to God-knew-where the next day, and at least this way Sam knew where his daughter was, even though he hated where she was.

"Any idea how long the body's been there?" he asked as Sam headed toward Bearsville.

"No." A man of few words before his daughter was discovered holding hands with Enid in the Tinker Street Cinema, Sam was positively Trappist now.

"Any idea how the—"

"No. I figured we'd wait and see what the coroner had to say." Sam shifted his unlit cigar from one side of his mouth to the other, chewing on the end with a ferocity that told Thor to stop asking stupid questions.

The hippie was dressed in well-worn jeans and had a fringed leather vest over his flannel shirt, moccasins on his feet, and a leather thong around his neck.

"Pretty hot for a long-sleeved shirt," Thor remarked, wiping sweat from his sunburned brow. Big, blond, and Nordic, he suffered every summer, but this one was especially brutal.

The coroner pushed his way through the bystanders with his medical bag in one hand and a fishing rod in the other.

"He didn't die here," Foley said after a cursory glance. "Body was moved."

"Hey, I've seen that guy!" A small, balding man pointed at the body. "He was at the post office about a week ago. Said his name was Quinn, and he was staying out at the old Thompson place on Meads Mountain—you know, where those hippies are. The ones with that purple van."

Sam stood frozen, his face a mask. Thor took a deep breath and let it out in a long sigh.

He knew the Thompson place, all right. It was where Bobbie Tate lived.

An hour later, Thor flipped on his left-turn signal and waited for traffic to pass before turning left and making his bouncing way up a steep gravel trail off Meads Mountain Road, about four miles before the Buddhist temple at the top.

Eighteen trees later, a rutted, signless dirt road opened; he cut another left and dropped his speed, taking the second and then the third right fork, moving upward until he caught a glimpse of dirty white paint.

"Shit." Doppler ran the window down and tossed out his butt. Thor said nothing, just hoped the damn thing was fully extinguished. "Look at the state of that place. Damn dirty shame, house like that going to hippies."

"It needed a few coats when old man Thompson was alive, as I recall."

"Hey, the man had arthritis, he couldn't take care of the place. These kids just don't give a shit, live like animals. No wonder somebody died out here, the shit they get up to. Drugs. Group sex. Never had this garbage till they had that damn rock concert."

This was a litany Thor had been hearing for too long and really didn't want to hear again. He gunned the car up the last stubborn bit of hillside and pulled up sharp, kicking the gearshift into park and slamming on the emergency brake.

"Holy shit!"

Thor's eyes followed Doppler's pointing finger. In the meadow behind the house stood a tall, white tepee.

"Think that's where Tonto lived?" Doppler asked.

The man in the barn looked exactly like Jesus Christ—if Jesus wore jeans and worked a pottery wheel. Hair and beard the color of mahogany, mild brown eyes, bare feet in sandals—put a white robe on this guy and churchgoing Woodstock would say it had seen a vision.

He stopped the wheel, taking his foot off the pedal and cupping the wet clay in his hands until it subsided into a mass ready for reshaping.

"Who are you?" Doppler spoke without removing his cigarette from his lips.

"I'm Scott. Scott Andrews." The Jesus face grew guarded, wary, but Thor had to admit, he'd probably look the same if he'd ended up on the wrong side of Doppler.

"We need to talk to you and your pals," Doppler went on. "Get 'em all together; we'll talk in the kitchen."

Doppler turned without waiting for an answer. He stepped from the barn to the back of the house, swung open the screen door, and walked into the kitchen as if he'd been invited to dinner. Showing that he knew the house, felt at home there, and was going to by God be in charge.

Thor followed. He'd never been inside the old farmhouse, but doubted that the hippies had made it any worse than it was when a drunken old man had lived there.

To his surprise, the kitchen sported a new coat of cream-colored paint and had handmade green stenciling on the walls. Mismatched, old-fashioned kitchen tools and canisters sat on the counters: a red-handled pastry cutter like the one his grandmother used, a faded ceramic dog-shaped cookie jar, hand-thrown bowls and pots, a cutting board striped with different shades of wood. It was homey and inviting, cluttered but clean, speaking of careful purchases at junk stores and yard sales coupled with handmade things.

The commune residents made things to sell at the crafts cooperative off Route 28A. Thor, grandson of artists, had pictured crude, shapeless masses of clay, tie-dyed T-shirts, macramé pot hangers—useless objects made by clumsy hands. But the stained-glass piece in the window, the glazed pot on the hand-rubbed kitchen table, all spoke of a love of materials and an attention to detail that impressed him.

Scott came into the room, followed by a dark-haired woman wearing a long patchwork skirt and a light-skinned black woman with a shiny, oiled Afro. "I told the guys," he said. "They're coming in."

The women were Mandy and Patrice.

Doppler turned to Thor. "Which one's the lezzie?"

"Neither," Thor replied. The girl who'd seduced Bobbie Tate was a light-skinned blonde with a slender figure and an exhibitionist's way of showing it off.

The women looked at one another, naked fear on their faces.

Was the fear because they knew the dead man, or because all hippies hated and feared all pigs? It was too soon to tell.

"We just found a body in the woods," Thor said, carefully moving his eyes from one face to another. "Someone said the man might have belonged to your commune."

"He had on a leather vest," Doppler added, "and it looks like he died of a drug overdose."

Many times in Thor's professional life he'd had the urge to strangle Doppler, and this was one more to add to the list. He glared at the man and added, "Right now we just want to identify the guy, notify any family he might have."

Again, the two women exchanged looks but said nothing. A man with long, curly hair and a lush beard came in, introduced himself as Leo, and told them Enid was in town buying supplies. No one answered the questions Doppler kept peppering them with until Warren entered the room, and all eyes turned to him.

He was pasty-faced and clean-shaven, with long, straight, lank hair and heavy, dark-rimmed glasses. Buddy Holly gone flower child.

"What are the pigs doing here?" His voice was reedy, but his tone expected answers and expected them now.

"They found a body somewhere, and they think we know something about it," Scott replied.

"We don't. So you can leave now," Warren said, challenge in his cool gray eyes. "You can take your kid with you if you want," he added. "We're not keeping her against her will or anything."

"Nobody said you were," Thor replied mildly. "And she isn't my daughter."

"Who lives in that tepee out back?" Doppler jerked his thumb toward the kitchen window, where the tent dominated the view.

"Oh, we take turns using it," Warren said. "It kind of belongs to all of us, like everything else out here."

Thor left the kitchen stonewalled and frustrated.

"Lying sonsabitches," Doppler muttered. Thor cut him off with a brusque wave. A little girl about six, her hair the same maple syrup color as Mandy's, sat in a tire swing, her bare feet scuffing the ground.

Thor signaled Doppler to stay back and approached the child. He knelt down on the grass near the swing and said, "That looks like fun. Who put it up for you?"

"Scott."

"What's your name?"

"Katie." The child gazed directly up at Thor with candid blue eyes.

"That tepee is pretty neat," Thor said. "Do you sleep in it?"

"No, that's where Quinn sleeps. He's an Eskimo, and he lives in a tepee. My mom makes him soup because he's sick. Really sick, throwing up and everything."

"When's the last time you saw Mr. Quinn?"

"Not for a while, because he's so sick. Mom says I have to be quiet and let him sleep, even in the daytime. He stays in his tepee all the time, and Patrice brings him my mom's soup. He won't let anyone else come in."

"He never slept in the house?"

Katie shook her head. "Not at night. Sometimes in the day."

"He slept inside during the day?"

"Sometimes. He'd go to Enid's room and that's why Bobbie sleeps in my room. Because she didn't like him going to Enid's room."

"Hey, what are you doing talking to her?"

Thor turned; Warren stood on the back porch, an outraged expression on his face. "You get out of here now, and don't come back without a warrant. We know our rights."

For a moment, Thor thought Doppler was going to make a fight out of it, but in the end they had no choice but to leave, to let Warren have his temporary victory.

Back inside the car, Doppler said, "The dead guy didn't look like an Eskimo."

Thor sighed. Sometimes he felt like an interpreter. It wasn't that he was a hippie, just that he did live in the actual twentieth century and listened to WDST on his car radio.

He explained to Doppler what he'd later have to explain to Sam Tate, that Quinn the Eskimo was a character in a Bob Dylan song, and his name came from dealing cocaine. That was enough for Sam. He got on the phone to the sheriff in Kingston, asked for a full tox screen on the dead man. Then he called the most anti-drug judge in Ulster County and got a search warrant.

"Take that place apart," he told Thor, and he didn't seem to mind at all when Doppler's mean little eyes lit up.

And what if they did find drugs? What if they had to arrest Bobbie?

As long as he'd known Sam Tate, he didn't know the answer to that one.

"No drugs?" Sam couldn't keep the amazement out of his voice. "Nothing, not a marijuana seed?"

Thor shook his head. The old house had four bedrooms. The biggest had a double mattress on the floor, covered with an Indian cloth. In one corner, an old-fashioned cradle on rockers had a handmade quilt tucked into it and a sleeping baby under the quilt. Mandy and Scott.

The second bedroom belonged to the little girl, Katie. The third bedroom was Warren's, the fourth Enid's, and Leo slept in the unfinished attic. Not one of the rooms had a bed in it. Mattresses, sleeping bags, homemade pallets of blanket and quilt lay on the floor like dog beds. They'd searched everything, emptied drawers, dumped clothes onto the floor, shredded sleeping bags.

"You tossed the place hard? I mean, you looked everywhere, right?"

"Nothing taped under the drawers, nothing behind the toilets, nothing in the heating ducts. We emptied out the flour barrels and dried beans, dumped spices out of the spice rack." Thor grinned. "Doppler even went after the compost heap, raked the whole thing, and came up empty."

His grin faded as he recalled the assault on the little girl's room. Dolls were slashed open, plastic toys broken against rocks, even the child's quilt, obviously handmade by her mother, was ripped end to end. When he'd protested, Doppler had replied, "Hell, that's where they'd hide the shit, knowing damn well a bleeding heart like you isn't gonna rip up a kid's stuff. Well, that's the difference between you and me, buddy."

Difference or no difference, they'd left empty-handed, both knowing full well that the commune used drugs but finding no evidence, not even a residue-filled hash pipe. Somewhere on the property, perhaps in a hollow tree, they might find dope and works, but for now, they had nothing. No evidence, no reason to suspect the hippies of anything more than getting an inconveniently dead guest off their property.

Even the tepee, fetid with the smell of sickness, had no telltale clues pointing to drug use, no roach clips, no hash pipe—nothing but sweat-stained blankets and a backpack filled with extra clothes.

"Did you—did you see Bobbie?"

Thor shook his head. "Mandy said she spends a lot of time out hiking, I suppose because Enid switched her attention to the dead man. She probably feels uncomfortable hanging around."

"I never should have named her Roberta," Sam muttered, and it took Thor a minute to realize what he was getting at.

"You think she's the way she is because of her name?"

Sam directs his gaze at the hunting scene on the back wall of his office. "Once her mother was gone, I just—I don't know, I just raised her the way my dad raised me. Took her hunting, taught her to fish, let her go on those Boy Scout hikes with you. She seemed to like it. It never occurred to me she liked it too much, that she'd want to be a boy."

A hundred memories fought for dominance in Thor's mind. Bobbie Tate at seven, adamantly refusing to wear a dress to church. Bobbie at ten, baiting her hook, tongue protruding from the corner of her mouth as she poked the metal through a wriggling worm. Bobbie at fourteen, outpacing Eagle Scouts up the slope of Mount Tremper.

Bobbie at sixteen, walking down Tinker Street holding hands with a willowy blonde, her face alight with pride and pleasure and a sexual awakening he'd never seen before, a glow that can only come from crossing the threshold to adulthood.

"She is who she is, Sam," he said, knowing the words were inadequate.

"I want her back the way she was before that bitch got to her."

Thor decided he wasn't going to be the one to tell Sam he might never get that Bobbie back again.

The first break in the case came two days later. "Guy was on some kinda mushroom shit," Doppler said, the unfiltered cigarette dangling from his lip dancing in tune to his rhythm. "Fuckin' hippies, always lookin' for some new way to get high."

"Yeah, fuckin' hippies," Thor agreed. Backup singer to Doppler's insistent pounding beat, the theme of which was always fuckin' this and fuckin' that. If it wasn't fuckin' hippies it was fuckin' summer people, fuckin' rich people, fuckin' white trash, fuckin' not-so-white trash, fuckin' bosses—

"They got a song about smokin' bananas, the hippies," Doppler continued. His eyes were flags: red, white, and blue, so raw they made your own eyes hurt just looking at them. "You heard it, Thor?

Smokin' fuckin' bananas." He shook his head, and a long block of ash dribbled to the ground, wind blowing it back onto his uniform shirt.

"So we're calling it an accidental overdose," he said, suddenly sick and tired of Doppler's shit.

"Seems like," Doppler said, stifling a yawn. He spat the butt onto the asphalt. Flecks of tobacco stuck to his thin, dry lips. His hand reached automatically for the soft pack in his shirt pocket, pulled out another, and shoved it into his mouth.

"So why are we on our way to see this tox guy? Why not just call it an overdose, close the file, and move on?"

Assistant Toxicologist Andy Grossmacher met them at the door. "Damndest thing you ever saw," he said with a wide grin on his freckled face. "Guy got himself high on Psilocybe, but what killed him was amanita."

"Wanna try that in English?"

"He was poisoned."

"I thought you said amanitas were everywhere." Thor hoped he didn't sound as whiny as he felt. Andy thought the use of local mushrooms pointed to the only local in the commune: Bobbie Tate. The thought of her deliberately giving someone deadly mushrooms had Thor's stomach tied in knots. She couldn't have turned into a killer before her eighteenth birthday.

"Not these babies. This is *Amanita verna*, and it doesn't grow west of the Cascades. Now, if they'd been *pantherina*," Andy goes on, a fanatic's glint in his eye, "then I could tell you what you want to hear. I still say they couldn't have gotten into the guy's stash by accident, but at least he could have brought them with him from the West. But *verna*, no, I'm sorry; those are Eastern mushrooms, they grow under beech trees, and they just happen to be out right now. I saw some myself last weekend on a hike I led up near Phoenicia. You know the trailhead just off—"

"Tell me again about hallucinogenics," Thor said, moving toward the window and gazing out on a perfect summer day that suddenly gave him no pleasure at all.

Andy's freckled face beamed with pleasure, almost as if the dead man had been murdered just to give him added fungus information. "He went for the best, I'll say that for him. You can get high with several species, you know. Not just Psilocybe. Around here, there's fly agaric, boletus—"

"Cut to the chase, Andy. What did the guy have, and where did he get it?"

The smile that split his companion's face was the one that earned him his childhood nickname: Raggedy Andy. "He had Mexican, man. The Carlos Castaneda stuff. When I was in Santa Cruz, I turned on with cubemis. Not bad, but this was Psilocybe mexicana, and you get it in Mexico and nowhere but Mexico. So now you have another reason why those amanitas didn't just wind up in his stomach by accident."

"If it wasn't an accident, then whoever killed Quinn had to know something about poisonous mushrooms," Thor said for the fifth time. He could barely look at his boss, knowing they were both thinking the same thing, and knowing Sam hated thinking it even more than he did.

"Hell, Bobbie's not the only person in this county who knows something about mushrooms, for Christ's sake."

"Right, Sam," Thor said with a nod. "But how many people in that commune know that Amanita verna grows on the north side of Slide Mountain during July and August?" He ran his big fingers through sun-lightened blond hair. "Hell, Sam, I took Bobbie on that hike with the mushroom guy from New Paltz. I was there when he showed her the destroying angels and told her how poisonous they were. You think anyone else in that commune knows that stuff?"

"They might," Sam replied, but he stared out the window at Tinker Street, not meeting Thor's eyes. "It's up to you to find out what they know. Dig until you get something."

He didn't have to finish the sentence: *Dig until you get something that proves my little girl didn't kill anyone.*

"There were two mushroom trips, okay? One was with all of us, like a ceremony," Scott said, taking charge of the gathering once Mandy had served iced herbal tea. "Quinn took his own trip two days later. Didn't offer any to the rest of us, said he had to get his head straight."

"I thought 'straight' meant not taking drugs," Thor was unwise enough to reply. Eyes were rolled.

"Okay," he conceded. "Quinn was the only one who took the mushrooms the second time. And that's when he started getting sick."

"Right," answered Scott. He seemed to have appointed himself spokesman for the group this time, odd since Warren had made such a point of being in charge before. "At first we thought it was normal. Most of us felt kind of weird after the mushroom feast."

"We didn't throw up, though," Mandy said quietly. "We should have known something was wrong."

"After Quinn got sick, what did you do?"

"I made him soup," Mandy said. "Vegetable broth. Sometimes I'd break an egg into it, stir it around, like Chinese egg-drop soup. That's all he ate for—until he died."

"At first we thought he was getting better," Warren said. "He threw up for a day or so, then got up and started walking around like he was OK. Then he had convulsions, went back into the tepee, and died two days later."

Thor nodded. That was precisely the pattern amanita poisoning took, according to Raggedy Andy.

He turned to Bobbie, who sat on the floor at the far end of the room, trying and failing to look invisible. "I know you picked them, Bobbie. You brought them here. Did you deliberately put them in Quinn's stash?"

"No," she said, her voice a sob. "I picked them. I—I don't even know why. I thought about taking them myself," she cried, staring hard at Enid, "but I didn't, and I didn't give them to Quinn, either. They were in my room, that's all."

"In your room?" Mandy turned disbelieving eyes on the sixteen-year-old. "In Katie's room, you mean. What if she'd found them? Are you crazy?"

"I think I sort of was," Bobbie admitted. "I had them wrapped in a bandanna on the top shelf of the closet, way in the back. I really didn't want Katie to get them."

"Who else would know they were there?"

"You don't mean you believe her?" Warren burst out. "Man, I knew it. Just because her daddy's a cop, you're going to let her off the hook and find a way to blame one of us."

"I didn't say I believe her," Thor replied in an even tone. "I'm considering all the alternatives."

Bobbie looked at him with brimming eyes. "What do you mean, you don't believe me? You think I killed Quinn?"

"Bobbie, please, I have a job to do here. What I believe isn't the question."

"It is to me. You—" She broke down, sobbing and hitting her thigh with an angry fist. "You were my best friend. You have to believe me."

Sam was right; he and Thor had both failed the little girl they loved so much. A teenager who called a thirty-year old detective her best friend wasn't normal. Bobbie was breaking his heart, just as he was breaking hers.

There was police work and there was friendship. He put his notebook on the floor, stood up, and walked over to where Bobbie sat huddled, all her energy consumed by racking sobs. He touched her hair, short, boyish, tomboy hair that curled slightly at the ends.

"I believe you. As Thor your friend, I believe you. As Detective Thorsten Magnussen, I have to consider you a suspect. So let me get back to work, okay?"

She nodded. Incredibly, even as she poured her entire soul into grieving for her lost innocence, she nodded.

"Very nice," Warren said, clapping slowly and ostentatiously. "The pig has a heart after all. Too bad she's guilty."

"You'd better explain that remark."

"I saw her go into the tepee." Warren cocked his head toward Bobbie. "After the mushroom feast and before Quinn went on his own trip. She looked around to see if anyone was watching, and then she crept inside. She was there a few minutes, and then came out."

Thor's heart felt too big for his chest. He'd believed her, but now—what innocent reason could she possibly have for going into the dead man's tent?

"Bobbie?"

She gasped for breath, sobs still shaking her body, tears still streaming down bright red cheeks. "I didn't put mushrooms in," she said brokenly, "I took some out."

"Why would you do that?"

"Quinn went on a trip to get his head straight, and I really needed to get mine straight too, so I thought I'd take some and—"

"You stole from Quinn's stash," said Enid. "I can't believe you'd do that."

"I didn't think of it as stealing," Bobbie replied. "But I guess it was."

"Of course it was," said Warren.

"Well, it's easily proved," Patrice said. "Just show the deputy the mushrooms, and he can get them analyzed and tell whether they're magic or poison, right?"

Thor nodded, but Bobbie said in a small voice, "I took them already."

"Oh, that's convenient," Warren replied.

"I went up to the mountain," Bobbie said, her voice growing stronger. "Up near the monastery." The Buddhist monastery, a fixture in Woodstock for many years, was a natural place for soul-searching, drug-enhanced or otherwise.

"I lay under a birch tree and I—I became one with it. I was the birch and the birch was me, and that's why my name is Birch now." She gazed with newfound serenity into Thor's eyes. "Call me Birch."

"Birch." No one on the planet could look less like a slender birch tree than Bobbie Tate, with her volleyball player's body and her Campbell's Soup kid face. "It's perfect."

She smiled a watery smile that had him believing now for good and all. She did not poison Quinn, she entered his tent to take mushrooms and not leave them—but there was still one more thing.

"Bobbie, I mean Birch, you must have known he was poisoned. Why didn't you get help?"

"I did," she said, giving Leo a quick, apologetic smile. "I asked Leo."

"How could Leo help?"

"He was a medic in 'Nam. He used to work for the Free Clinic in the East Village. He knows a lot about drugs."

"Not much about mushrooms," Leo replied. "But when Birch told me she thought Quinn might be poisoned, I gave him some ipecac, just to stimulate vomiting. It was all I could think of to do."

"Well, it worked all right," Warren muttered. "Guy was throwing up day and night for a couple days there."

"So you suspected he'd been poisoned," Scott said, "and you didn't tell anyone?" It wasn't clear whether his remarks were directed at Leo or Birch.

"I wasn't sure," she said. "I went to look at the destroying angels, and it didn't look like there were any missing, but they were all dried out so it was hard to tell. I didn't think—I guess I wanted to believe he was sick from something else. But I told Leo, just in case."

"Who else knew there were poison mushrooms in the house?"

"Everybody," Bobbie answered. "I said so when we all got high. Remember?" She looked from one to the other. "I talked about destroying angels and white death and how there were mushrooms and mushrooms. I remember saying it when we were all still in the same room."

"Well, I don't remember that," Warren said loudly.

"Was that what you meant?" Mandy was frowning. "I remember the white angel part, but I didn't know you meant mushrooms."

"Everybody's going to say they didn't understand," Patrice pointed out.

"Who could have gone into the tepee without arousing suspicion?"

"Any of the girls," Leo said with a wry smile. "Quinn was balling every one of them at one time or another. Enid, Patrice, Mandy—"

Thor raised an eyebrow and turned his attention to the woman in the patchwork skirt. "You and Quinn had something going?"

"Not really," Mandy replied, but her face was pink. "It was the mushrooms, that's all. I did something crazy while we were high. I never went into the tepee after that night."

Thor glanced at Scott. Another motive heard from; he doubted that even this placid potter would take Mandy's defection lightly.

"Patrice went in," Enid said, and her little teeth shone in the firelight. Malice charged her voice. "Mandy made broth, and Patrice took it in to the tepee. Quinn wouldn't let anyone else feed him when he got sick."

"Is this true?"

"Yes. I don't know why, but he told me to keep everyone else out," Patrice admitted. "I knew him from before, so I guess he trusted me."

"The real issue is who put poison into the stash, not who went to the tepee after he got sick," Scott pointed out.

"I'm not so sure about that," Bobbie—no, Birch—said in a faraway voice. "What if the mushrooms were okay? The ones Quinn took, I mean. What if the poison was something else instead?"

"That's crazy," someone shouted.

"You think I poisoned him with the soup?" Mandy said, her voice rising.

"Don't be stupid," Warren pronounced.

"She may be right," Thor said thoughtfully. "Getting poison into the kitchen and putting in into the broth would be easier than sneaking into the tepee without being seen."

"The broth was for Quinn," Mandy agreed with a slow nod. "I used it to make vegetable soup for everyone, but I saved the broth for Quinn. No spices, no big chunks—it was in its own special pot in the fridge."

"So anybody could have gone into the kitchen, dropped some amanitas into the soup, strained them out again, and left poison broth to be carried to Quinn?"

"Pretty dangerous," Scott pointed out. "Anyone might have eaten the broth. Katie might have—"

Thor thought Mandy was going to faint. She swayed slightly in her chair, eyes rolling back in her head. Unless she was a powerful actress, Thor decided she hadn't killed Quinn, and neither had Scott.

Who had? If Bob—Birch was telling the truth, the amanitas weren't in the stash of mexicana.

What if—Thor looked directly at Leo, who lowered his eyes and gazed into the wood stove's blazing fire.

"You gave him the ipecac because he was vomiting," Thor said. Leo nodded. "And you gave it to him because Bo—I mean Birch told you about the poison mushrooms," he added.

"Yeah," Leo agreed.

"Exactly when was that?"

"I don't remember exactly."

"Birch?" Odd how the name was becoming second nature.

"It was Saturday afternoon," she said in a small voice. "I didn't want to believe it, so I didn't mention it earlier."

Thor turned to Warren. "You said Quinn was throwing up a lot at first. What day of the week would that have been?"

"Thursday, Friday, something in there."

"The mushroom feast was Tuesday," Mandy said. "So Quinn took his own trip on Thursday."

"Here's what I think happened," Thor said, and the spreading red stain on Leo's averted face told him he was close to the truth. Not the world's most adept liar, Leo had committed a murder of opportunity, not executed a well-laid plan.

"Quinn was no more sick the day after his trip than you were. He started throwing up because Leo slipped ipecac into his food. Birch came forward and 'reminded' Leo about the poison mushrooms. That made Leo the unofficial doctor, which meant Quinn would take anything Leo gave him. So he soaked the amanitas in water and added that to the ipecac. Every day he gave Quinn a little more poison, and every day Quinn got sicker and sicker until he died."

"But why?" Birch turned disappointed eyes on the teddy bear man with the curly hair and beard. Her eyes widened and she whispered, "It was you who screamed. What did Quinn do to you?"

"We were all—everybody was having sex with everybody else," Leo said, his face burning and his voice a strangled cry. "I—I didn't want what Quinn was doing to me, but I couldn't stop him. He—he said later it was something I needed to explore, a side of myself I should—but I didn't want to. I hated him for making me do that!" Leo sobbed like a child, burrowed into the side of the sofa like a wounded bear.

When Thor had Leo handcuffed in the back of the black and white, he turned to Birch and said, "Can I give you a ride home?"

"Did Pop tell you to say that?"

"No, but I know he wants you—"

"He wants me to be something I can't be," she said, her voice steady and her eyes dry. "I love him, but I can't change who I am."

Later that night, the sky cracked open. Booms so loud babies woke crying, rain falling so hard that looking through the car windshield was like trying to see through a shower curtain, hard, pounding rain that washed away sins.

Sam felt his soul lighten as he rammed his way up Rock City

Road, straight the hell up, no switchbacks. Gutting it out, making his Ford Torino do the work God made a jeep to do. Going after Bobbie come hell or high water, he told himself with a manic grin.

He loved her, loved her no matter what, loved the way she cocked her head to one side and looked skeptically at him, forcing him to defend his position in an argument. Loved the way her short hair curled at the nape of her neck, loved the stubby little fingers with bitten nails, loved the husky tomboy voice, the shy, eager smile. He wasn't at all sure he could handle her sexuality, but he was goddamn going to try.

Making the turn spat gobs of mud into the bushes at the side of the dirt road and had his wheels spinning madly. He rocked back, then pushed ahead and plowed up the hill toward the lights of the Thompson place.

Making the dash from car to front door had him soaked to the skin. The tepee, battered by the fierce winds, had fallen in the backyard like a downed hot air balloon. He pounded on the door, water streaming from his hat onto the back of his neck.

A woman answered the door, a baby in her arms. She had long, straight, folksinger hair, parted in the middle.

She said nothing, just stood there looking at him. No fear, no objection to his presence, just a quietly sad smile on her round face.

"She's gone," the woman said at last. "Birch is gone. Scott took her to the bus two hours ago, before the storm broke."

"Gone? What do you mean, gone? Where could she go?"

"She said something about the East Village," the woman replied, shifting the weight of her baby onto her hip.

"How could you let a sixteen-year-old go to New York City by herself?" The words burst from Sam before he had time to hear them in his head and realize how strange they were, strange in their implication that the commune was responsible for her.

"I didn't want her to go," the woman said, "but Birch told us you wouldn't let her come home."

"I never said—I just said I didn't—I couldn't live with—oh, God, I didn't mean it like that! I never meant to send her away for good! I didn't mean—"

He raised a hand to his face, wiping tears away with quick, boyish swipes. The woman in the doorway put out a hand and gently rubbed his shoulder. He wrenched himself away and plowed through the mud back to his car. All the way back to Woodstock, the windshield wiper blades sang the woeful dirge, Too late, too late, Sam Tate was too late.

A Matter of Honor
by Jeremiah Healy

Kirkus *once described Jeremiah Healy as the most consistently successful writer of private eye stories since Ross Macdonald. During his lifetime, Jerry wrote 18 books—13 of them featuring private investigator John Francis Cuddy. Or "the Cuddy character," as Jerry insisted on saying, the former law professor in him feeling the need to stipulate that Cuddy was, indeed, a fictional character.*
And maybe Jerry was right to make the point. Cuddy was one of the most human of fictional private investigators. A modern knight of old helping those who couldn't help themselves, while still grieving his wife's loss so keenly that he communed with her graveside.

More than half of Jerry's sixty short stories also featured Cuddy —stories that have been called "miracles of resourcefulness, economy, and compassion." Crippen and Landru published two collections of those short stories: The Concise Cuddy *in 1998 and* Cuddy Plus One *in 2003.*

The "Plus One" was a Mairead O'Clare short story. Jerry had started the legal thrillers featuring O'Clare under the pen name Terry Devane and couldn't resist giving folks a taste of the new books.

A master marketer, always, our Jerry.

*Neither of the compilations, though, included this story—*A Matter of Honor. *Originally published in* Ellery Queen Mystery Magazine, Honor *is a particular favorite of mine with roots in Iceland, a place Jerry and I visited together.*

Although he moved on to the legal thrillers, the Cuddy series remained Jerry's favorite and he was, in fact, working on a new Cuddy when he died in 2014. I know he'd be honored that he and Cuddy — sorry, "the Cuddy character"— are included in Crippen & Landru's 25th anniversary anthology.

ONE

The woman sitting in a client chair across my desk from me laid her handbag in her lap and said, "First thing, I come to Boston now from Iceland."

I had to admit, it was an attention-getter.

Then again, so was she. About twenty-five, her eyes shone a pale, haunting blue and her hair a steely blonde, drawn back into a ponytail. The facial features leaned to the handsome side of pretty, but to the smart side, too. Her clothes seemed a little summery for even a sunny October day, though. And, when she'd entered through the door stenciled with "JOHN FRANCIS CUDDY, CONFIDENTIAL INVESTIGATIONS," and I'd stood to greet her, the top of her head was even with my brow, and I go nearly six-three.

"My names I will spell for you."

I drew a legal pad toward me and let a pen hover in my hand above it.

She nodded solemnly, as though about to start a prayer. "F-R-E-Y-D-I-S is the first, pronounced fray-dees. In Iceland, we are most named for our father, and so K-A-R-L-S-D-O-T-T-I-R is the last, pronounced karls-dot-tur."

Simple enough: Karl's daughter. I wrote down the names, and, since it seemed important to the woman for me to get them right, I read both back to her as well. Then, "Ms. Karlsdottir, what can I do for you?"

She shook her head. "In my country, we have many traditions. One is to use first names and perhaps middle names, so please: If you can call me "Freydis," and I can call you 'John Francis'?"

"That would be fine."

Another nod. "Iceland, you have been there?"

"Never."

"You should. There is a direct flight—Icelandair—from here to our airport, Keflavik near to our capital, Reykjavik. Which is aid to a second tradition, from the Vikings of ancient days. Our people will—the word we use is 'sail.'" To go away and come back with skills from job or things for the enriching of our island, yes?"

"I understand."

"My father did just so, to England, and his younger friend the same, but the friend, Hogni Ragnarsson, came here."

"Can you spell that one for me, too?"

Karlsdottir did, and I felt slightly pleased with myself that I'd phonetically gotten it right without her.

She reached into her bag. "Hogni lives in not-so-good neighborhood in your Boston, John Francis, so all we have is postal box for address." Rummaging now. "But when we send him letter, it returns with no delivery."

Karlsdottir sighed heavily and looked at me with those Alaskan huskie eyes. "Sorry. The 'jetlag,' yes? I cannot find the envelope."

"And, I take it, you cannot find Mr. Ragnarsson, either."

A bleak smile. "That is true."

"Freydis, is there a reason you came all this way to look for him?"

She gave me a third solemn nod. "My father is now dead."

"I'm sorry."

"No need, please. He was sick with the prostate cancer that went to his bones."

I'd had an older uncle who'd suffered that particularly cruel and painful passing. "A difficult way to die."

"There is no easy way, I think. But my father left an—'inheritance'?"

"In his will or estate documents?"

"Yes, John Francis. An inheritance to Hogni."

"And you want to get that to Mr. Ragnarsson."

"I must. My sister and I are the only family to do this duty, and she is younger and sick herself, in hospital." Karlsdottir swiped her right index finger under both eyes, like a miniature squeegee for escaping tears. "So, I have the obligation. As a matter of honor."

I put down my pen. "Freydis, have you tried the Icelandic Consulate here in Boston?"

"There is not one."

"Our police, then?"

A firm shake of the head now. "When Icelandair woman tells me we have no consulate here, I ask her, what I should do? She tells me police in the United States are not like ours, who function as 'guides' for tourists and do not carry with them guns."

My turn to nod. There wouldn't exactly be an avalanche of help from the Boston department if Karlsdottir didn't even know where the guy lived in terms of our police districts.

She said, "The Icelandair woman tells me to find a private investigator. Like you, John Francis."

"She knows me personally?"

"Oh, no. Sorry. You are the most close one to my hotel."

I've received more ringing endorsements. "Look, Freydis, this could become expensive for you."

"My father was not a rich man, but with my own inheritance from him, several thousand dollars is not the problem."

"Have you looked in a telephone directory for metropolitan Boston?"

"At your airport. The directory is odd to me, because it has the last names, not the first names, in sequence of alphabet. But no Hogni."

If our White Pages threw her.... I picked up my desk phone. "Let's see if I can save us some of my time and your money."

For a change, Karlsdottir didn't nod, but she did wait politely as a buddy of mine at Verizon confirmed no number for Hogni Ragnarsson, landline or cell, listed or unlisted.

I cradled the receiver. "Do you have any idea where your father's friend might work?"

"No, John Francis. And I am worried true for Hogni. We have not heard from him in many months now."

"And that's unusual?"

"Impossible. Icelanders always maintain contact—with families, with friends—forever."

Family, duty, honor. Quite a trifecta.

"Okay." I quoted Karlsdottir my daily rate, which didn't make her blink. She dipped back into the handbag and found her cash right away.

As Karlsdottir slid two days' worth of retainer across my desk, though, she fixed me with those haunting eyes. "One more thing, please?"

I took her money. "Yes?"

"I will come with you."

"With me, Freydis?"

"Just so. In your vehicle, or the trains. The ways you will seek for Hogni."

"Wouldn't you rather play tourist?"

Finally, a smile that wasn't bleak, and pushed her back over the line from handsome to borderline beautiful. "The air flight was on my cost, the hotel is on my cost, and you are on my cost. The weather is good, and if the police cannot guide me in your city, I will go with you."

I thought, *there are far worse ways to spend your day, John Francis.*

TWO

Outside the state office building blocks from mine on Tremont Street, Freydis Karlsdottir said, "We have walked this far, and I cannot enter with you?"

"It's not that you cannot enter. It's more that my expert inside will get nervous if somebody's with me."

Karlsdottir pawed the concrete with her shoe like a bridled horse unhappy to be restrained. "What you do, John Francis, it is perhaps not...'legal'?"

"Not exactly. But it's very efficient, and no one gets hurt."

She glanced around. "Then I will go back to the small place of graves by the church you called King's Chapel."

"I'll meet you there, Freydis."

* * *

"So, Jimmy, how're you doing?"

"I'd be doing a lot better, I didn't think you're gonna ask me to do what I think you are."

I rested my rump on the edge of his computer hutch. It's never been entirely clear to me exactly what Jimmy's real job is nor which agency of the Commonwealth he actually works for. But he has a genuine talent for finding all sorts of things via the computer. A good thing, too, because at six-one, one-thirty, and a dress code like Jughead in the old Archie comics, Jimmy doesn't make the sort of first impression that would have private companies vying for his services. And he also loves to bet the greyhounds at the Suffolk Downs dog track, which means fresh cash—in this case, some of Freydis Karlsdottir's retainer—is always welcome.

Jimmy quickly scanned the room—probably for the unlikely presence of a supervisor actually at work—and then cut to the car chase. "All right, Cuddy, what do you want from me?"

I set down a sheet of legal pad, the name "Hogni Ragnarsson" block-printed on it and a fifty-dollar bill beneath it.

Jimmy glanced down. "Screwy name. Swedish?"

"Icelandic."

"You mean, like the Vikings?"

"Some of them, anyway."

"What's this particular Viking done?"

"Nothing, far as I know. But I need a residential or business address for him."

Jimmy palmed the fifty from under the sheet and swung around to his keyboard. "See what I can do."

After clacking and tapping for a while, he said, "No record of a driver's license or car registration."

"I think Ragnarsson came overseas to work."

More clacking, the screen on his monitor zipping images left and right and up and down like a video game. "Let's try the Department of Revenue then, see if he filed—damnit!"

"What's the matter?"

"Shut up a minute, let me cover my tracks here."

I'd never seen Jimmy upset with his computer before. It was like watching ice-dancers at the Olympics when one seemed to blame the other for a spin-out.

"Jesus," he said finally. "That was close."

"Can you explain it in English?"

"At your level of software comprehension? Let's just say that the Commonwealth's tax collectors put in a new burglar alarm, and it almost caught me climbing in their back window."

"Can you keep going?"

"Yeah, but not with Revenue. You say maybe the guy worked, let's try the Eye-Ay-Bee."

As in "I.A.B.," or Industrial Accident Board, the state agency that processes employee claims for injuries suffered on the job.

More clacking and tapping, but slower this time around, like Jimmy didn't want to trip another alarm.

"Ah," he said, "now we're cooking."

I bent over his shoulder toward the monitor's screen. "Construction site accident."

"Four months ago."

Which might explain the incommunicado status that worried Karlsdottir. "I don't see an address for our boy."

"No," said Jimmy with a smug edge in his voice, "but here's one for the construction company's headquarters, the construction site itself, and even the poor Viking's lawyer."

Jimmy doesn't like to print things from his computer for me, so I began taking down the information on the sheet of legal pad. "You're worth your weight in gold, my man."

Jimmy sniffed. "You don't mind, I'll take my height in gold."

* * *

When I returned to the cemetery outside King's Chapel, I didn't see Freydis Karlsdottir, so I went through the massive, fortress-like doors and into the stark little church itself. I spotted her about six rows up, just sitting as opposed to kneeling, so I moved alongside her pew.

She looked up, but not startled. "It is like a church in Iceland, this."

"How so?"

"White, clean. And…simple. A place to be reminded that one person is perhaps not so important in the world."

"Interesting observation."

Her eyes changed focus. "You found data about Hogni?"

"Indirectly. We need to go for a drive."

The beaming smile as she rose from her bench. "I like you for my guide, John Francis."

THREE

From the passenger's seat in my old Honda Prelude, Freydis Karlsdottir said, "I do not understand why we go first to construction place and not to lawyer?"

I maneuvered around some orange traffic cones, which, since Boston's "Big Dig" road-and-tunnel project began, have become as much a part of our local scenery as the cobblestones at Quincy Market. "Even my computer expert couldn't find a residential address for Mr. Ragnarsson in the Massachusetts official records. Before I approach a lawyer who might be suspicious of us, I'd like to have a little more background on your father's friend."

In my peripheral vision, I caught a frown. "Hogni's inheritance would be 'suspicious' to his lawyer?"

Now I looked over, noticing that her English was improving as she used it more with me. "In this country, Freydis, people are wary of unexpected gifts. Not in Iceland?"

The bleak smile. "So many of us there know each other—are 'related' by distant blood to each other—that we have few surprises." Even the bleak smile faded now. "An expression on our island is, 'Who are his people?,' which means the man's family history. We are much guided by our history."

I dredged up what I could from a college course on European History. "Here in the United States, we learned about your Leif Eriksson discovering North America before Christopher Columbus."

A grunt, which took me a moment to realize stood for Karlsdottir's laugh. "Only a very small part of this history, John Francis. Iceland held its first parliament, avoided civil war over religions, and discovered North America, all before the year one-thousand after Christ."

Deciding my own heritage didn't pose a real comeback to that, I concentrated on my driving.

Karlsdottir warmed to her subject. "We have the stories of such things told by our sagas, books of ancient days in an institute of culture, the pages to be read through boxes of glass. Our men of Iceland left to explore in their ships, with atgeir and sax."

"Sorry?"

"Ah, no. I should be sorry. The 'sax' is a sword, short with only one side made sharp."

I thought of a pirate's cutlass.

"And the atgeir is…when you put the blade of the hatchet on a short-also spear?"

"Halberd, I think is the word in English."

A nod. "Hal…berd. Good. But when our men are away, the women must grow strong to work the farm, even to become war chieftains to defend the home."

"Makes sense."

Karlsdottir nodded. "If in ancient days someone did a crime of violence, the family of the victim takes the blood vengeance. Later days, the criminal was made 'outlaw,' to receive no food or water, horse or aid from any other Icelander. Three years for less crime, forever if bad crime. But now, even for beating of wife or taking of children for sex, no real punishing for 'outlaw.'"

I thought about Boston's horrendous priest-rape scandals, somewhat resolved by recent settlements totaling nearly a hundred million dollars. "Modern civilization has a blind-spot about some things, Freydis, but eventually, justice kicks in."

"Justice." She turned to me, then turned back. "Perhaps, John Francis."

* * *

"Hey, you can't come through that gate without a hardhat. And a pass."

There was a slight Southern lilt to the man's words. Outside the open gate in the chain-link fence, Freydis Karlsdottir turned to me, a confused expression on her face. "What is…'pass?' Like for the entering of airplane?"

"Stay here and let me handle it."

I walked halfway to the burly black guy who'd challenged us, in a hardhat himself. Despite the dusty bluejeans and a torn flannel shirt, he held a clipboard in one hammy hand, and I drew the impression of a foreman, not a laborer. "This young lady and I would like to ask some questions."

"Don't have time for questions, man." He waved the clipboard at the skyscraper-in-progress behind him that was producing one hell of a symphony. Assuming jack-hammers, welding equipment, and nail-guns were your idea of orchestral instruments. "Got an 'unparalleled tower of luxury condominiums' to build."

If the guy was cynical enough to quote company hype, a bluff might work. "Look, it's about one of your workers who got injured here. You can answer my questions now, conveniently, or traipse into a lawyer's office for a few days of depositions. Your choice."

A disgusted expression for me, then an appraising one as he looked to Karlsdottir. "It's the guy from Iceland, right?"

"Good guess, Mr....?"

"Monroe. Lionel Monroe."

I took out my leather ID holder and showed him the laminated copy of my investigator's license.

Monroe shook his head. "Mr. Cuddy, anything like this is supposed to go through the office folks first. They say okay, then I can talk to you."

Seemed a reasonable policy, though not very helpful for my purposes. "It's not about the comp' claim. We're just trying to locate Hogni Ragnarsson."

"Hogni," with a grunted laugh, nearly like Karlsdottir's. "All the whites on this site who make fun of Afro first names like 'Latrell' or 'Deoncey,' and this guy's is 'Hogni.'" Another look to Karlsdottir. "She family of the man?"

"No. Just trying to give him something from a friend of his."

Monroe used the thumb of his free hand to push back the cuff of his shirt. "Watch says I got five minutes, but outside the gate, or the boss'll have my ass for a 'significant safety violation.'"

We moved shoulder to shoulder back to where Karlsdottir waited.

I said, "This is Mr. Monroe, and—"

He cut me off with a sidelong look as he spoke to her. "Hogni, he told me you Icelanders like first names, right?"

The beaming smile from my client, and I sensed we had Monroe won over.

She said, "Yes. And Freydis is mine."

Karlsdottir stuck out her right hand, and, after slapping his palm against a blue-jeaned thigh, he shook with her.

"Then I'm Lionel. Now, what can I tell you?"

"Where Hogni now lives in your city?"

Monroe continued ignoring me to focus on her. "Don't know, Freydis. I recollect that he used a post office box," another wave of the clipboard back toward the building, "but I never ran into him outside the site here."

The P.O. box might at least indicate Ragnarsson's local neighborhood. "Lionel, do you—"

He snapped his head toward me this time. "I told Freydis she could use my first name, not you."

Didn't want to lose him. "Sorry, Mr. Monroe."

"I mean, like, it's their custom to use first names, not ours, right?"

"Right."

"Okay." Monroe huffed out a breath and returned to Karlsdottir. "Let me tell you all I know about Hogni, and then you both be on your way."

"Yes?" she replied, in a tone that implied she was also trying to keep him talking.

"We're not a union shop here, and your Hogni was big and strong enough, I thought we could use him. Went fine for maybe a week. Matter of fact, he went on about how in Iceland everybody works account of it's your way. Two, three jobs even, stuff being so expensive on an island because everything's got to be imported. Hogni told the boys stories about eating horse steaks and smoked eels and—what did he call it? Oh, yeah: 'wind-dried puffin,' that cute little bird looks kind of like a duck crossed with a penguin."

"Our tradition from ancient days."

Another huff. "Then one morning I hear him on our coffee break, asking the other guys questions about what happens, you get yourself hurt on the job. And, what do you know, next afternoon, Hogni takes himself a fall. I saw it, would have hurt anybody, but before the end of the week, man's filing for workers comp', claiming he can't move on his leg."

Like a huge pigeon, Monroe bobbed his head forward. "Freydis, I'm sorry if he's a friend of yours, but I don't think that 'work ethic' stuff from back home sunk into Hogni too well." Now to me. "Okay, that's it."

"Not quite, Mr. Monroe."

"Say what?"

"Do you remember the local post office where Mr. Ragnarsson rented his box?"

A final huff. "No. You can call the company office and ask, but I'll tell you now, they won't give it out." Lionel Monroe turned away from us. "'The privacy rights of our employees are paramount.'"

* * *

Back in the car—and the bumper-to-bumper traffic—I said to Karlsdottir, "You must be pretty tired, the jetlag and all."

She blinked a few times, then rubbed the heels of her hands over both eyes. "For true, but also we must see Hogni's lawyer, yes?"

"We're a little late in the day for that, Freydis. Can I buy you dinner—or whatever other meal your body clock's telling you it wants?"

"My body…clock?"

"Do you feel like lunch instead of dinner?"

"Ah. No, John Francis. My…body clock makes the sound for dinner."

"'Chimes.'"

I sensed the confused look without turning toward her. "The sound a clock makes on each hour. We say it 'chimes.'"

The silhouette in profile of her solemn nod. "A lovely word. It is to the ear as the sound it describes."

I agreed, though I thought we might save 'onomatopoeic' until the morning.

* * *

"You are a good guide for restaurants as well, John Francis."

I'd brought her to Silvertones, a restaurant and bar roughly halfway between her hotel and my office, so I could leave the Prelude in a parking space I rent behind the building. Silvertones is in a cavernous basement and serves mainly comfort food, but it's well prepared by the husband-and-wife team who run the place, and not knowing much about Icelandic fare beyond "horse/eel/puffin," I'd hoped Karlsdottir could find something on their menu that she'd like.

Over a second glass of wine, and halfway through our meals, my new client hooded her eyes, I thought at first from fatigue. Then she said, "The African man at the construction fence. He stood…above you?"

I recalled the "first-name" exchange. "Stood up to me, Freydis."

"Just so." A sip from her glass. "Confrontation. But what made him offended?"

How to provide her a short version? "Africans first came to this country as slaves, kidnapped from their villages over there."

"This I know of."

"Their white masters here would give them first names, but broke up—separated—families to sell them. At auction."

Karlsdottir's eyes grew wide. "As in a…place of market?"

"Yes." Fast forward. "More recently, there were many aspects of discrimination, and one was for a white person to call a black person by a first name instead of 'Mr.' or 'Ms.' and the last name."

"As though still the black person is a…slave?"

"Or that would be the insult the black person would assume." I tried to lighten things a little. "Different in your country, eh?"

"As to the tradition of first name, yes." The bleak smile, and she seemed to really be crashing on our differential in time zones. "About the slavery and the race, not so different, perhaps. In ancient days of the Vikings, my people raided and pillaged in their boats to the south, bringing women—and girls—of Ireland back to our island, as slaves and forced wives. And my father told me that when NATO first came with an Air Force base at our Keflavik just fifty years past, the Iceland government required no black soldiers be sent to us. But we have grown. One family in twenty in my country—the word is 'adopt,' yes?—the Vietnam people who leave by boat after your war there is over."

And it had been my war, all right. But one in…? "Freydis, five percent of your population adopted those children?"

"I tell you before, John Francis: We believe in family. And courage, to do the right thing. I carry the name of a woman from the Saga of Eirik the Red. That Freydis was pregnant but joined battle with her men against the Native Americans who fought us in your 'new world,' yes? When the natives attacked her, she lifted the sword of a killed Viking, pulled her clothing down to display one of her breasts, and hit the side of the blade against it." Karlsdottir mimed smacking herself there with the palm of her right hand. "The natives run away from Freydis then."

The things you learn. But Karlsdottir now used her hand to stifle a yawn, and I thought it was time to call it a night. "Can I walk you to your hotel?"

A tired, but beaming, smile. "Please, yes."

I settled our tab, and we climbed up Silvertones' internal stairs to the street. Two more blocks, and we were at the entrance to her hotel.

Karlsdottir turned to me and said, "In the duty-free shop, I purchased a bottle of brandy. Would you share some with me?"

"In your room?"

"Just so, John Francis."

"I don't think we should."

The eyes hooded again, though differently. "My name is Freydis, but I am not pregnant, and I will not defend myself with a sword." Now the trace of her beaming smile. "Also, I am not so tired as you may think."

"I'm flattered. And honored, Freydis. But even if you were not a client, I lost my wife to cancer, and I still grieve for her."

Those ghost eyes welled with tears. "Grieve I know of, John Francis." She turned halfway to the entrance. "So, I go to my bed, and you go to yours."

Yes, but not yet.

* * *

The cemetery staff is pretty good about leaving the gates open at night, so that people with demanding work schedules can still visit. I walked up the hillside to her row and then to her stone, knowing I could find it even on a starless night.

"No flowers, John? I guess the honeymoon really IS over."

I looked down at the etched letters that would forever form "MARY ELIZABETH DEVLIN CUDDY," even though the absence of light made them unreadable. "I tried, Beth. The florist shops were all closed."

"What made you so late?"

I told her.

"The woman comes all the way from Iceland to find this 'Hogni,', but she doesn't have the envelope with his P.O. box on it?"

"She couldn't find it, and besides, there are other ways."

"I don't know, John. Doesn't feel right somehow."

I looked down at the harbor. A police boat was out with its distinctive blue running lights, but otherwise a quiet autumn evening.

"Well," I said, "worst thing, I'm helping a stranger keep a promise to her dad."

"My poor widower and his sense of 'promise'."

I thought back to Freydis Karlsdottir's "brandy" offer, and now it was my turn to nod solemnly.

FOUR

"What's that?" I said the next morning, still behind the wheel, Freydis Karlsdottir not allowing the teen-aged doorman outside her hotel to help with a rectangular wooden case—about long and wide enough to hold a croquet set—that she clutched to her chest.

"Part of Hogni's inheritance." Karlsdottir inclined her head to the trunk of the Prelude. "We can put this in your boot?"

I'd long ago disabled the lid release next to the driver's seat, so I had to get out to open it, the doorman doing his best to keep a straight face over the old fart in the old car picking up this exotic beauty of a hotel guest.

After Karlsdottir laid the case carefully into the trunk, and we were on our way, she turned to me. "If you have the mobile telephone, John Francis, we call Hogni's lawyer first?"

I slipped my right hand into the side pocket of my suit jacket and flashed the little Nokia at her. "We could. However, I've generally found that it's best to surprise people."

"Surprise." The beaming smile as she turned forward again. "Perhaps not in Iceland, but in America, 'surprise' works good, yes?"

* * *

The lawyer's office proved to be a flat-faced store-front in a four-story building on the main drag of East Boston, a traditionally Italian-American neighborhood that had become a mixing pot—if not melting pot—of first-generation immigrants from a number of different countries, even continents. As I parked on the opposite side of the street and we got out of the car, a Delta airliner on its landing path roared low enough over our heads that you could almost expect tire-tracks on the roof of the Prelude.

Karlsdottir reflexively ducked and blurted out something that wasn't recognizable. Then, "I hope we are near to your airport."

"Very close."

She looked around at the evident, if modest, apartments above the commercial level. "How do the people sleep with such noise?"

I thought about smaller, slower planes rattling the window frames of my family's rowhouse in South Boston when I was growing up. "It's an acquired skill."

We crossed the street to the Law Offices of Michael A. Nuzzo. His picture windows were pasted with decals reading "SE HABLA ESPANOL" and I guessed similar messages from several other languages. Inside the doorway stood three desks and as many young women behind them forming their own miniature United Nations. The placards in front of them were printed with "ITALIAN," "SPANISH," and "CAMBODIAN," small cribs of clear plastic holding business cards nearby. Ringing the floor space around the reception area were four-drawer file cabinets. Lots of them.

The first two women were on the telephone, leaving the third—staffing the Cambodian station—to look up at us from a computer screen.

A professional smile before, "May I help you?"

I said, "We'd like to see Mr. Nuzzo, please."

"Is he expecting you?"

"No," I showed her my ID, "but he'll want to see us nonetheless."

The smile wavered, but she took my license holder in one hand while she hit a number on the telephone pad with her other. Swinging in the swivel chair away from me, she spoke softly into the receiver, then nodded and turned back. "That door."

There were only two at the back of the reception area, and one had the familiar symbol for a unisex restroom. Karlsdottir followed me to the second, and I knocked just as its handle turned.

The door swung inward, showing a background of manila files stacked in teetering towers on the floor and against two walls. The short man looking up at me was about forty, with black hair beating a retreat above his temples, leaving a little tuft of wayward strands at the crown and a moat of scalp around it. Nuzzo wore a dress shirt and suit pants, but no tie, and his belly sagged over his belt. In his hand he had a cellphone.

"What's this all about?"

"Sorry," I said. "You on a call?"

He looked down at the cellular. "No, the damned thing's not working. Won't even tell time."

I stuck out my own hand. "John Cuddy."

He shook it without obvious enthusiasm. "Michael Nuzzo."

"And this is my client, Ms. Freydis Karlsdottir."

He seemed to appraise the tall woman whose shadow loomed over him. "Well, come on in."

Nuzzo had to move another pile of files from one of his own client chairs to give both of us places to sit. As we did, he moved around his desk and dropped the useless cellular on top of it. "What can I do for you?"

"We're looking for a friend of Ms. Karlsdottir's father."

"What makes you think I know him?"

Him, not "this person" or other ambiguity. "You represent the man on a Worker's Compensation claim."

"Hey," gesturing toward the files, "you got any idea how many comp' cases I do a year?"

It seemed a bit of a non-sequitur, but I've always felt you learn more by letting attorneys in any speciality talk. "You want to tell us?"

Nuzzo gave me a sour look. "When I got out of law school fifteen years ago, you could make a good living off comp'. Hell, in ninety-one, there were over forty-thousand claims filed with the Commonwealth state-wide. Then Governor Willie 'May he burn in hell' Weld, a blue-blood who never did manual labor a single day in his life, got the legislature to cut benefits from sixty-seven percent of the weekly wage to sixty, and the benefit period from five years down to three. And now there's less than half as many claims filed as back in ninety-one."

Karlsdottir broke in with the question I was about to ask. "But you must keep a list of all workers you help and the place they live, yes?"

Nuzzo stared at her. "Confidential."

That seemed a little over-protective, since we'd already told him we knew he represented our boy. "Hogni Ragnarsson."

The lawyer didn't flinch or even squint at the unusual name. "Confidential."

Karlsdottir leaned forward in her chair. "I have from my father an inheritance for Hogni."

Nuzzo perked up. "Inheritance?"

I said, "The reason we're trying to find Mr. Ragnarsson."

"Well," a pursing of the lips. "You could make out a check to me, and I could pass it on to him."

"If you represent the man," I said.

Nuzzo shot me another sour look.

Karlsdottir shook her head. "I must give this to Hogni for my family. It is a matter of honor."

Nuzzo stood up. "Then I guess this conference is over."

My client started to speak, but I squelched her by rising also. "Thanks for your time."

"Don't mention it."

As we left his office, I put a finger to my lips so that Karlsdottir would hold her peace. On our way past the Cambodia desk, I thanked the woman while plucking one of Nuzzo's business cards from its plastic crib.

Out on the sidewalk, Karlsdottir tugged on my coat sleeve. "John Francis, why did you not—"

I motioned her to move with me beyond the angles of sight allowed by the picture windows. Then I took out my cellphone and dialed that buddy of mine at Verizon again while crossing the street toward the Prelude.

"Who do you call?"

I shook my head as I heard my friend pick up. "It's John Cuddy."

"Twice in one day?" came back from a transmitting tower somewhere.

"Another favor, yeah. Right about now, there's a call going out on"—I glanced down at Nuzzo's card and read off the ten-digit office number—"and I need to know the address it's going to."

"Cuddy, you make a better enemy than a friend."

"I'll wait patiently."

As I did, we reached my car, and Freydis Karlsdottir treated me to her beaming smile.

FIVE

It took us less than five minutes to reach the address, also in Eastie, that my friend gave me. The number belonged to the payphone in a rooming house, one that had seen better days, now that we were pulling up outside it.

"Hogni is like me," said Karlsdottir, giving another solemn nod. "He goes to the professional most close to him."

I set the parking brake as my client said, "Please, to open the boot?"

As we both moved around to the back of the car, Karlsdottir added, "John Francis, already you have been such a good guide to me, I should see Hogni alone, yes?"

I keyed the lid, but she reached in before I could help her take the wooden case out. "Hey, Freydis, we've come this far together, I'd like to meet the guy."

Karlsdottir clutched the case to her chest, nodding uncertainly now.

We began walking up the path to the rooming house's front door. About halfway there, it flew open, and a tall, red-headed man burst onto the stoop, looking down at the steps and limping down them, too, with a duffle-bag in his left hand. The door—maybe on a spring—slammed behind him as he hit the path and looked up to see us.

And to freeze.

Which is when I found myself on my knees, registering that I'd been struck over my right ear, the pain expanding geometrically through my skull. As I lost even that precarious balance and pitched forward, I managed to get my palms out in a modified push-up to break the rest of the fall, ending up on all fours and low to the ground.

Karlsdottir's voice above me said, "John Francis, I am so sorry."

The red-headed man yelled her first name, then a string of what I guessed to be Icelandic.

With that, Karlsdottir strode around and in front of me, tossing a short, broad sword toward his feet and brandishing an axe on a short handle with a spearpoint at its business end.

In English, cutlass and halberd.

Karlsdottir yelled back at Ragnarsson, "Hogni," and then her own indecipherable statement.

He dropped the duffle bag, but made no move for the sword, instead limping backward with his hands up in stop signs and baying in Icelandic.

She advanced on him in a herringbone pattern, first angling left, then right, the halberd held with both hands like a batter in baseball stalking a pitcher who'd just plunked him at the plate.

Ragnarsson, cringing and babbling now, tripped over the last step of the stoop and fell backward, his head nearly at the closed door, crying out in pain but also, I thought, pleading.

It did him no good.

Karlsdottir arrived over him, and brought the axe down like she was felling a horizontal tree, the blade on impact making a sickening "thock" as Ragnarsson fell silent.

I closed my eyes, thinking I'd just witnessed an example of what "smote" means.

When I opened my eyes again, Karlsdottir was kneeling in front of me, her hands empty but Ragnarsson's blood spattered over them as well as her face and clothes.

"Freydis...?"

"John Francis, true I am sorry. But Hogni in Iceland did rape on my young sister while he was to be caring for her in his house, as I was caring for my father in ours. My sister is in mental hospital forever from the attack of Hogni, yet the courts ordered him to jail for no time. And so he comes here, to escape me." Karlsdottir's eyes drifted northeastward. "I promise to my father as he dies I will take blood vengeance for my sister, because I am the only one of our family who can do just so."

I shook my head, the consequent pain nearly blocking my words. "But the inheritance…?"

Freydis Karlsdottir's bleak smile. "In our tradition, inheritance and vengeance are two sides of the same road, John Francis."

I think I said, "A matter of honor," just before blacking out.

Death Row
by Michael Z. Lewin

My Crippen & Landru story collection, The Reluctant Detective and Other Stories, *was published in 2001. Doug was a total pleasure to deal with — responsive, intelligent, knowledgeable and quick.*

He knew my work. There was a story he suggested that I didn't want to include (not good enough) and one I submitted that he asked me to omit. No problem both ways. I really wish that Doug's manner of working had been an industry standard in the course of my career. Let's just say it hasn't been; I've been lucky to get one of the adjectives above, much less all four.
And it's been a pleasure meeting and talking with Doug about other things and other people many times, at conferences and at Detection Club events in London.

He also particularly liked a couple of my funnier stories with Dan Quayle as detective. Remember Dan Quayle? Looks a bit better than he used to, doesn't he?

The story in this collection doesn't feature Danny, but "Death Row" is true. Well, true to the extent that there really is such an institution in a pub in Bath.

The real pub isn't called The Sun and Moon. It's called The Star and it's been a licensed public house since 1759. That's not the oldest boozer in Bath, but it's a special place and, of course, I had to go there and do some research as I was writing the story.

The story was first published in Ellery Queen's Mystery Magazine, *and that fact hit the papers here in Bath. I'd like to say that's because murder in this ancient and beautiful city is so rare but that's not entirely true. What's rare is a story set in a local pub. Except for the ones told around the tables (or overheard by shy and retiring folk such as I.) No, I'm not claiming this is as a true crime tale, but there is a Death Row.*

Although I'm American by birth, I've lived in England nearly fifty years. But even now by no means all my oeuvre is set here. For instance, my newest book, Alien Quartet, marks a return between soft covers (and in electronic formats) of my first fictional character. Albert Samson is a PI based in Indianapolis, first published in 1971... The book contains four linked stories, all also previously published in EQMM but never before put together in book form.

No space ships in Alien Quartet: apologies for those seeking yet more novelty from me in the mystery genre. But a still-sensitive, sometimes reflective private eye. One of the stories won a Shamus, another a nomination.

Big thanks too to the redoubtable Jeffrey Marks who has put this collection together with such courtesy and efficiency.

"But it's my only chance," Morrison said. "It's my last chance."

Katy drank from her pint. Then she shook her head slowly, dismissively. "What do you need to be on television for anyway? I've never been on television. I don't feel less a person because of it."

"You'd avoid being on the tele, if what you've been telling me all these years is true."

"Oh it's true all right." She dropped her eyes. "And I can't even tell you most of it."

"So you always say," Morrison said. He finished his own pint as Katy's head snapped up, a frown on her face. "And I'm not disbelieving you. I'm not. You've lived one hell of a life. One that would put most men to shame. One that puts me to shame. But that's not point. The point is that here I am, seventy-eight years old, and I've never been on the television and now I got a chance and all I'm asking for is a little help."

"A little help is what you call it?" Katy rubbed her face.

"It'll be like riding a bike," Morrison said. His wry expression silently added, "if what you've been telling me all these years is true."

"I still don't get why it's so damned important to you."

"It's television," Morrison said. "It's the modern age. Everything is on the tele. Everybody is on the tele. You're nothing if you haven't been on tele. Unless, of course, it's your personal choice. But my grandkids, I can tell by the way they look at me, they think I'm a slug because their mother thinks I'm a slug but if suddenly, there I was, on the TV, then that'd all change. There'd be some respect in their eyes. I've been waiting all my life to see some respect in my grandkids' eyes."

"Your grandchildren are twenty-two and twenty-eight, Mo. And when was the last time you even spoke to the twenty-eight-year-old?"

"OK, Colin's a DJ or impresario or whatever queer thing he's went and made himself. But there's little Becky."

"Who has two kids of her own and lives in a council house."

"So maybe it's my great-grandkids I want some respect from."

"When's the last time you saw them?"

"If I was going to be on the tele I could call Becky up, tell her when, visit her. Maybe we could watch it together with the greats. It could be the start of a whole new phase of my life. I could be a real grandfather to these ones. I could teach them things. I could tell them stories. And they'd listen because they could tell their friends that's my great-granddad and he was on the TV news."

"You really believe it makes that much difference to them?"

"It's television. What else do they know at their ages."

"What's their ages?"

"Four and five."

"You sure?"

"Or thereabouts."

Katy sighed. She drank from her beer, finishing it. "You want another?" She stood up. "Same again?"

"And why are we sitting out here?" Morrison said. He gestured around the small garden.

"Because it's a nice evening?"

"Instead of in there. You see anybody else out here because it's a nice evening?"

"Just as well, considering what you're asking me to do."

"It's just that it's not that nice a evening, that's my point," Morrison said. "Only tourists would sit out here else by choice."

"You're just after the ten percent discount."

Morrison shrugged. "I'm not a rich man. But that's not the point."

Katy carried his glass and her own to the back door of the public house.

"It's not the point."

She lifted her shoulders in a shrug, knowing he would see it as she headed indoors for the bar.

"It's not the point," Morrison said to himself. "I got me a chance to go on the television and all I'm asking is a little help."

A few minutes later a young couple came to the door of the garden. The woman pointed to the other table and asked, "Is that table taken?"

"Yes," Morrison said. "A family. With grandkids. Sorry."

The young couple retreated into the interior of The Sun and Moon. A moment later Katy came back out. She glanced back, probably seeing the retreating couple. "They wanted to be alone," Morrison said. "Didn't want a table next to some old codger."

Katy sat down. "And his old lady friend."

"You're not old."

"I'm as old as you."

"No you're not."

"Because I'm eleven months younger? That's near as makes no difference at our age, Mo."

"You don't look it."

"Thanks, I suppose."

"And you don't act it. You move like a gazelle."

She laughed. "How would you know how a gazelle moves? Especially an arthritic one."

"You're going to tell me you know about gazelles? All that glamorous life you've led. Adventures this part of the world and that."

Katy tilted her head as if she might contest the idea that she'd had adventures. Instead she said, "Hardly glamorous."

"You been all over the world. Where have I ever been? Not even on the tele."

"I haven't been that many places."

"Africa?"

"Well…"

"Far East?"

"Sitting in an Army office most of the time."

"Sitting. Oh right. Not doing anything. I believe that. And the earth is flat."

"It is."

"What is?"

"The earth. Flat."

He stared at her, his hand around his new pint.

"In places." She laughed.

"Ha-bloody-ha," he said. He lifted his glass. "Cheers."

They touched glasses. They both drank.

"I know you can't tell me all what you did," Morrison said. "Not even now. Not even when there's nobody I could tell it to anyway."

"I signed the Official Secrets Act," Katy said. "There's a lot don't take that seriously now, but I do. It's an oath."

"And I respect you for that."

"I'll tell you this much though," she said after a deep drag on her drink. "If I was a young woman now, the adventures I could have, same kind of career, they'd leave what I actually did in the dust. They're in the SAS now, you know."

"Who?"

"Women. There's about nothing that the blokes in the Army do that the women don't do now." She shook her head.

"There's some been killed in Iraq," Morrison said. "Women. Soldiers."

"The risk is part of what they pay you for."

"Anyhow, you wouldn't have been much good undercover against the Mau Mau. Or in Korea. Or Suez."

"The SAS isn't about undercover. It's about getting in there to do a job and then getting out again without being caught."

"Or Malaya." He drank.

Katy sat quietly.

He said, "Northern Ireland..." He looked at her. "You could have been over there. You were over there."

"Strictly in an administrative capacity," she said. "But if it was going on these days, the job I could have done as a woman... There are things women can do that the men couldn't. They've finally learned that." She sighed, a sigh for the glamour and adventure she'd missed out on because she'd been born at the wrong time.

"The Falklands. The two Iraqs," Morrison said. "There's always some bloody war or another. If it isn't us fighting as ourselves, it's as part of the UN. And women are in them all these days."

"You're not wrong about that. But you know what?"

"What?"

"You know the demilitarized zone they left in Korea after they stopped? Barbed wire across the whole peninsula, however many miles wide?"

"What about it?"

"It's nature reserve now, good as. They've got species thriving in there that are rare in the rest of Korea. It's all because they're safe in that strip across the country because nobody's allowed in there. I read about it the other day."

Morrison smiled. "War is good for something then."

"Unresolved war is. Speaking of which, did you know that the Second World War didn't end till 1989?"

Morrison's eyes narrowed.

"It's true," Katy said.

"That's silly."

"The war was against Germany, wasn't it? The whole of Germany. Well, it wasn't till the Berlin Wall came down and Germany was reunited that the war against Germany – the whole of Germany – could officially end." She lifted her glass. "It's true."

He scratched his head. "You're full of information tonight," he said with some admiration.

"I just read. Keep my eyes and ears open."

"And it keeps you young. I'll bet if I was to tell my great-grandkids that, about the war, they'd be impressed. I'm sure they would. They could pass on true facts that their great-grandfather told them to their pals. And it's not as if they're going to have their great-grandfather around forever now, is it?"

"Seventy-eight isn't that old these days."

"Farty Freddy's ninety-two," Morrison said.

"My point exactly."

Morrison was silent for a moment. Then he asked, "How are they in there?"

"Where?"

"Don't play dumb," he said. "It doesn't suit you. On the bench, of course."

"They're fine."

"All present and correct."

"Freddy's there."

"And all the others?"

"Bert and Mike."

"Not Jack?" Morrison's eyes lit up a little.

"Don't get excited. They haven't called for an ambulance. There was a drink in his place. I'm sure he just went to the gents."

Morrison nodded, having a natural sympathy for any man past a certain age who needed to go to the gents. "Freddy talking to himself?"

Katy nodded.

"And farting?"

"There was… an air about him."

"He doesn't even change his clothes, you know. He'd still smell, but not half so much if he'd at least bloody do that."

"I don't know why you want a place on the bench so badly."

"Yes you do."

She looked around, although they were alone in the small garden area. The habit of caution built up over a lifetime? "If you want it so badly, why don't you do it yourself?"

"I don't have the expertise, do I?"

"A frail old geezer like that. How much expertise does it take?"

"I've thought about it, Katy."

"Well then. Resolve is half the battle."

"That sounds like something written over a coat of arms. Or on a medal."

"If you want it done so badly, why don't you just do it?"

"He'd never let me in his flat."

"That's the problem?"

"He lives down the road. He doesn't even have to cross a street to get to the pub and back. If he had to cross a street it would be a different matter altogether."

"It would?"

"I could rent a car. I could take him at the intersection."

"Do you have a driver's license these days?"

"I could steal a car."

Katy rolled her eyes.

"It doesn't matter, does it? Freddy shuffles home. Two minute walk, takes him fifteen minutes. Doesn't even cross a street."

"Fifteen minutes?"

"OK, six or seven. But the point is, he walks along a busy road, but doesn't cross it. The only thing he does in his whole life is walk to the pub and back. Everything else they bring to him."

"Who brings what to him?"

"I told you, he doesn't have kids. Had a boy once – he'll tell you about it if you get close enough to talk to him."

"Thanks but no thanks."

"Boy got run down himself. Decades ago. Now he's got nobody. Social services bring him his shopping, take him to the doctor. They ought to bloody see he changes his clothes and gets fumigated, but no such luck."

"You're absolutely sure he has no family?" Katy said.

Morrison blinked. "Yes." He began to ask why she'd asked but instead said, "He'd let you inside, no problem. A bit of disguise in case someone saw you at the door but he'd just take you for one of the social service busybodies."

"Disguise, not getting caught, none of that would be a problem," she said.

Morrison nodded. If what Katy'd been saying about her life and her background was even half true... But did she still have the bottle?

"The problem would be figuring out why on earth I would want to take out an old man like that?"

"Air pollution?"

"Seriously."

"As a favour to me?"

"That's the problem, see, Mo. You say it's all about getting yourself on the tele."

"I've explained that."

"Your Becky isn't going to let you back in her life just because your face is on the box."

"The reporter would talk to me. I'd say something about her. I'd wave to her. And the kids."

"If you really wanted to do something to get a place back with her, you'd sell that house of yours. Give her some money. Get her out of the hole she's in."

"Sell my house?"

"If you really wanted to do your granddaughter and her kids some good, that's what you'd do."

"They already get it in my will."

Katy shrugged.

Morrison snorted. He thought it was quietly to himself, but it was a sharp sound, louder than he expected. Then he said, "OK, I'll do it. I'll sell the house."

"Really?"

"If you'll just get me on the tele."

* * *

Charlene Brockman, of "Today In The West," said, "And now we have a story that we thought was going to be a light-hearted tribute to our postal service."

"Oh yes?" Paul Worthy, her co-host, asked rhetorically.

"But it's been coloured by unexpected tragedy. Nadia Norris got the details for us this afternoon."

The young and attractive face of Nadia Norris came up on the screen. "I'm standing outside The Sun and Moon public house in Bath," she said. "It's one of the city's oldest and most traditional pubs. And they really do value their traditions here."

The picture changed to a wooden bench inside the pub. "And this is one of them. This simple bench, the closest seating to the bar, is known as 'Death Row'. Now that isn't meant to be as chilling a name as you might think. It's just that space on the bench is traditionally reserved for the pub's oldest regular customers. The Sun and Moon's landlord, Keith Waters knows the story."

The camera drew back to include the face of the landlord, who said, "It was called 'Death Row' long before I came to the pub, about eight years ago. But we were happy to continue the tradition and show a bit of respect. So our oldest regulars get a special bench – the closest to the bar, so they don't have to walk so far. And they also get a little discount off their drinks."

Back to Nadia. "It's been such a tradition at the pub, and so well-known, that they even get post." She held up a card. "Here is the latest delivery, a postcard from a member of the staff who's on holiday in Scotland. Look, all that's on the address is Death Row, Bath."

The camera closed in on the postcard, showing the brief address.

"Yet," Nadia said, "the card was delivered to the pub only two days after it was posted. I've got Howard Hilsomely, the postie for the street here to explain how it happened."

The camera turned to Hilsomely who said, "When the card came into the sorting office some of the new lads thought it was a creepy joke. But a lot of us know about Death Row and the pub has been on my route for years. So, no problem."

"Not rain or sleet or snow or the most minimal of addresses can stop the Royal Mail," Nadia said, now back inside the pub. "And when you got the card, Keith, what did you do?"

"I thought people might be interested in knowing what a fine postal service we still have here," the landlord said. "So I invited Howard in and rang you folks at 'Today In The West'."

"Cheers," Howard, the postie, said, lifting a glass.

"However," Nadia said, "before we could get our camera crew over to Bath to cover the story, the Sun and Moon's Death Row was hit by tragedy."

"It's a bit of a blow," Keith said, again on camera. "Our oldest member of Death Row, Freddy Loriner, unfortunately died in his sleep day before yesterday. He hadn't been well, and he was ninety-two." Keith lifted a pint. "Here's to you, Freddy, mate."

"Without becoming morbid about it," Nadia said, "you must be used to occasional deaths among the members of Death Row."

"Of course," Keith said, wiping foam from his lips. "One reason we carry on the tradition is to make the last years of our older customers a little more comfortable. But, when it does happen, well, we know we've done our bit."

"And what happens when a spot on the bench becomes vacant?"

"The existing members shuffle along – we keep people's places in strict order of age."

"And the new place?"

"Goes to the next oldest regular on the list."

"You keep a list?"

"Oh yes."

"So who has filled Freddy's place?"

"Well, unfortunately, that's another sad story. The next regular on the list was Morrison Mason. Unfortunately Mo was hit crossing the road on his way home just last night. It was a hit and run and he was killed immediately, poor old bloke. I know he was particularly looking forward to meeting you today, Nadia."

Nadia turned to the camera. "So our light-hearted story has a tinge of tragedy." She held up a photograph. "If any of our viewers in Bath, or driving through Bath last night, saw this man at the corner of Lansdown Road and the London Road, and saw what happened, we – and the police – would be very grateful for the information."

"So would we," said Keith, off camera.

"But tradition is tradition," Nadia said. "Although traditions do evolve over time."

The camera pulled back.

Nadia said, "I have Katy Butterworth here with me. And I have to say, you don't look nearly old enough to qualify for a place on the bench, Katy."

"Thank you," Katy said.

"But you are, aren't you, the newest member of Death Row?"

"I am, and proud of it. Although it's awful that poor Mo wasn't able to take his place for more than the one night. I know for a fact that it meant a lot to him. And I know that if he'd been able to appear on your programme he'd have sent his love and best wishes to his granddaughter, Becky, her two kids, and to his grandson, Colin."

"You're seventy-seven years old, Katy, if you don't mind my saying so."

"That I am."

"How do you stay looking so young?"

"Clean living. Regular exercise. And a pint or two of Keith's excellent ale."

"And you are – this is right, isn't it? – you are the very first woman ever to take a place on Death Row, aren't you?"

"I believe I am," Katy said. "It's a pleasure and a privilege. In its way, the fulfilment of a lifetime's ambition."

A Crippen & Landru Checklist

Published in 1994
- John Dickson Carr. *Speak of the Devil*

Published in 1995
- Margery Allingham. *The Darings of the Red Rose*
- Marcia Muller. *The McCone Files*

Published in 1996
- Edward D. Hoch. *Diagnosis: Impossible*
- Patricia Moyes. *Who Killed Father Christmas?*
- Bill Pronzini. *Spadework*

Published in 1997
- Michael Gilbert. *The Man Who Hated Banks*
- Edward D. Hoch. *The Ripper of Storyville*
- H. R. F. Keating. *In Kensington Gardens Once . . .*
- Margaret Maron. *Shoveling Smoke*
- James Yaffe. *My Mother the Detective*

Published in 1998
- P. M. Carlson. *Renowned Be Thy Grave*
- Jeremiah Healy. *The Concise Cuddy*
- Peter Lovesey. *Do Not Exceed the Stated Dose*
- Bill Pronzini. *Carpenter and Quincannon*
- Peter Robinson. *Not Safe After Dark*

Published in 1999
- Doug Allyn. *All Creatures Dark and Dangerous*
- Lawrence Block. *One Night Stands*
- Ed Gorman. *Famous Blue Raincoat*
- Ellery Queen. *The Tragedy of Errors*

Published in 2000
- Hugh B. Cave. *Long Live the Dead*
- Michael Collins. *Fortune's World*
- Joe Gores. *Stakeout on Page Street*
- Edward D. Hoch. *The Velvet Touch*
- Clark Howard. *Challenge the Widow-Maker*
- Marcia Muller. *McCone and Friends*
- Carolyn Wheat. *Tales Out of School*

Published in 2001
- Lawrence Block. *The Lost Cases of Ed London*
- Max Allan Collins. *The Kisses of Death*
- Susan Dunlap. *The Celestial Buffet*
- Ron Goulart. *Adam and Eve on a Raft*
- Edward D. Hoch. *The Old Spies Club*
- Michael Z. Lewin. *The Reluctant Detective*
- Peter Lovesey. *The Sedgemoor Strangler*
- Ross Macdonald. *Strangers in Town*

Published in 2002
- Christianna Brand. *The Spotted Cat* ("Lost Classics")
- Charles B. Child. *The Sleuth of Baghdad* ("Lost Classics")
- Michael Gilbert. *The Curious Conspiracy*
- Peter Godfrey. *The Newtonian Egg* ("Lost Classics")
- Wendy Hornsby. *Nine Sons*
- Stuart Palmer. *Hildegarde Withers* ("Lost Classics")
- Craig Rice. *Murder, Mystery and Malone* ("Lost Classics")
- Georges Simenon. *The 13 Culprits*
- Raoul Whitfield. *Jo Gar's Casebook*
- Brendan DuBois. *The Dark Snow*

Published in 2003
- Jon L. Breen. *Kill the Umpire*
- Hugh B. Cave. *Come Into My Parlor*
- Liza Cody. *Lucky Dip*
- William DeAndrea. *Murder – All Kinds* ("Lost Classics")
- William Campbell Gault. *Marksman* ("Lost Classics")
- Jeremiah Healy. *Cuddy – Plus One*
- Edward D. Hoch. *The Iron Angel*
- Gerald Kersh. *Karmesin* ("Lost Classics")

- C. Daly King. *The Complete Curious Mr. Tarrant* ("Lost Classics")
- Helen McCloy. *The Pleasant Assassin* ("Lost Classics")
- Bill Pronzini & Barry Malzberg. *Problems Solved*
- Eric Wright. *A Killing Climate*

Published in 2004
- Anthony Berkeley. *The Avenging Chance* ("Lost Classics")
- Joseph Commings. *Banner Deadlines* ("Lost Classics")
- Margaret Maron. *Suitable for Hanging*
- Kathy Lynn Emerson. *Murders and Other Confusions*
- Erle Stanley Gardner. *The Danger Zone* ("Lost Classics")
- Margaret Millar. *The Couple Next Door* ("Lost Classics")
- Mickey Spillane. *Byline: Mickey Spillane*
- T. S. Stribling. *Dr. Poggioli: Criminologist* ("Lost Classics")

Published in 2005
- Terence Faherty. *The Confessions of Owen Keane*
- Dennis Lynds writing as Michael Collins. *Slot-Machine Kelly* ("Lost Classics")
- Edward Marston. *Murder – Ancient and Modern*
- Gladys Mitchell. *Sleuth's Alchemy* ("Lost Classics")
- Philip Warne. *Who Was Guilty?* ("Lost Classics")
- Ellery Queen. *The Adventure of the Murdered Moths*

Published in 2006
- Detection Club. *The Verdict of Us All* (An anthology in honor of H. R. F. Keating)
- Erle Stanley Gardner. *The Casebook of Sidney Zoom* ("Lost Classics")
- Edward D. Hoch. *More Things Impossible*
- Amy Myers. *Murder, 'Orrible Murder*
- Ellis Peters. *The Trinity Cat* ("Lost Classics")
- Rafael Sabatini. *The Evidence of the Sword* ("Lost Classics")
- Julian Symons. *The Detections of Francis Quarles* ("Lost Classics")

Published in 2007
- Lloyd Biggle. *The Grandfather Rastin Mysteries* ("Lost Classics")
- Max Brand. *Masquerade* ("Lost Classics")
- Mignon G. Eberhart. *Dead Yesterday* ("Lost Classics")
- Ross Macdonald. *The Archer Files*
- Walter Satterthwait. *The Mankiller of Pooejegai*

Published in 2008
- John Dickson Carr and Val Gielgud. *13 to the Gallows*
- Richard Lupoff. *Quintet*
- Peter Lovesey. *Murder on the Short List*
- Hugh Pentecost. *The Battles of Jericho* ("Lost Classics")

Published in 2009
- Anthony Boucher and Denis Green. *The Casebook of Gregory Hood* ("Lost Classics")
- Victor Canning. *The Minerva Club* ("Lost Classics")
- Vera Caspary. *The Murder in the Stork Club* ("Lost Classics")
- James Powell. *A Pocketful of Noses*
- Robert Silverberg and Randall Garrett. *A Little Intelligence*
- S. J. Rozan. *A Tale About a Tiger*

Published in 2010
- Erle Stanley Gardner. *The Exploits of the Patent Leather Kid* ("Lost Classics")
- William Link. *The Columbo Collection*
- Philip Wylie. *Ten Thousand Blunt Instruments* ("Lost Classics")

Published in 2011
- Vincent Cornier. *The Duel of Shadows* ("Lost Classics")
- Loren D. Estleman. *Valentino*
- Elizabeth Ferrars. *The Casebook of Jonas P. Jonas* ("Lost Classics")
- Melodie Johnson Howe. *Shooting Hollywood*

Published in 2014
- Charlotte Armstrong. *Night Call* ("Lost Classics")
- Edward D. Hoch. *Nothing Is Impossible*

Published in 2015
- Phyllis Bentley. *Chain of Witnesses* ("Lost Classics")
- Anthony Berkeley. *The Avenging Chance, Enlarged edition with one additional story* ("Lost Classics")
- Marilyn Todd. *Swords, Sandals, and Sirens*

Published in 2016
- Patrick Quentin. *The Puzzles of Peter Duluth* ("Lost Classics")
- Frederick Irving Anderson. *The Purple Flame and Other Detective Stories* ("Lost Classics")
- Detection Club. *Motives for Murder, A Celebration of Peter Lovesey on His 80th Birthday*
- James Yaffe. *My Mother, The Detective, Enlarged edition with one additional story*

Published in 2017
- Edward D. Hoch. *All But Impossible: The Impossible Files of Dr. Sam Hawthorne*
- Anthony Gilbert. *Sequel to Murder: The Cases of Arthur Crook and Other Mysteries* ("Lost Classics")

Published in 2018
- James Holding. *The Zanzibar Shirt Mystery and Other Stories* ("Lost Classics")
- Elaine Viets. *A Deal with the Devil and 13 Short Stories*
- Edward D. Hoch. *Challenge the Impossible, The Last Casebook of Dr. Sam Hawthorne*
- William Brittain. *The Man Who Read Mysteries* ("Lost Classics")

Published in 2019
- Peter Lovesey. *The Crime of Miss Oyster Brown and Other Stories*
- Q. Patrick/Patrick Quentin. *The Cases of Lt. Timothy Trant* ("Lost Classics]
- *Silver Bullets: The 25th anniversary of Crippen & Landru Publishing*

Crippen & Landru has published a series of short stories as holiday gifts for subscribers and other supporters. Except for the first one, all the pamphlets are newly written for Crippen & Landru:

Margery Allingham. Room to Let, A Radio Play. 1999.
Peter Lovesey. The Kiss of Death, A Peter Diamond Mystery. 2000.
Marcia Muller and Bill Pronzini. Season of Sharing, A Sharon McCone and "Nameless Detective" Story. 2001.
James Yaffe. Mom Lights a Candle. 2002.
H.R.F. Keating. Majumdar Uncle, An Inspector Ghote Story. 2003.
Joe Gores. No Crib for His Bed, A DKA Files Story. 2004.
Peter Robinson. Blue Christmas, An Inspector Banks Story. 2005.
Edward D. Hoch. The Christmas Egg, A Simon Ark Story. 2006.
Margaret Maron. Io Saturnalia! 2007.
Edward Marston. Hogmanay Homicide. 2008.
Liza Cody. Mr. Bo. 2009.
Kathy Lynn Emerson. Lady Appleton and the Yuletide Hogglers. 2010.
Loren D. Estleman. Wolfe in the Manger, A Claudius Lyon Story. 2011.
Barbara and Max Allan Collins. writing as Barbara Allan. Antique Slay Ride. 2014.
Amy Myers. Tom Wasp and the Winter's Rage. 2015.
Marilyn Todd. Bull's Eye, A Claudia Seferious Story. 2017
Elaine Viets. The Scrooge Society. 2018.

To honor writers recognized at Malice Domestic Conventions Crippen & Landru has been privileged to be associated with Malice Domestic in issuing chapbooks containing previously unpublished or little-known material. They are given to each person in attendance at the convention.

Ellery Queen. The Adventure of the Scarecrow and the Snowman. 1998.
John Dickson Carr. The Detective in Fiction and Harem-Scarem. 1999.
Arthur Conan Doyle. The Surgeon of Gaster Fell. 2000.
Rex Stout. By His Own Hand. 2001.
Tony Hillerman. Chee's Witch. 2002.
Elizabeth Peters. Liz Peters, PI. 2003.
Erle Stanley Gardner. Early Birds. 2004.
Ellis Peters. Let Nothing You Dismay! 2005.
Craig Rice. I'll See You in My Dreams. 2006.
Georgette Heyer. Night at the Inn. 2007.
Peter Lovesey. The Homicidal Hat. 2008.
Nancy Pickard. Dr. Couch Saves a Bird. 2009.
Edward D. Hoch. The Killdeer Chronicles. 2010.
Sue Grafton. The Lying Game. 2011.
Lee Goldberg. Mr. Monk and the BBQ. 2012.
Aaron Elkins. A Slight Mistake. 2013.
Kathy Lynn Emerson. The Tell-Tale Twinkle. 2014.
Ann Cleeves. The Soothsmoothers. 2015.
Sarah Caudwell. Malice Among Friends. 2016.
Martin Edwards. Acknowledgments. 2017.
Robin Hathaway. Does Thee Murder? 2018.
Donna Andrews. The Birthday Dinner. 2019.

And we published one chapbook for a Bouchercon convention:
Edward D. Hoch. Bouchercon Bound. 2001.

Afterword

I believe Kate Stine first introduced Doug to me at a conference over 20 years ago. He was finishing his definitive biography of John Dickson Carr, and I was researching my biography of Craig Rice. I cheered when his biography was nominated for an Edgar, and after my biography was published, he asked me to edit a collection of Craig Rice stories for Crippen & Landru. I was thrilled to participate and fell in love with the publishing house.

Besides our shared enjoyment of Golden Age Detection authors, we also shared a passion for education. Doug was a professor, where I teach middle school. Over the years, we chatted about books, many of which he'd published.

I had been introduced to mysteries at an early age. I'd read my first Agatha Christie (*The Underdog and Other Stories* – of course a short story collection) at the age of 14 and started collecting first editions over the years. I have a complete collection of the American first editions of Agatha Christie now, and I've expanded my collection to include signed copies of Craig Rice, Anthony Boucher and Ellery Queen, all of course American first editions. Due to the volumes that Crippen & Landru has produced, I've added Patrick Quentin/Q Patrick/Jonathan Stagge to my list of collectibles as well. It makes for a full, but happy house.

In the summer of 2014, I volunteered to help Doug get the Crippen & Landru website back in shape. I had twenty years as an IT specialist in a previous life, so that didn't seem like a daunting task. The site had a problem with its SSL certificate, in case anyone is dying to know.

After the certificate issue was fixed, I saw some other ways to improve the site. By October, I'd upgraded the website to include a variety of different functionalities, email notifications, reviews, search capabilities and more. By December, I'd added information on upcoming books, and I'd added pages for eBooks too. At some point during all the improvements, I was hooked.

I spent the next two years upgrading the website and creating a number of eBooks for our readers. I still enjoy these tasks. Sometime during this time period, Doug named me as the Director of Development, a title I thought more than sufficient since I enjoyed everything about Crippen & Landru.

Fast forward to 2018, and I took the reins of Crippen & Landru. Doug has stayed on as Senior Editor. It's been scary, wonderful, and amazing all at once. Doug and I have mapped out a cornucopia of mystery collections over the next four years, and I can't wait to be able to introduce you all to familiar authors and new-to-you writers.

Jeffrey Marks
Cincinnati, OH
June, 2019

SILVER BULLETS

Silver Bullets is printed on 60-pound paper, and is designed by Jeffrey Marks using InDesign. The type is Perpetua, a serif typeface design by Eric Gill between 1925 and 1932. The cover is by Joshua Luboski. The first edition was published in two forms: trade softcover, perfect bound; and one hundred fifty copies sew in cloth, numbered and signed by Crippen & Landru's two publishers. Each of the clothbound copies includes a separate pamphlet, *The Long Arm of the Paw*, a short story by current publisher, Jeffrey Marks. *Silver Bullets* was printed by Southern Ohio Printers and bound by Cincinnati Bindery. The book was published in July 2019 by Crippen & Landru Publishers, Inc., Cincinnati, OH.

Crippen & Landru, Publishers
P. O. Box 532057
Cincinnati, OH 45253
Web: www.Crippenlandru.Com
E-mail: info@crippenlandru.Com

Praise for Crippen & Landru Publishers

This is the best edited, most attractively packaged line of mystery books introduced in this decade. The books are equally valuable to collectors and readers. [Mystery Scene Magazine]

The specialty publisher with the most star-studded list is Crippen & Landru, which has produced short story collections by some of the biggest names in contemporary crime fiction. [Ellery Queen's Mystery Magazine]

God bless Crippen & Landru. [The Strand Magazine]

A monument in the making is appearing year by year from Crippen & Landru, a small press devoted exclusively to publishing the criminous short story. [Alfred Hitchcock's Mystery Magazine]

]

Subscriptions

Subscribers agree to purchase each forthcoming publication, either the Regular Series or the Lost Classics or (preferably) both. Collectors can thereby guarantee receiving limited editions, and readers won't miss any favorite stories.

Subscribers receive a discount of 20% off the list price (and the same discount on our backlist) and a specially commissioned short story by a major writer in a deluxe edition as a gift at the end of the year.

The point for us is that, since customers don't pick and choose which books they want, we have a guaranteed sale even before the book is published, and that allows us to be more imaginative in choosing short story collections to issue.

That's worth the 20% discount for us. Sign up now and start saving. Email us at crippenlandru@earthlink.net or visit our website at www.crippenlandru.com on our subscription page.